PRAISE FOR

The Frontman

"In this funny, fresh, heartwarming debut novel, Bahar takes us back to a formative time and place, the late '70s, early '80s, when the sound of possibility was coming through the speakers of every dashboard, and introduces us to Ron, our hapless, earnest, lovelorn hero, struggling to come of age against the pressures to honor his Jewish heritage—in the Midwest."

—Nicola Kraus, best-selling coauthor of *The Nanny Diaries*

"A humorous, smart, and engaging portrait of one boy's coming of age in 1980s Nebraska, *The Frontman* takes the reader on a rollicking rollercoaster of teenage ups and downs, with all the thrills, fears, ecstasies, and agonies that entails. You'll ride along with Ron as he tries to balance the hopes and wishes of his immigrant parents against his own—all the while rooting for him to finally make it work with the girl of his dreams."

—Josh Reims, television writer and executive producer of ABC's *Mistresses*

"In the tradition of Philip Roth's *Portnoy's Complaint*, *The Frontman* is a fresh, musical look at faith, family and fidelity through the lens of a first generation Jewish protagonist. Ron Bahar's debut novel is hilariously funny and gut-wrenchingly emotional (you'll have to read the book to understand that)."

—Ed Decter, screenwriter of *There's Something About Mary*

"Imagine being the only Jewish high schooler in Lincoln, Nebraska. In Ron Bahar's semi-autobiographical debut novel, he shares his unconventional coming-of-age story, and the result is a delightful mix of heart, wit, and hilarious insights. Growing up in a culture of rules and order, we are quickly engrossed in Ron trying to manage the expectations of his parents while being true to himself, and in the process, discovering who he really is and what he really wants. It's a celebration of family relations, the healing power of music, and identity."

—Holly Bario, President of Production, DreamWorks Studios

"No one makes me laugh the way Ron Bahar does—it's been happening since we were writing sketches together in junior high school and continues to this day. Ron has this uniquely intelligent, honest, hilarious take on life that I've always admired and tried to emulate. He's got a way of finding the funny while making himself vulnerable, which makes you laugh and care at the same time. That rare combination of heart and hilarity is executed masterfully in his writing of *The Frontman*, an honest and, at times, heartbreaking look at the time in our lives when we're trying to figure out who we are and what we stand for."

—Mark Gross, comedian, writer/producer, CBS television

THE FRONTMAN

THE FRONTMAN

A Novel

BY

RON BAHAR, MD

Published by SparkPress, a BookSparks imprint,
A division of SparkPoint Studio, LLC
Tempe, Arizona, USA, 85281
www.gosparkpress.com

Published 2018
Printed in the United States of America
ISBN: 978-1-943006-44-1 (pbk)
ISBN: 978-1-943006-45-8 (e-bk)
.
Library of Congress Control Number: 2017956185

Book design by Stacey Aaronson

To Laurie, Ophira, Ezekiel, Zillah, Iris, Ethan,
and Matthew Bahar,
who allowed me to use my imagination.

———

To the late Eric Peterson,
who made me laugh until it hurt.
Rest in peace, my friend.

———

To the late Donna West, the smartest, funniest,
most empathetic teacher an impressionable,
insecure boy could ever have.
Rest in peace, my mentor.

Conflict, whether professional, religious, cultural, or personal, is universal, and so is our responsibility to resolve it.

Listen, in order, to all of *The Frontman*'s referenced songs using the Spotify app. Simply search for the profile "feelgoodz" and click on the playlist entitled *The Frontman.*

AUTHOR'S NOTE

While this book is primarily a work of fiction, it is interspersed with autobiographical stories and characters. Permission has been graciously granted from all living persons whose real names are used in sometimes compromising situations. Any additional similarity to real persons, living or dead, is purely coincidental.

PROLOGUE

*"Won't you take me back to school?
I need to learn the golden rule"*

—THE MOODY BLUES' "THE VOICE," FROM THE ALBUM
LONG DISTANCE VOYAGER, RELEASED JULY 23RD, 1981.
IT PEAKED AT NUMBER FIFTEEN ON US BILLBOARD'S HOT
100 SONGS.

This spot is perfect!" I declared, holding the kite.

"No, it's not," answered Benjie. "When I did this last year at Holmes Lake, there was a lot more open space."

"Well you're twelve and I'm eleven, so I don't think either of us is going to drive there, and no one's at home right now, so this is all we've got."

"I know, I know. But these things were a dollar and ninety-nine cents at Treasure City, so I don't think they're very strong. If one of them gets caught in a tree, that's *it*."

"I don't feel like waiting until we can get out to Holmes Lake. This is the first day where there's no snow on the ground and there's enough wind to keep these things up in the air. Let's just stay here and try."

Benjie surveyed the upper yard of Maude Rousseau Elementary School, with its mix of jungle gyms, a basketball court, tetherball poles, gravel, backstops, and still-leafless

Nebraska cottonwood trees. "This isn't going to work," he announced. "Let's go to the lower yard." He walked with determination down the concrete stairs to the soggy, but uncluttered, field below.

I stopped nervously at the top of the stairs. "Benjie, you *know* this is a bad idea. The power lines are right there," I said, knowing that once he set his mind on something, there was no changing it.

"Oh, don't be such a wimp," he responded adamantly. "We've got plenty of room."

"It's just . . . see, look at the package the kite comes in—it says right here—'Parental guidance recommended when flown by children—'"

"'—eight years and younger!' You're not a baby! Would you just *calm down*? If you want to be a weenie and get your kite stuck after five seconds, that's fine . . . but watch this!" He then proceeded to find a pitcher's-mound sized, slightly rounded, relatively dry spot from which he could launch the Gayla keel-guided *Super Bat*, about twenty yards from the power lines. He continued his assessment and realized he needed help. "Ron, come here. I want you to hold the kite in front of me and let it go while I hold the string."

"I'm not doing it . . . I'm a *weenie*, remember?"

"Okay, I'm sorry, you're not a weenie . . . you know I was just kidding . . . please, just do it. I promise it'll be fine."

I knew, even as an eleven-year-old, when I was being manipulated, and the idea of caving turned my stomach. However, Benjie was the closest thing I had to an older brother. He shrugged his shoulders, turned up his palms, and raised his eyebrows. "Fine," I answered, exasperated. I protested meekly by tiptoeing deliberately across the lower yard toward him to avoid soaking my white canvas All Stars.

I took the kite from his hands and retreated carefully,

away from school and toward the power lines, with the westerly winds. "Keep going . . . *please*," he implored.

I turned around and looked up; I was standing directly below the power lines. "No! Back up!" I yelled.

"I'm *not* backing up!"

"Well I'm *not* moving!"

"Shit. Okay, then let go . . ."

"No!" It was too late to object. Benjie had tugged on the kite string just hard enough to loosen my grasp. Super Bat, with its cheap, plastic-winged body and bloodshot eyes, was already airborne when a bona fide gust of Midwestern wind propelled it into the power lines, with both the string and Benjie attached.

"Benjie, let go!" I begged. "You'll get electrocuted!"

"No way! I'm not giving up now. I just need to pull on it a little—"

Before he could either finish his thought or free Super Bat, Benjie collapsed to the ground. His entire body quivered while his arms flailed briefly, and then he lay motionless.

"*No!*" I screamed, as I ran frantically toward him. Before I could reach his lifeless body, I tumbled into a soup of gravel, dormant grass, and mud. Undeterred and desperate to perform a fifth-grade version of CPR, I quickly rose to my feet and dove at Benjie. I grabbed him by the shoulders and began to shake him hysterically. "Benjie, Benjie!" No response. I tried again. Nothing. My efforts, and I, were useless. Prostrate, with my filthy hands covering my filthy face, I began to sob.

I heard the sound of giggling next to me. I looked in Benjie's direction. Though his eyes remained shut, he was again quivering, this time with laughter. He eventually opened his eyes and cracked up.

"Benjie, you're alive! But why are you laughing? You

could've died!" I leapt to my feet with arms outstretched, ready to hug him.

"No, I couldn't," he answered confidently. He then waved at me with both hands. "I'm wearing my dad's electrical gloves that I tucked into my jacket." There was no way I was going to get hurt." He was now standing and guffawing.

"You mean you *planned* this?"

"Yup."

"You're a . . . you're a . . . " I started.

"A *what*?" he asked, smiling.

"You're a *fucker*!" I exclaimed. I had never used the word "fucker" before, but it felt entirely appropriate.

"C'mon, Ron. It was a joke!"

"You're a *fucker*!" I repeated. "A big, crazy *fucker*!" I seethed as he calmly walked to the string and played with it until *Super Bat* wriggled free and fell to the ground. He then, for effect, slowly un-tucked and removed the long black rubber gloves, picked up the kite, and walked back to me. "I'm not a fucker and you know it," he added. "I'm your best friend, and someday you'll laugh about it, too. Lighten up!"

"No!" The only thing left quivering was my lower lip.

"You really *are* mad, aren't you?" he asked, somewhat surprised.

"Yes! That was the meanest thing anyone's ever done to me."

Benjie stared at me, then paused before finally saying, "Well, I swear I'll make it up to you one day."

CHAPTER 1

"You don't drink don't smoke – what do you do?
Subtle innuendos follow"

—ADAM ANT'S "GOODY TWO SHOES," FROM THE ALBUM
FRIEND OR FOE, RELEASED OCTOBER, 1982.
IT PEAKED AT NUMBER TWELVE ON US BILLBOARD'S HOT
100 SONGS.

W hat the hell are you wearing?" asked Mark after he opened his front door and inspected Sundar's outfit. "You look like a bellhop!"

"It's a Nehru jacket. My uncle sent it over from India; it's all the rage over there," answered Sundar, as he carefully unbuttoned his royal blue tunic.

"Oh yeah, that's right," added Tommy, toasting Sundar with his tenth beer. "I saw Sean Connery wear one of those as James Bond in *Dr. No*. I think you look like the fuckin' ambassador of cool." He then turned to Mark. "And what do *you* know, anyway? I've seen some of those ridiculous outfits you've come up with. There's a reason you're the class clown."

All three smiled. Sundar made himself at home on the living room couch, leaning back and confidently placing his hands behind his head. He was so goddamn comfortable in his own brown skin—and everyone always agreed with Tommy— Sundar actually *was* "the fuckin' ambassador of cool."

Mark Gross had perhaps the most permissive parents on

Earth, so naturally, gatherings at his home were frequent and uninhibited. He relished his role as both the host and the life of the party, but that night he could do little to steal the spotlight from Tommy, who, only three hours earlier, threw the game-winning touchdown for the Lincoln Southeast Knights' football team.

"It really wasn't that big a deal," explained Tommy to Julia Turner, *The Hottest Girl to Ever Walk the Face of the Planet*. "My receiver was open, I threw the ball to him, and he scored. It's that simple."

"It's not that simple, Tommy. Don't be modest," she said. Her body language spoke volumes. She wasn't just fawning, and she wasn't even just eye-fucking; she was sloppy drunk and practically mounting Tommy right there on the family ottoman. Sundar and I had to look away to avoid the appearance of voyeurism.

I grabbed the keys from Tommy as we left Mark's house several hours later. "Ron, I promise you, I drive better when I'm buzzed."

"No fucking way, Tommy," I responded. "Get in the passenger seat while we wait for Julia to finish peeing. I'm driving your car, my friend. And, hey, at what point do you transition from buzzed to shit-faced and incapacitated?"

"Good question, Ron," he replied with a thoughtful grin. "Buzzed is the stage where I feel everything, and everything feels better. Shit-faced is where I wish I would feel nothing and regret that I wasn't satisfied at buzzed. Beer, mushrooms, vodka, weed, mescaline, gin . . . I don't discriminate."

Tommy casually puked in Mark's driveway then promptly stumbled into his black, two-door '82 BMW 320i, specially delivered from Chicago to Nebraska because of the state's lack of German auto dealerships. Admittedly, part of me wanted to drive the car, most importantly wanted to be *seen* driving the car. "Ron, I don't understand," he said to me, "How do you have such self-control? You never, ever, ever do shit. Did you even have one drink tonight?"

"Nope," I answered, now regretting that I had raised the subject.

"Jesus, Ron! It'll never be 1982 again, and I'll never be a high-school senior again. I basically get good grades, but I have way more fun than you do. You can have a drink every now and then, and you don't have to get an A in every class, bro. You can still become a doctor. You have plenty of time to prove yourself in college. Don't you kinda wanna be me?"

My mind raced. In addition to being wealthy, Tommy Hanson was handsome, clever, and athletic, as though Thor was ripped from the pages of a comic book and transported directly to Lincoln, both to befriend me and to torture me with jealousy. "Yes," I said. "I would *kinda wanna* be you."

"How are you so fucking mature?" he asked with a hint of slurred speech and a touch of spittle.

"I'm not. I'm just a chicken shit." The words stung as they left my mouth.

Before Tommy could respond, we were both mesmerized by the sight of Julia sauntering around the car to Tommy's window. She did rock those Jordache jeans. With her long, purposely-tussled blonde locks, she performed a perfect hair flip as Tommy rolled down the window to toy with her. "Well, aren't you going to give me a ride?" she asked.

"Uh . . . yeah." Despite his inebriation, Tommy skillfully shoved a handful of Tic Tacs in his mouth, opened the passenger door, faked sobriety, popped out, let her slide into the backseat, and followed her inside. I doubt she even noticed me, her chauffeur. She then sat on his lap, and he winked at me as if to say, "I'm not too shit-faced for *this*." Even in his compromised state, Tommy was a living, breathing aphrodisiac.

They started making out. The combined scent of their alcohol and his Drakkar Noir cologne was nauseating. I was humiliated, but Tommy possessed the ability to charm his way out of any perception that he was a dick. I drove them to Tommy's empty estate at Pine Lake. His older sister, Susan, was living at the University of Nebraska's Zeta Sigma Omega sorority house downtown, and his parents were on their annual golf junket in Florida to avoid the early frost of October. Mr. Hanson had made his fortune as an executive in Omaha's thriving insurance industry, and work was now an afterthought. After the two of them staggered out of the car, Tommy waited until Julia was a few paces ahead before turning to me, smiling coyly, and whispering through the open passenger window, "Be a friend, don't tell anyone about this. After all, I am a gentleman."

"Sure thing," I said, smiling weakly. "And I'll bring the car back tomorrow."

As I drove home in the Beemer, I thought out loud about the injustice of it all. "How the fuck is it fair that tonight, he stars in a high-school football game, drinks like a fish at a post-game party, gets an escort in his chariot, and spends the night alone at home with Ms. Bodacious?"

I parked the Beemer a few blocks away from my house and sat in the driver's seat before closing my eyes and smelling the scent of the leather seats. I was envious of both Sundar and Tommy, and I was ashamed that I was envious. Embarrassed and alone, I stepped out of the car, locked the door, and walked home in the dark.

CHAPTER 2

"I just can't help but feeling
I'm Living a life of illusion"

—JOE WALSH'S "A LIFE OF ILLUSION," FROM THE ALBUM
THERE GOES THE NEIGHBORHOOD, RELEASED MAY, 1981.
IT PEAKED AT NUMBER THIRTY-FOUR ON US BILLBOARD'S
HOT 100 SONGS.

The next morning, Saturday, my alarm went off at 8:00, far too early for the weekend. While my friends were sleeping off the aftermath of the previous night's debauchery, I dragged myself out of the shower, soaking wet, and wiped the fog off the mirror. I looked at my naked self— my hairy, swarthy, scrawny naked self. I was different. I didn't just appear different. I *felt* different.

Growing up in Lincoln in the 1980s, I was the only Jew in my class. I was the only one who looked Middle Eastern, the only one who shaved by age twelve, and the only one whose family spoke Hebrew at home. I wasn't a particularly good athlete, and I was continually compared to my two older, *really-fucking-smart* sisters.

To the casual observer, my ethnicity was difficult to identify. My blonde-haired, blue-eyed, Israeli-born, half-Polish, half-Belarusian mother conceived three children with her Indian-born husband of Iraqi-Jewish descent. Sadly, the end product of my disparate and "interesting" lineage was not a portrait of "rugged good looks." Instead, it was an unfortunate and ironic mix of Lou Ferrigno's head and Bill Bixby's body, neither Incredible nor Hulky.

As part of my Saturday morning ritual, I toweled off, plugged in my Sony Walkman, pressed play, and began to alternate between karaoke and lip sync, this morning to the music of Billy Idol. At the risk of sounding cocky, I was an exceptionally gifted singer, and, unlike my abilities as a student, I never had to work hard at it; my voice came naturally and effortlessly, and I never took a lesson. If my parents didn't pressure me to pursue a career in medicine, they would surely have wanted me to become the cantor at our temple.

Despite being told more than once by old Mrs. Goldberg that I had, "the voice of an angel," I would rather have pursued a life of crime than become a member of the clergy. I was wildly proud of my heritage and the risk my parents and grandparents took in uprooting their lives so that their children and grandchildren could have better ones. Though the spirituality and parables of Judaism fascinated me, its rituals and services bored me to tears, leaving me to resent my father's early morning "call to prayer."

"Ronnie, move it!" my father commanded, as he pounded on the bathroom door. "We're leaving for synagogue in five minutes . . . and what is that garbage you're singing anyway? Using your voice for anything other than religious purposes borders on sacrilege."

While I ignored my father's proclamations, I understood that we remained at an impasse. So instead of concentrating on music, I appeased him by focusing on my application to six-year medical schools that would allow me to matriculate directly out of high school. "Full steam ahead," he would say. "Anything less is a sinful waste of time."

Music was indeed my comfort food. Though my own skills were limited to my voice, I did play a respectable air guitar during karaoke-lip sync:

"I'm dancing with myself
when there's no-one else in slight . . ."

I was the youngest of three children. The oldest was my sister, Zillie—yes, Zillie—short for Zillah. Try growing up with a name like that in the Midwest. My parents didn't mean to torture her. She was named after my maternal grandmother, and was born in Israel, where the biblically derived moniker was perfectly acceptable. It was, therefore, imperative that she grew thick skin; there would be no other means to survive the nickname "Godzilla," which haunted her for the twelve years she lived in Nebraska. Mercifully, my parents grew to understand this cruel reality before they named their younger two children. It was no accident, then, that in choosing a college, Zillie sought only East Coast melting-pot schools, where assimilation was not necessary and where visiting Lincoln would be conveniently inconvenient.

Those born in Israel are described as "sabras," a reference to the cactus-borne fruit that is prickly on the outside and soft on the inside. Zillie personified this description; while her brutal honesty was painful, her loyalty was unrelenting.

She called me early that morning to shoot the shit, and while she made me run late, she offered me both solicited and unsolicited advice. "Ronnie, stop trying to please everyone," she explained. "If you want to become a doctor, become a doctor, and if you want to sing, tell everyone to fuck off."

"Okay, okay," I answered dismissively.

"Don't 'okay, okay' me! That's patronizing! And, by the way, I will *always* have your back, dumbass."

My middle sister, Iris, was home from college at the University of Illinois. I was certain she attended engineering school to pander to my engineering-professor father, but it turned out she was just wired differently and more successfully than I was. I loved Iris, but she had no patience for her baby brother. Though she was quite familiar with my Saturday morning bathroom customs, and though she was about as enthusiastic about going to temple as I was, she was not one to procrastinate. My sisters and I shared one of the two bathrooms in our three bedroom, one-story stone house, and I had gotten used to feeling like an only child when both of them had departed for college. Iris thumped loudly on the door. "Ronnie, give it a rest! We're going to be late!"

"That's the idea," I responded.

Now my mother had reached her limit and took it upon herself to extricate me with a lighter, but more urgent knock. "Ronnie, hurry up! I put your clean panties in your room!"

Chills ascended my spine. "Jesus, Mom, I asked you never to use the words 'Ronnie' and 'panties' in the same sentence. I wear *underwear!*"

"What does Jesus have to do with your panties?" she responded, lost in translation. "We have to leave!"

My concert had concluded. I left the bathroom, dressed, and ran to the kitchen to shovel dry cereal down my gullet in an attempt to prevent starvation at the seemingly eternal services. After only a few bites of Frosted Flakes, a repetitive honk emerged from the car. I was generally not allowed to drive until the end of the Sabbath, when three stars in a hopefully cloudless sky signified the end of its traditional observance (thus leaving Tommy's car down the street to avoid conflict) and the beginning of a new week. However, according to my parents' interpretation of Jewish law, the "convenience loophole" superseded this rule so that we could then drive *specifically* to services. On cue, I would run out, plead with my father to stop waking the dead, and jump in the car. I never begrudged my parents. I simply and genuinely didn't understand them. Most things never changed.

CHAPTER 3

"Mm, but it's poetry in motion
And when she turned her eyes to me"

—THOMAS DOLBY'S "SHE BLINDED ME WITH SCIENCE,"
FROM THE ALBUM *THE GOLDEN AGE OF WIRELESS*, RELEASED
MAY 10TH, 1982. IT PEAKED AT NUMBER FIVE ON US
BILLBOARD'S HOT 100 SONGS.

I had perfect grades, but in order to achieve them I studied endlessly. To complicate matters, my sleep hygiene sucked. After studying until 3:00 a.m., I would wake up at 7:00 a.m. each weekday and drag myself out of bed to shit, shave, and shower. "Breakfast" typically consisted of shoving those same dry Frosted Flakes directly from the box into my mouth with one hand while precariously steering and racing my '70 Plymouth Duster to school with the other. My mom hated that I didn't eat "like a real human being." I do indeed remember summers in Israel, where my grandfather would meticulously prepare cucumber and tomato salad with freshly baked bread, a slice of farmer's cheese, and a giant glass of milk. Best food ever. I agree that only the latter meal represented human food, but I was simply trying my best to behave like an American teenager.

I was always exhausted. Despite the exotic lure of nonkosher food, the thought of consuming subsidized school lunches featuring mystery meat wrapped in stale Midwestern tortillas repulsed me. Because I lived so close to school, I often ran home during lunch to think and eat. And eat. And eat. I could finish an entire box of Kraft Mac & Cheese in one sitting. The key was to strike the right balance of milk, butter, and starch to maximize adolescent-male satiety, while avoiding nausea. Paradoxically, Kraft managed to create a cheap and delicious alternative to human food. After school, cross-country practice would ensure that the thousands of calories I devoured would be burned, and my bony physique would persevere.

Once I reached home, I was spent. My legs twitched. After a half hour with my parents, Dan Rather and the *CBS Nightly News* at the dinner table at 5:30 p.m., I would sleep for about an hour. I would then awaken, still groggy, and watch a mindless show to help rouse me. The 7:00 p.m. time slot was critical. Monday night's selection—no, not *Family Ties* (8:00 p.m.), and no, not *M*A*S*H"* (8:30 p.m.), but *Square Pegs*, was a taunting metaphor for my life. I would procrastinate a couple of hours more with phone calls and Peanut M&M's, and then finally begin the slog of homework that would last until the wee hours of the morning. Calculus. Chemistry. English (I pretended to be well-rounded). Then I would crash and wake again at 7:00 a.m. The harrowing cycle would continue until Friday night.

THAT'S disgusting," said Amy.

"No it's not. It's fucking awesome," I responded.

Amy Andrews and I had originally met in fifth grade, at a time when our fathers worked together closely in the faculty senate at the University of Nebraska. Her father, Steven, was a professor of English, and my dad a professor of electrical engineering. The two of them shared a passion for their work and an absent-mindedness for the rest of the world at large: a match made in heaven. Amy's mother, Carol, also a member of the English faculty, bared the additional, sexist reality of equal work for lower pay, along with her presumptive responsibility as the primary caregiver to her only child.

My mother regularly and happily invited Amy home with me after school; she was thrilled to have someone apply peer pressure to her distractible, impressionable, and occasionally lonely son.

As a winner of multiple teaching and societal awards, Steven Andrews was tremendously popular with both students and faculty alike. He was smart, charming, and handsome—my mom thought he looked like Ryan O'Neal—perhaps too charming and handsome. During the spring of our sixth grade, he was caught by a suspicious Carol while having a brief, but torrid, affair with a professor from the Spanish Department. Steven and his Latina lover shared a penchant for Jimmy Buffett music, and he and his literal "Mexican Cutie," Dr. Sonia Mendes, were caught naked, sipping margaritas in a room at The Lincoln Airport Howard Johnson.

The subsequent and ugly divorce proceedings resulted in a permanently scarred and untrusting Amy, who spent many days (and nights) in 1977 and 1978 with my family while Steven and Carol duked it out in attorney's offices and, eventually, in court. The Andrews depended on the discretion of my parents, who reserved judgment in Amy's presence. "It's a disgrace . . . both the affair *and* the divorce," repeated my father on a near daily basis.

"You don't just leave each other . . . you work things out," my mother would add, completing their mantra. My parents cared deeply about Amy, and so protected her through silence beyond the family circle. God knows they understood how it felt to be outsiders.

———

FROM my naïve standpoint, I just didn't get it. The Andrews seemed like the perfect little family. Carol was sweet, funny, and attractive, in an *I-can-see-where-Amy-gets-her-good-looks* sort of way, and Steven doted over the two of them whenever I saw them together. And wasn't adultery a Top 10 sin?

For the most part, divorce was both relatively uncommon and frowned upon in Lincoln in the late '70s. Steven was vilified in the community to a degree to which he felt he could no longer function socially or professionally. He eventually departed Lincoln for a tenured position at the University of Michigan, abandoning Amy both physically and emotionally. Amy wore her parents' failed marriage as a badge of shame. The disappearing invitations to the homes of family "friends," along with acquaintances who feigned empathy with lingering, pathetic stares, crushed her spirit. I caught her on more than one occasion crying silently in front of the television or a book, and offered comfort in a manner unique to an awkward seventh grader. "Amy, it's . . . it's fine," I finally said, while patting her back stiffly during a particularly bad evening.

"No, it's really not." She looked up and studied my face. I nearly looked away; I was petrified that she would discover through my eyes that I thought she was beautiful. "Can we bake cookies?"

"What?" I answered, utterly thrown.

"Cookies."

"What kind?"

"Chocolate chip . . . Nestle Tollhouse. We can also do that thing where we replace some of the chips with Peanut M&M's." She looked down and sniffed. "I know you like them."

"Um . . . I suppose so. Why now?"

Her eyes returned to mine. "Because you've been really nice to me, and because Peanut M&M's make me happy." She wiped a tear with the palm of her hand and forced a smile.

I smiled back. Mine was unforced. "Me too. Okay, lemme get Iris. She's good at—"

"No," she interrupted. She grabbed my hand before I could leave the room. "Just us." She held on to my hand a moment longer than was necessary. My eyes scanned the length of my goosebumped arm as I wondered exactly how and why that weird phenomenon occurred. Yes, I understood we were talking about cookies, but at the time, it was the hottest thing I had ever heard in my life. Goddammit those cookies were delicious.

I continued to lust after her throughout puberty. She and I would do homework together, especially during the first year of her parents' separation, but her presence was some-times more of a hindrance than a help; I would not-so-secretly stare at her for hours. Though our time together dissipated once the Andrews' custody arrangement had been settled, my passion for Amy only grew.

Even at the tender age of twelve, however, I understood that, to my parents, Amy represented the ultimate forbidden fruit: the non-Jewish girl to the Jewish boy. With regard to my feelings, I knew they knew, and they knew I knew they knew.

Fuck.

Amy was ridiculously smart and naturally curious. Like her parents, she was a voracious reader, and, coupled with her near photographic memory, she made school appear effortless. If she weren't so goddamn nice, girls would have universally despised her. She had almond-shaped hazel eyes, and during high school she wore a thick mane of feathered brown hair. When she smiled, my adolescent, hormonal eyes actually thought she sparkled. Fall and spring were the best times to see her during the school year, because she had spectacular legs and, when it was anywhere above sixty degrees outside, she exposed them in alluring fashion by wearing denim shorts. Despite her sex appeal, her easy-going personality, her intelligence and her genuineness made her the type of girl you bring home to mother. Unless, of course, your mother was Israeli and thought it was reasonable that her red-blooded American son should only date Jewish girls in a desert of Jews.

AS an underclassman, I had taken Frank Dupuis' courses in biology and botany. During senior year, he taught anatomy and physiology, and I was his best audience. His unbridled enthusiasm for seemingly mundane subjects—the lifecycle of a jellyfish, or the formation of one milliliter of urine in a human bladder—was infectious. He wore his pocket protector proudly; he was so uncool he was cool.

He was plump and disheveled, and he continuously readjusted his wire-framed, rectangular glasses. However, despite his nebbishy exterior, Frank's interior brimmed with his interest in the complexities of human interaction and how these interactions related to animal behavior. He could easily have forgone teaching to pursue a career in adolescent psychology. His interest likely stemmed from the early days of his relationship with his wife (then girlfriend), whom he courted unconventionally by impressing her with his knowledge of ferns. Not exactly Richard Gere and Debra Winger in *An Officer and a Gentleman*, but love assumes many forms. When Sheila met Frank, he was a graduate student at the University of Nebraska, and she worked at Azalealand as a florist. The rest, including the birth of their daughter Fern (yes, Fern), is history.

Mr. Dupuis and I spoke often, and though we had talked frequently about my religion and my ability to sing, we never discussed Amy. Initially, there was no need; he sensed my attraction to her. I'm not sure why; perhaps it was the fact that I continued to gawk at her, hopefully in a non-creepy fashion. He had a policy of seating kids in alphabetical order, and though it had been his practice for years, I swear he did it specifically so that I, Ron Bahar, might sit next to Amy Andrews. In addition, I think he may have ensured that students were assigned special twin lab tables with extra-wide tops that hid the erections of young men, which could sprout even with a respectable gust of wind, let alone sitting next to a girl like Amy.

Frank finally tired of my plodding approach toward Amy and eventually took me aside one day after class. "You like her, don't you?" he asked.

"Excuse me?" I responded, surprised and a little flustered.

"Ron, don't be coy with me . . . do you want my advice, or not?"

"Well, sure . . . but I don't think you'd understand."

"Why wouldn't I understand?"

"Because you're not—"

"Not what? Seventeen? I actually was at one time," he said, smiling.

"No, because you're not Jewish," I answered bluntly.

"You're right, I'm not Jewish . . . and I'm not black or Hispanic either . . . but that doesn't mean I don't know what it feels like to be alone in a crowd in Nebraska."

I immediately felt deeply embarrassed for my previous statement. He was right . . . on all accounts.

"Ron," he continued, "Did you know that only about five percent of all mammals mate for life?"

"What? What do mammals and mating for life have anything to do with me?"

"I'm getting to my point. Wolves, beavers, bats, and humans are among the only ones who do. Wolves have alpha
males, beavers go off on their own to find a mate and build a
new colony, and male bats literally sing to females who fly by
to try and serenade them . . . some of these animals even risk
their lives in the process. But humans . . . humans do *all* of
these things as part of their search for their one true love.
It's part of what makes us human. Biology can be incredibly
romantic, don't you think?"

"Well yes, but—"

"Go experience life, Ron—all of it. Be an alpha male, go
find someone, and go sing."

MR. Dupuis unwrapped the formaldehyde-infused frog he
had dissected earlier in the day. He then gave his students a
literal tour of blood and guts, from mouth, to esophagus, to
stomach to small intestine to large intestine, and finally to
the amphibian analogue of the anus: the cloaca. He didn't
allow his students to leave his last class of the day until all
of us memorized this route, including the role of its major
tributaries, the liver, the gallbladder, and the pancreas.

"Okay, it's awesome, but it's disgusting," Amy declared.

As she and I walked down the hall together after class, I
considered Frank's odd, yet inspiring illustrations and rec-
ommendations and decided once and for all to take the "you
only live once" approach.

"Amy?"

"Yes?"

Holy shit, this is actually going to happen, I thought.
Go Ron. Fuck yes. After years of daydreaming, sex is im-

minent. I fucking rule! Amy, you have no idea how long . . .

"Ron!" exclaimed Amy, interrupting my trance.

"Huh?" I asked, returning to Earth.

She smiled, almost conciliatorily. "You were going to ask me something and then you spaced out . . . what is it?"

"Um . . . nothing." *What a fucking loser.*

I spent the rest of the day mentally masturbating over my ineptitude. I was humiliated by my inability to speak honestly to someone I cared about so intensely, someone who craved that honesty so desperately. Of course I'd had opportunities over the years to tell her how I really felt, but inevitably I would succumb to my own fears. What a jackass I was. I ran surface streets during cross country practice that afternoon and, despite the general sparsity of traffic in Lincoln, my lack of focus nearly caused me to collide with two cars, a pedestrian, a stray dog, and one very angry man on a Harley near Pioneers Park.

After practice, I wandered toward the Duster with my head down, trying to make sense out of what had transpired. Just before I reached the car, I bumped into something. Someone. Before looking up, I smelled the unmistakable scent of Faberge Organic Shampoo and Conditioner . . . you know, the one that Heather Locklear used in those commercials, the one that intoxicated me every time I leaned to the opposite side of my lab table.

"Hey," Amy said as I looked up. "It's *me*. You don't have to be so shy. I know how you've felt about me for years. I know your situation is a little 'complicated'—so is mine—but I feel the same way and I'm right here. I'll be around when you're ready for me." She smiled. I smiled back. She leaned in dangerously close to me, and squeezed my hand. Our lips nearly touched, but we didn't kiss. I grinned widely as she stared at me with those hazel eyes. She was breathtaking. I was smitten.

She let go of my hand, turned around, and walked toward her '76 white VW Rabbit. She knew I was staring at her. I jumped in the Duster and drove home, exhausted as usual, but very, very happy. The only feeling more exciting than a first crush is the realization that the sensation is mutual. Social status and religion play no part in this strange and wonderful collection of emotions.

CHAPTER 4

"When you get so sick of trying
Just hold on tight to your dream"

—ELECTRIC LIGHT ORCHESTRA'S "HOLD ON TIGHT,"
FROM THE ALBUM *TIME*, RELEASED JULY, 1981.
IT PEAKED AT NUMBER TEN ON US BILLBOARD'S HOT
100 SONGS.

had wanted to become a physician since preschool and, though my ambition was precocious, my patience was not. I was all about the goal and not about the process. I did love biology and physiology. Of course, I wanted to understand how twenty-three chromosomes could nearly flawlessly pass down information from tens of thousands of genes to the next generation. Of course, I wanted to know how a fertile, amorous male could navigate the miraculous process of seeing an attractive, aroused fertile female, mount an erection, spread his seed, and approximately nine months later, witness another human pop out of said-female's vagina. Unfortunately, however, I approached school only as a means to an end, and I didn't want to waste one joule of energy outside the confines of the classroom. I would save the love of learning for another time; I was on a mission.

I was a scholastic parrot. I repeated everything and invented nothing. Perhaps that's why karaoke and lip sync appealed so much to me. My intellectual curiosity was limited to the minimum memorization necessary for me to absorb and subsequently regurgitate information to garner As on a report card.

I wasn't particularly proud of my approach, but I was proud of my determination. At the time, my deepest secret was a fear of being exposed as an intellectual fraud, and to avoid this shame I would study harder than anyone. And it worked. Mr. Dupuis and my college counselor, Mr. Evans, together recognized my "strength," and encouraged me to apply to accelerated medical school programs, only perpetuating my twisted view of education. I skipped the chapter on the Socratic method.

I was the product of a perfect storm of Jewish guilt and the Indian dream of upward mobility.

ZILLAH Rosenbaum was born in Poland in 1901, the fourth child of seven in an Orthodox Jewish family in Warsaw. After finishing high school and dabbling in chemistry at night school, she worked diligently at a local bank through the stock market crash of 1929 and into the Great Depression years of the early 1930s. Zillah eventually received a small severance pay in 1933, but saw no future for herself in her native country. Instead, with a pioneering spirit, she used the money to travel by boat to Beirut, and from there by taxi to Palestine. Her parents and siblings would all later perish, either in the Warsaw Ghetto or in the gas chambers of Treblinka.

Zalman Rodov was born in Marina Gorka, Belarus, in 1897. He studied horticulture in college, and subsequently served as a local government administrator. In 1926, he was caught carrying Zionist literature and was immediately sent to a Soviet prison camp in the Ural Mountains for four years. After his release, he was exiled, shortly before Stalin enacted a policy of murdering such "subversives." He found his way to Palestine in 1930, where he later studied and eventually practiced land surveying. On the side, he smuggled in Jewish refugees at night from the shores of the Mediterranean. He was also a member of the Haganah, the Jewish paramilitary group, which would eventually become the nucleus of The Israel Defense Force.

Zillah and Zalman married in 1935, and Ophira, their first of two children, was born the next year in the coastal city of Haifa. Ophira was shy, skinny, and studious. Despite their limited means, the Rodovs spent half of Zalman's salary fostering their children's education in private school. After high school, Ophira enlisted in the army, where she served for two years and attained the rank of corporal in the Israeli Air Force. She then attended teachers' college before teaching seventh and eighth graders for two years.

HANNAH Gabbay was born in 1908 in the city of Baghdad. She moved to Mumbai (then Bombay) in 1918 after the conclusion of World War I, when the British occupation of Iraq allowed the departure of many Jews to brighter pastures in England, Southern Asia, and Australia. Though she initially attended Jewish day school, she left after a prank, in which classmates locked her in a closet with a boy. She spent her high school years at The Convent of Jesus and Mary.

Silas Bahar was born in 1905 and moved from Baghdad to Mumbai in the same exodus of 1918. After attending an Iraqi Jewish high school, he started a career in the printing business and eventually opened his own press at the age of forty. When Hannah was seventeen years old, she married

Silas' older brother George. George died of pneumonia only six months later. Hannah was devastated, but, according to custom, Silas married her the next year.

Ezekiel Bahar, their third of ten children, was born in 1933. Eze, as he was known to all, was mischievous yet devoted. He would surreptitiously place stink bombs in front of neighbors' doorsteps. However, he would also take the blame and a Catholic school priest's whipping for the wrongdoings of a younger brother. Eze completed his studies at Saint Mary's High School in 1948, twelve years before its most famous alumnus, rocker Freddie Mercury.

Eze was also self-reliant and ambitious, even at the ripe age of sixteen. In 1949, only one year after Israel precariously declared its independence, he informed both his family and The Jewish Agency for Israel of his dream to emigrate, or make *aliyah* (literally "ascent," in Hebrew), to the fledgling state. When, at the last moment, an Afghan family relinquished its seats on the plane that would take them later that day to Tel Aviv, the agency called for volunteers. Eze had only a moment to decide. He immediately accepted the offer, and, after his mother tearfully consented to his departure, he grabbed his pre-packed suitcase and left. When Silas returned from work later that afternoon and found out what had happened, he raced to the airport to say good-bye to his son. The plane had already taken off, with Eze on board. Eze and Silas would never see each other again.

Sixteen and alone. Once in Israel, Eze spent two years at The Mikveh Yisrael ("Hope of Israel") Agricultural School in the town of Holon. He then enlisted in the army, rose to the rank of staff sergeant, and worked for the Israeli Intelligence as part of his three-year commitment. During his conscription, he was not renowned for his skills in the field, and in fact at one point overturned a jeep and broke his arm. However, his aptitude for math and physics was noticed by his superiors, who encouraged him to pursue a college degree. Shortly after his military stint, he attended engineering school at Israel's Institute of Technology in Haifa.

IN 1957, Ophira met Ezekiel through one of his classmates; it was love at first sight. They were engaged within six weeks and married within six months. Though they had little money, they were happy. She taught and he studied. Zillah and Zalman treated Eze like a son, and he loved them like his own parents. Zillah died of breast cancer in 1959, and her namesake, my sister Zillie, was born three years later. That same year, my parents made the decision to move their new family to the United States so that my father could complete his graduate studies.

To this day, my mother regrets that decision.

My father became a star graduate student at The University of Colorado at Boulder. Upon receiving his PhD in electrical engineering in 1964, the same year Iris was born, his chairman offered him a junior faculty position to stay as an assistant professor. I was born the following year, and my family remained in Boulder until 1967, when the Chairman at The University of Nebraska contacted him about a promotion to come to Lincoln. In considering the move, my parents, who had originally planned to return to Israel immediately after he was awarded his diploma, were heartened by the promise of a small but tight-knit Jewish community in the Cornhusker State. The Bahars would pack their bags for Lincoln and move there that fall.

MY father's professional ascent was meteoric; he became a full professor before the age of forty. I could tell you that his work involved such scintillating topics as "transient response from irregular structures and inhomogeneous anisotropic media," and "transform techniques for boundary value problems." I could also tell you that he penned a chapter on "radio wave propagation over a non-uniform overburden" in the all-time-nerd bestseller *Electromagnetic Probing in Geophysics.* I literally had no idea what he actually did.

I knew my father was brilliant, but did he and my mother make the right decision in moving to Nebraska? Essentially all of the select few Middle Eastern or Asian highly educated adult males who moved to Midwestern college towns in the 1960s or '70s were either professors or physicians. My father met both cultural criteria, but was his transplantation truly the fulfillment of a dream?

While my father plugged away with his career, my mother never adjusted. He ignored the long, cold winters and simply worked. My mother, on the other hand, never felt comfortable, either with the temperature or with the people. When I was ten, she returned to school to earn a master's degree and concentrated, of course, on Jewish History and the Middle East. She did so to fill the void and numb the pain she felt for "abandoning" her past.

If we were to remain in Lincoln, Zillie, Iris, and I would justify my parents' diaspora through their children's educational success and fidelity to Judaism. We, in fact, carried dual citizenship with the United States and Israel. Did the three of us feel the pressure of living up to the legacy of our ancestors, who sacrificed and suffered so much so that future generations could live freely and robustly as Jews?

Yes.

Rule number one: Perfect report cards were expected,

not desired. My parents didn't even attend parent-teacher conferences. While I was an excellent rule follower, I saw no reason to work beyond what was expected from me at school. With my goal of reaching medical school, and despite my impatience, I had become an expert at delayed gratification. Conversely, I had no idea what it meant to live in the present. Sadly, I would be amazed when my sisters would read non school-assigned books. Whom were they trying to impress, anyway?

Rule number two: Never date a non-Jew. As there *were* no Jewish girls for me to date, it was the ultimate paradox for this horndog. Not that anyone should feel sorry for me (well, maybe they should), but what the fuck? Why did I need to suppress my love for the opposite sex, and, for that matter, my ability to be the musical frontman anywhere else but at my Bar Mitzvah?

CHAPTER 5

"Sometimes love don't feel like it should
You make it hurt so good"

—John Cougar's "Hurts So Good," from the album
American Fool, released July 10th, 1982.
It peaked at number one on US Billboard's Hot 100
songs.

Sundar Rajendran was my only classmate of Indian heritage. Naturally, his father, Somasundaram, was a physician. Also, naturally, Sundar and his younger brother, Babu, intended to follow suit. Sundar and I shared the first-generation bond that few others in our nearly homogenous community felt. Of course our languages, religions and food differed—I spoke Hebrew, practiced Judaism, and lived in a house that smelled like roasted eggplant. He spoke Tamil, practiced Hinduism, and lived in a house that smelled like curry.

I loved that smell; I would salivate the moment I stepped into the Rajendran's home. Sundar's mother, Prema, fried some badass samosas. The scent also reminded me of my grandmother. An accomplished cook herself, Hannah Bahar taught me the true meaning of spice, and that ketchup was indeed *not* a food group, even in Nebraska. "*Acha, dahling,* try it with a little yogurt sauce," Granny would say in her singsong accent, music to my ears, and a symphony to my gut.

I also loved visiting Sundar's father, who was both my mentor and my own physician. Dr. Rajendran was the first pediatric gastroenterologist in the state of Nebraska. I was fortunate to have easy access to him, given my career goals and my diagnosis of irritable bowel syndrome, better known as IBS.

Two events exacerbated my IBS symptoms: taking tests and talking to girls. Both scenarios manifested in a cruel combination of insomnia, sweat, flatulence, and diarrhea. Very attractive.

In a direct breech of doctor-patient confidentiality, Sundar would insert himself into any health-related conversation I had with his father. I was like a human physiology experiment, and, as a future pre-med himself, Sundar wanted to know exactly what made me tick. He was also a nosy *sonofabitch*. We were close friends, and, I had to admit, beyond the discomfort and embarrassment, I found it pretty fucking funny.

Dr. Rajendaran spoke professorially yet paternally. "Ron, clinical depression involves the abnormal transmission of the neurochemical serotonin in the brain. Irritable bowel syndrome involves the abnormal transmission of serotonin in the intestines. So it's as though your intestines are depressed, and IBS-related symptoms are significantly exacerbated by anxiety. New research suggests that the use of antidepressants will help your brain help your gut. We should talk to your parents about possible treatment options. I'm concerned about you, son. What's going on in your life that could be stressing you out so much?"

"You mean other than his blue balls and the fear that he won't get into medical school? " snickered Sundar.

"Stop it, Sundar. I'm serious."

"So am I," he answered.

Sundar embraced the prairie. All of it. School came easily to him, and so did the women. His conquests were legendary: Smart girls, hot girls, athletic girls, farm girls . . . it didn't matter. "I invented tall, dark, and handsome . . . the women love the brown man," he liked to say while looking in the mirror, mock-flexing like Arnold Schwarzenegger, in spite of his slight frame.

"I see the dark, but I don't see the tall or the handsome," I'd answer. Fucking lothario. I was deeply jealous of his freedom from repression; he owned his appearance and everything attached to it. Our parents' odysseys overlapped, but our courage did not. He brimmed with confidence; I withered with apprehension.

"It's all in the attitude, amigo . . . all in the attitude," he said, still flexing, but now adding a fake grimace. I had to laugh. "Dude, you gotta get over this fear of girls or you're gonna shit your pants when it matters most."

"Sundar, please!" pleaded the good doctor.

I knew he was right. I wouldn't medicate myself; *drugs were for crazy people*, I thought. But how would I emulate Sundar's 'attitude?' There were only so many times I could tolerate the sudden rumbling of my abdomen in the middle of an exam. There were only so many times I could stand in a crowded room, talk to an attractive girl, fart, and accuse others of colonic impropriety. I barely escaped social suicide on too many occasions.

"Sundar is not so eloquent, but he makes a good point," said Dr. Rajendran. "You must *trust* yourself."

CHAPTER 6

*"I'm not waiting on a lady,
I'm just waiting on a friend"*

—The Rolling Stones' "Waiting on a Friend,"
from the album *Tattoo You*, released August
24th, 1981. It peaked at number five on US
Billboard's Hot 100 Songs.

Turn up the distortion to ten. Just the distortion," he said.

"I can't. Your parents will freak out," I answered.

Benjie stared at me then rolled his eyes, exasperated. "This isn't *your* house. My parents don't care."

"Whatever you say." I delicately adjusted the distortion knob from seven to ten. I didn't dare touch the volume, gain, treble, middle, or bass knobs. God forbid I even look at the reverb knob. Benjie was a free spirit, but not about his Yamaha Solid State G100-212 amplifier. It complemented his guitar, a mahogany Gibson SG, perfectly.

Benjie felt that his guitar, his amp, and he were somehow inextricably linked, and who was I to disagree? He had started strumming at age twelve, and, unlike most boys his age, he was not satisfied with learning the first few bars of Deep Purple's "Smoke on the Water" or Boston's "More Than a Feeling." Instead, within two months, he was able to flawlessly play complicated riffs from such '70s classics as

The Allman Brothers Band's "Jessica," and REO Speed-wagon's "Ridin' the Storm Out." He especially loved the latter song because it involved the use of a siren. Rock and roll.

BENJIE was Iris's age, and the two of them shared every educational experience together, from Jewish preschool onward. So, like Iris, Benjie had already graduated high school earlier in the year, in the spring of 1982. Unlike my sister, however, he decided not to leave town.

Bob Hirsch, the wealthiest Jewish businessman in town and owner of the decidedly un-kosher fast-food chain, The Salty Hog, had been admiring Benjie's musical skills since he'd heard him play a tribute to Peter Frampton at Tifereth Israel Synagogue's talent show in ninth grade. I swear, "Baby, I Love Your Way" never sounded so good. So in the summer of 1981, Bob called Benjie directly and offered him $1,000 if he and the three other members of his band, The Well Endowed, would play Top 40-ish music at his son Josh's Bar Mitzvah. To a seventeen-year-old Lincolnite in 1981, $250 was a lot of money. Benjie would otherwise jump at the opportunity, but he worried about "compromising the integrity" of the band by playing cover music.

"Dad, should we do it?" Benjie asked his pragmatic father, Sheldon.

"*Benj*, that's the dumbest question you've ever asked. You think there's no virtue in making an honest buck for your talent? You're goddamn right you should do it!"

Keyboardist Nick Ramsey left the band due to "artistic differences," if that concept is possible for a teenager. He was immediately replaced by Peter Syrett. Peter's father, David, pianist for the Lincoln Symphony Orchestra, also understood the value of a dollar. Therefore, to preserve their honor, Benjie, Peter, drummer Johnny Burke and bassist Jeff Sorensen, agreed to have two iterations of the same band: The Well Endowed, which played only original music, and a second group, which played only what was heard on KFMQ, *the* local FM pop station, and KLMS, its AM rival. The boys even gave the cover band a separate name: The Repeats.

Could the vested corduroy suits and powder-blue chiffon dresses of the Bar Mitzvah circuit mesh with the teen-hipster musicians of Lincoln, Nebraska?

Money spoke loudly, both to The Well Endowed and to The Repeats. While The Well Endowed was popular in its own circle, it had never garnered more than about fifty fans at any single setting, including Lincoln's most famous *up-and-comer* venue, Duffy's Tavern. The night of Josh Hirsch's Bar Mitzvah, however, would be different. The Hilton rocked three hundred screaming fans that night. Offers from upcoming Bar and Bat Mitzvahs, including those from Omaha, Des Moines, and Kansas City, started pouring in.

Something else enticed The Repeats that night. To the girls in the crowd, it was as though Rick Springfield, Bob Seger, Foreigner, Hall & Oates, and The Police had all shown up to play for them, especially after the kosher Manischewitz wine was pilfered from the adult tables. The combination of alcohol, music, and hormones was simply too much for Dana Hirsch, Josh's older sister. The band's rendition of Seger's "Against the Wind" made her lose all inhibition. After the gig, she treated Benjie to his first blowjob in the cramped back seat of his 1966 burgundy Mustang. She told him she loved his "majestic" Jew-fro (it was, indeed, magnificent).

The three other Repeats also fared well. Though The Well Endowed had an inkling that performing music live was an aphrodisiac, they had no idea until the Bar Mitzvah that a big crowd would make them feel like the fucking Beatles during the British Invasion. Any concerns they had about "selling out" dissolved with the influx of money and girls.

"Something happens when you have a guitar in your hands, a wad of money in your pocket, and mob of girls in front of you," Benjie would later say. "You have this power over them. It's palpable. I could be the world's ugliest man, but if I can sing or play guitar, it just doesn't matter. Look at Gene Simmons or Keith Richards. Now those are some ugly motherfuckers. Women line up just to have a chance to 'do the deed' with them. And the money's not always a part of the story. I know plenty of guys with no cash who get some serious tail just for playing the part."

The Repeats didn't just conquer the Jewish circuit. Once word of the band's vibe had spread, the boys became the hottest thing at weddings, graduations, proms, home-comings, and fairs alike. While The Well Endowed continued to perform at small venues, like Little Bo's, to perform their original music, the boys knew where their bread was but-tered. Benjie put college on hold to see how things would go. And the beat went on.

BENJIE and I had been best friends since early childhood. We hid nothing from each other. I understood his dream of becom-ing a successful musician, and he understood my obsession, if not dream, with becoming a doctor. He all but felt my fear of failure, my sources of guilt, and my need to please my family. I all but felt the rush *and* the catharsis of his performances.

We shared everything about Judaism: Bar Mitzvahs, Holocaust stories, the miracle of Israel, and having the rabbi kick us out of Hebrew School class together for uncontrollable laughter at the emission of a silent fart. I taught Benjie how to swear in Hebrew, and he taught me how to sing in front of a crowd, but up to this point only facing the congregation, and not the rest of the world.

THE Yamaha hummed slightly as the volume was cranked, but the music that emanated from it was always clear and powerful. "Ronnie, you know that new Modern English song?"

"'I Melt with You'?" I asked. "Of course. Not only do I know all the words, but I can air guitar the shit out of that thing."

"Okay, I want you to listen to this and tell me what you think . . .

Moving forward using all my breath, making love to you was never second best . . ."

Fucking rock star. I understood. Honestly, he made cheesy profound.

"Well, what do you think?" he asked.

"Dude, I think I'm hard for you."

"Exactly. I think I'm hard for myself."

We both laughed, hard.

Then he looked at me, intently. "Now you sing."

"What the fuck are you talking about? I don't do the real thing," I answered.

"What the fuck are *you* talking about? It's just me. Go ahead," he said.

"Okay, okay." I grabbed his real microphone. No mirror, air guitar, or lip sync this time.

I started again from where he left off, tentatively at first, but by the chorus . . .

God that felt good.

CHAPTER 7

"I'm floating
in a beam of light with you"

—A FLOCK OF SEAGULLS' "I RAN (SO FAR AWAY),"
FROM THE BAND'S DEBUT, EPONYMOUS ALBUM, RELEASED
APRIL 30TH, 1982. IT PEAKED AT NUMBER THREE ON US
BILLBOARD'S HOT 100 SONGS.

would do anything to spend time with Amy: make unnecessary locker visits, linger after classes when I knew she would show up the next period, time my arrival at school so that my Duster would coincidentally park next to her Rabbit. For PE, I even took disco dancing instead of wrestling, so that I would have the chance to touch her instead of a sweaty teenage boy. Despite the merciless ridicule I endured for that decision, I would consider it, on balance, unmitigated genius.

By mid-October, 1982, I called Zillie to discuss my dilemma. "Honestly, I don't know what to do," I complained. "I've had a thing for Amy for years. And now I know she likes me, but I don't want to go behind anyone's back . . . this just sucks."

To say Zillie and I saw the world differently is an understatement. "First of all, you didn't need to tell me you were hot for Amy. I think the fact that you drool every time she's around gives it away." Thankfully, she couldn't detect my blush over the phone. "I just don't understand you, Ronnie. This is your life. You're only going to be a horny seventeen year old once. Don't blow it. Remember when I started dating Brian Cook my junior year of high school? Mom and Dad found out, right? And what happened?"

"A lot of yelling, screaming, and crying," I responded.

"No, no. I mean, what happened after that?"

"Nothing, I guess. You kept dating him. They were really pissed until you dumped him."

"Exactly! Life goes on, Ronnie. I love my parents just as much as you do, but fucking *carpe diem*! They put you in Nebraska, so you have to live like a Nebraskan . . . at least until you leave for med school."

"*If* I leave for med school. I haven't gotten in yet."

"Jesus Christ, Ronnie, your pessimism is part of the problem. Everything will be fine. Listen, I gotta go. Big econ test tomorrow. My parting words . . . don't be a coward. Live a little." Click.

HALLOWEEN was on Sunday night that year, so the parties fell the night before. Tommy's parents were out of town, as usual, and the Hanson Tudor Estate, which itself looked like a haunted house, would need little decoration to become the site of this year's festivities.

Jason from *Friday the 13th* and Princess Leia dominated the costumes. In an attempt at originality and Jewish pride, I went as Moses. My vision of him was always that of Charlton Heston. You know, *The Ten Commandments* movie version, in which he instantly aged about fifty years after beholding the burning bush. My cotton-ball beard was excellent, if I may say so myself. To avoid confusion with Santa Claus, I fashioned two pieces of Hebrew-inscribed construction paper to serve as my tablets; an old pool cue made a perfect staff. Naturally, I wore my leather-strapped Gali-brand Israeli sandals. Along with my dad's Star-of-David blue bathrobe, I believe I did my people proud.

Though several girls dressed as black cats, I knew instantly which one was Amy. As I had stared at her butt a thousand times over the years, there was no mistaking her silhouette created by the fog and early Christmas lights outside the house in the makeshift beer garden. It was magical.

Sundar had driven me to the party. Though he didn't share my obsession with Amy, he certainly understood the lust. "If you stare any harder, your balls might burst. Go talk to her, for God's sake," he said, smirking.

Of course he was right. Up to this point, my tactile experiences with girls consisted of an occasional game of Spin the Bottle or Seven Minutes in Heaven, the latter of which generally consisted of about six and a half minutes of awkward conversation, followed by a lackluster hug and peck on the cheek. Saliva was rarely shared.

I approached Amy and her best friend, Christine Evans, my college counselor's daughter. "Ever spent an evening with a prophet?" I asked, putting one arm around each girl in a weak attempt at cool. "I envision you will," I added, carefully raising an eyebrow for dramatic effect.

"Oh God," Chris replied, simultaneously smiling, rolling her eyes, and walking away. Like Amy, Chris was attractive, smart, and intuitive. On her way to the Wapatui bowl (essentially a "kitchen sink" of liquor and fruit juice), she actually winked so that only I could see. *I love you, Chris,* I thought. Naturally, Sundar followed her like a lap dog.

Amy and I stared at each other and grinned. I was so nervous, my heart nearly leaped from my chest. Two aspects of the evening were in my favor: the air was cool enough to keep my palms from sweating, and the music was loud enough to muffle the sound of my rumbling abdomen. I prayed I wouldn't fart.

God answered by quieting my generally untamed colon. He even added the sweet scent of applewood from the nearby bonfire. Nice touch, dear Lord; A Halloween Miracle.

The chilly, windy weather conditions prompted the kids to congregate around the flame, and the free flow of alcohol only enhanced an already celebratory mood. "The heat feels so good," said Christine, whose sexy pioneer woman costume had rendered her barelegged and goosebumped. She stood with palms out, warming herself slowly to the rhythm of outdoor music. Tommy's giant-ass JVC RCM-90 boom box did indeed "boom" and reverberate as it played Bow Wow Wow's "I Want Candy."

"I know a guy who's tough but sweet . . ."

"Hey, that's my theme song, baby!" declared an excited and decidedly drunk Tommy. "Wait! I got one more!" he then added, now laughing. He ran inside the house to his prized cassette collection. As "I Want Candy" ended, he stumbled in his return with a copy of Asia's self-titled album. He changed the tape and cranked track number one:

"I never meant to be so bad to you
One thing I said that I would never do . . ."

Tommy raised an Anchor Steam beer bottle—only the best would do—above his head, and started to chime in. By the time the chorus arrived, the entire crowd was singing along.

Everyone was focused on the campfire, except for Amy and me. She looked directly at me with those enormous, shimmering eyes, and smiled so completely that I nearly melted despite the cold. Before I could kiss her, I tried to channel Benjie's energy, Sundar's bravado, and Zillie's resolve. I simultaneously battled Jewish guilt. On a less syrupy note, I channeled Tom Selleck. Yes, TV's *Magnum PI*. Dude was a stud, and he looked as though he smelled really good. Thank you. All of you. I removed my beard. We kissed. And kissed. And kissed. No bottle spinning. No seven minutes. This felt different. We fit perfectly. The rest of the world disappeared, if only for a moment.

Just then, Mark Gross, dressed as Superman, grabbed a fire log from its non-burning end. The opposite one glowed yellow, giving it the appearance of a giant cigarette . . . or of a giant burning penis.

"Look, my dick's on fire!" he yelled.

Wildly drunk, he laughed, spun, and fell, right into one of the Princess Leias. This surreal sexual collision of intergalactic royalty would have been funny, if not for the fact that the dress of Leia, this time portrayed by Liz Olson, was set afire.

I'M fairly certain Amy and I were the only sober attendees. I ran for the water hose and Amy had Liz roll around in the dirt. By the time I returned, poor Liz was covered in debris. The water extinguished the remaining smoke, but Leia's hair buns had transformed into mud pies.

Judge White, Tommy's next-door neighbor, thundered into the backyard to determine what the commotion was all about.

"Tommy, what the hell is going on?" he roared. "I have half a mind to drag your parents back from Florida just to bail your sorry ass out of jail."

"Please, Judge, I can explain everything," he answered.

"Only a few friends were supposed to stop by, and things just got out of hand. I'm telling you the truth."

Tommy deserved an Oscar for his performance. Judge White and Tommy ended up sampling his honor's best bottle of scotch together. An embarrassed Liz would come inside to shower and dress in Tommy's sister's pajamas. And, of course Tommy and Liz had sex later that night. Order was restored.

Before I departed with Amy, I approached Sundar to explain my situation. Before I could speak, he put his hand up as a gesture to keep me from doing so. He then laughed and said, "Dude, you don't need to explain. Go live the dream."

Amy and I made small talk before reaching her mother's house. Carol Andrews was out for the evening, so we were alone. We made out on the couch. The power of puppy love cannot be underestimated. I felt a series of hormonal surges pulsating inside my body, as adrenaline and testosterone fought valiantly for attention.

After a few minutes, Amy came up for air. "Ron, there's something I want to talk to you about."

"What?" I asked, confused.

"Promise me I can trust you?"

I thought she was joking, so I followed suit. "I'm sorry, I can't promise you anything," I answered, chuckling.

"Don't laugh!" she implored, now visibly upset. "If we're going to be together, I need to trust you."

"What are you *talking* about? Of course you can trust me."

"No, I mean *really* trust you. I've been through too much since my parents split to be able to rely on any male, whether it's my father or a boy."

A single, plump tear formed at the corner of her left eye and began to drip down her face. I wiped it carefully with the index finger of my right hand. "Amy, I would never do anything to hurt you. You know that, don't you?"

"Ron, I used to trust everyone, especially my dad."

I didn't answer; instead I held her close. We sat silently and I closed my eyes as I concentrated on the beat of her heart and the smell of her hair. I actually felt myself falling in love.

Moments later, Carol Andrews pulled into the driveway. Amy and I quickly reassembled ourselves, but the lustful atmosphere was still obvious. "Hi, guys," said Carol in an inquisitive tone. Call me paranoid, but I think the good Dr. Andrews gave me the *mess-with-my-sensitive-daughter-and-I'll-rip-your-balls-off-and-serve-them-to-my-dog-for-breakfast* look.

"Hi, Dr. Andrews, I was just leaving," I answered. I tightened my robe, grabbed my beard, mumbled an awkward good-bye, and left.

I must have looked ridiculous running three miles through the streets of Lincoln in my dad's bathrobe and sandals, especially after I had reattached the beard to avoid recognition. But I needed to clear my head and I thought the pace might help.

Once home, I walked up the front porch; my dad was standing in the doorway, wearing his post-evening-out uniform: undershirt displaying a hint of potbelly, tighty-whiteys, black socks, and red wingtip shoes. I knew from the look on his face that Carol had already called my mom. Given that Carol understood my parents' stance on interfaith dating, and given the pain of abandonment she had shared with Amy, I knew I was fucked.

He rarely raised his voice, so when it happened, I knew I was in for it. "You're playing with fire!" he yelled before stomping off to bed.

Shit.

CHAPTER 8

*"We slip and slide as we fall in love
And I just can't seem to get enough of"*

—DEPECHE MODE'S "JUST CAN'T GET ENOUGH," FROM THE ALBUM *SPEAK AND SPELL*, RELEASED SEPTEMBER 7TH, 1981. IT PEAKED AT NUMBER TWENTY-SIX ON US BILLBOARD'S HOT 100 SONGS.

After that odd, beautiful, and stressful night, Amy and I made every excuse to spend time with each other under the guise of "school activities"—football games, bird watching with Frank Dupuis, French Club meetings (I studied Spanish), etc. Amy and I were inseparable, and it was understood, unofficially or not, by classmates and siblings alike, that we were "together." Our time away from school was another story.

In spite of being overprotective, Carol Andrews was an open-minded Presbyterian. However, like the nuns at Saint Mary's of Mumbai, she was respectful of the religious restrictions of others. My parents and Carol agreed that, as good students with good parents, Amy and I were positive influences on each other, and should therefore be encouraged to study together. Conversely, any relationship outside this circle was strictly forbidden.

Yeah, right.

In a state like Nebraska, with all its elbow room, clandestine meetings were not difficult. From my house, it took only a short drive by car to reach an isolated park, bucolic country road, or cornfield. We had many brief but memorable rendezvous. Though I did not deflower Amy during these encounters, I came breathtakingly close. We made the conscious decision to remain technically abstinent, but we did burn a lot of calories doing everything else along the way. Our bodies matched remarkably well. It's interesting how fast one learns what goes where.

The Duster was far more accommodating than the tiny Rabbit. My father's sister Elaine once told me that Plymouths were like Indian immigrants—they were cheap, reliable, practical, and modest. The engine always started, but the car had no air conditioning and sported only an AM radio. The front row had neither an armrest nor a center console, so a third passenger could be wedged there, up close and personal. Though the seats did not recline, the entire front row could be adjusted in one piece. Therefore, without great effort, the Duster could be transformed into a bachelor pad, Indian-style.

One particular Tuesday, we parked a few miles south of town along US Route 77. It was dusk, but I could still see how stunning Amy looked in what little light remained. She didn't need to try hard either: jeans, Keds, ponytail, and an oversized red sweater with one shoulder unintentionally exposed in a tantalizing, pre-*Flashdance* look. Easy access.

Ignoring the outside temperature, we rolled down the windows. That year the corn was harvested until the end of November, and the scent of the freshly cut stalks was intoxicating. I'm not kidding.

I began to ramble. "I love this smell, but my favorite comes from eucalyptus trees. They remind me of Israel. Did you know they're not indigenous to that part of the world?

They were brought in from Australia by the Jewish National Fund and planted along the Mediterranean Coast to drain the swamps . . ."

"That's great, Ron," she interrupted, smiling. Then she rubbed me, the right way. Literally. I stopped talking and kissed her.

KLMS was playing Grover Washington, Jr.'s "Just the Two of Us."

"I see the crystal raindrops fall, and the beauty of it all . . ."

Yes it was sappy, but it was fantastic. I stopped kissing her, contorted my best faux-serious face, raised an eyebrow, and chimed in. This time she didn't interrupt me; she just smiled and waited for me to finish singing. "Someday you'll appreciate that voice of yours," she said finally.

"I do, I swear. It's like a cool bar trick . . . everyone's surprised in the end."

"I'm not joking!" she insisted.

"Yeah, yeah. It's a gift, I know," I said, laughing.

"Ron, some people are lucky enough to have one special talent, like running a four minute mile . . ."

"Clearly, you're not talking about me . . ."

"Okay, okay, like becoming a doctor . . ."

"Again, not me . . . I haven't even finished high school yet, and becoming a doctor's not even a talent . . . it just means you know how to work hard."

"Working hard *is* a talent . . . anyway, lemme finish, I'm on a roll," she declared, no longer facing me but instead looking out onto the seemingly endless and hypnotizing rows of corn. "You were fortunate enough to have a second talent . . . your voice . . . don't waste it." She leaned back into my arms; I wished I could freeze time.

"Whatever you say, Amy."

She turned to me, shoved me playfully, and kissed me once more before we left.

CHAPTER 9

"It's the terror of knowing
What the world is about"

—QUEEN AND DAVID BOWIE'S "UNDER PRESSURE," FROM THE
ALBUM HOT SPACE, RELEASED OCTOBER 26TH, 1981.
IT PEAKED AT NUMBER TWENTY-NINE ON US BILLBOARD'S
HOT 100 SONGS.

In true Bahar fashion, my parents and I researched how I
could complete medical school in the shortest time possible.
Typically, students would spend four years with under-
graduate studies, and an additional four in medical school.
There were five American medical schools that would allow
me to finish both in six years: The University of Missouri-
Kansas City, The University of Miami, Northeastern Ohio
Medical University, Penn State/Thomas Jefferson, and The
University of Wisconsin-Madison. My list was set. Though
Kansas City was the closest to home, my mother liked the
idea of Wisconsin the best.

"Madison is not too *farrr* away, and it will have a lot of
Jewish girls for you to meet," she said, unabashedly. "I also
heard they have a lot of kids who turn into communists there,
but you can stay away from *them*."

Even if I were taking my mother's words seriously, I was
entirely too focused on Amy to think about other girls.

I received my first application envelope—Wisconsin's—on November 22nd, 1982, ripped it open, and rifled excitedly through its contents. I nodded confidently to myself as I read through words like "submit your transcript" and "letter of recommendation." However, when I reached page six, my heart sank as I digested the following:

"For the applicant: in 500 words or less, describe why you want to become a physician."

Okay, I thought. *I'll just wait for the rest of the applications and complete only the ones that don't make me have to write a fucking essay.* No such luck; envelope after envelope teased me with sections I could have written in my sleep, but then tortured me with an eventual, "Why?" Well, why the hell *not?* Applying to medical school was something I *did*, not something I *explained*. *Why* did I need to describe anything to anyone? My dad was an Indian engineering professor and I was on track to become my class' valedictorian—end of story.

FORGET calculus or physics; English was by far my most difficult subject. Composing any term paper was, for me, nothing less than torture. My world was black and white, concrete and sequential. Now I had to concisely, but eloquently, justify my career goal to some old white men who had already read every variation of *"My Struggle and Inspiration for the American Dream."*

Fuck.

On the other hand, this painful exercise did force me to re-evaluate my aspiration. What aspiration? Wasn't it manifest destiny? I could invent a story about saving the life of my ten-year-old foster-child neighbor by performing CPR and being inspired to become a pediatrician. How about, after stumbling on an article about a parasite called Cryptosporidium in the October 2nd, 1980, issue of the *New England Journal of Medicine*, I made it my life's goal to become a gastroenterologist and eliminate vomiting and diarrhea for all mankind?[1]

Fuck.

I turned to my English teacher, Sandra Donovan, for advice. I couldn't help but marvel at her appearance; she had the face of a plump, bespectacled librarian, the hair of the claymation character Heat Miser, and the body of a Weeble doll, all braced precariously on high heels. Ms. Donovan was intelligent and compassionate, and she had high expectations for herself as well as for her students. She completed her doctoral degree in education while teaching full time. Though she appeared to have a soft spot for me, perhaps because of my own high expectations, she didn't let me off the hook when I sent her a draft of my personal statement.

"Ron, don't take this the wrong way, but this is atrocious," she said, bluntly. "Don't give me a laundry list of your accomplishments. Look at what you wrote here: 'I have achieved a perfect grade point average with rigorous coursework in a competitive environment . . .' Ron, I hate that. I know you have the capacity to complete medical school. I want to know *why* you want to complete medical school."

If you say why *again, I'm going to fucking lose it,* I thought.

She crumpled my paper and threw it in the wastebasket beside her desk. "Come back when you have a story to tell me."

SHE was right. For the next few evenings, I slogged, word by word, to tell a flowery tale of the evolution of my love for medicine. "With my every heartbeat, I feel my love for all things human germinate. I become tachycardic at the mere theorization of my potential erudition of the surgical modus operandi . . ."

Ms. Donovan rolled her eyes and groaned audibly at my "second first draft." "Do me a favor, Ron, please come back after school with your thesaurus," she implored, more than requested. I dutifully complied, still hoping she would agree I was on to something.

"May I have that?" she asked, as I returned to her classroom later that day. She took the book, stared at the faded maroon *Merriam Webster* cover, ran her fingers up and down its spine, almost lovingly, and looked up.

"Don't you *ever* disrespect and abuse the English language like that again," she said, quite seriously. "Ron, you're a smart kid. *In your own words*, tell me about yourself! Tell me what makes you tick—what you dream about, what makes you happy, what makes your blood boil—and then *show* me what you're going to do with these sensations and that brain of yours to make a difference in this world! You may have your thesaurus back when you complete your personal statement." She placed the book on her own shelf, turned around, sat at her desk, and resumed grading papers.

She sensed after a moment that I had not yet left the room. I could only stare at her, speechless. She glared at me and removed her reading glasses, allowing them to dangle by the gold chain around her neck. She paused for a moment before asking, "Will there be anything else?"

I realized at that moment that I had no idea what I was doing.

I drove directly home, stomped into my room, threw my backpack on the floor, and locked the door. I was incredibly tired, but this afternoon I could not sleep. Though I had not cried for years, I felt the tears streaming silently down my face.

After about two hours of self-pity, I scraped myself off the bed, sat at the Smith Corona Coronet Electric, and started typing. Remarkably, I never used the eraser cartridge. The words flowed.

The next morning, I nervously entered Ms. Donovan's room, stood in front of her, and handed her my statement. "Long before I became interested in a career in medicine, I was interested in music. It was my first love . . ."

She finished reading, took the thesaurus off the bookshelf, and handed it to me.

"Nice to finally meet you," she said, now smiling.

CHAPTER 10

"Although it doesn't matter
You and me got plenty of time"

—FLEETWOOD MAC'S "HOLD ME," FROM THE ALBUM
MIRAGE, RELEASED JUNE 18TH, 1982.
IT PEAKED AT NUMBER FOUR ON US BILLBOARD'S HOT
100 SONGS.

loved Thanksgiving. I loved that the entire country could
share it, and no single religion could claim it as its own. I
loved that there was no Thanksgiving ham, but instead a
potentially kosher turkey. I loved that the autumn leaves
were already raked, but that I had no lawn to mow and no
snow to shovel. I loved that cross-country season was over
and I could spend more time after school fondling my girlfriend (I began to take far fewer naps) and eating the dozens
of Peanut M&M's cookies she baked me. I loved that my favorite cover band would be playing two nights later at Kimberly Bennett's wedding.

Kimberly Bennett had recently graduated from UCLA
with a degree in political science. She happened to be brilliant, and was accepted to Georgetown's Law School during
her senior year. She had political aspirations and deferred
matriculation to work for the Reagan administration as an
aide in the office of Attorney General William French Smith.
She was hot shit in Washington, but she was still "Kimmy"

back home, and she was about to marry her high school sweetheart, Scott Campbell.

Scott *was* actually hot shit at home, but in a nice way. You wanted to hate him, but you couldn't. Though he was the best athlete Lincoln Southeast High School had produced in a decade, he was not your stereotypical, towel-slapping, noogie-rubbing caveman. Most of his teammates reveled in merci-lessly ridiculing the Dungeons and Dragons players, stealing their dice and characters during lunch. Scott, instead, bristled at the thought and would browbeat the thieves into returning the items . . . with an apology. His decency was legendary, and his story was passed down from class to class. Scott was the rare hero to the torturers and tortured alike. He was al-most too good to be true. Thinking of him now still makes me uncomfortable. As a high-school football star in his senior year, he turned down scholarship offers from USC, Alabama, and Notre Dame to stay at home and play free safety for the Nebraska Cornhuskers. His illustrious gridiron career peaked during his junior year of college, in which he achieved All-American status. His hope of being drafted by the National Football League was dashed when he blew out his left knee during spring practice prior to his senior year. Few athletes of the early 1980s could recover from such injuries. He therefore made the conscious decision that he would concen-trate on academics and Kimmy.

Scott and Kimmy dated on and off in college; neither could completely shake the other. Kimmy's wholesome beauty, combined with her sharp wit, made her an irresistible novelty, pursued by LA surfers, trust-funders, writers, and actors alike. Scott's rugged good looks and athletic excellence made countless "Lady Huskers" swoon. Nonetheless, Kimmy left her heart in the prairie, and Scott worked tirelessly to pave her way back.

Scott completed a combined degree in business and finance, and was accepted to the MBA program at George Washington University in DC. Kimmy, always the rationalist, initially discouraged the move, worrying that he would eventually regret uprooting himself for her. Scott, always the hopeless romantic, threw caution to the wind, and headed east.

Scott was not a stalker; he was simply in love. After spending his last dime financing an engagement ring at Borsheim's of Omaha (eventually purchased by perhaps the world's third most famous Nebraskan, Warren Buffett), he returned triumphantly to DC to propose. It was early April, 1982, at the height of cherry blossom season, so he sent Kimmy to the blossoming National Mall on a scavenger hunt to search for Nebraska paraphernalia: an ear of corn at Ulysses S. Grant's statue, and a toy Husker football in front of the Air and Space Museum. Kimmy started at the capitol building, but instead of having her head straight west, Scott penned a note directly on the football for her to take a left at the Washington Monument in order to get a view of the Tidal Basin, the Jefferson Memorial, and those cherry trees, in all their glory.

Though it was chilly in DC, Kimmy's heart melted. She knew what was coming, but she assumed that Scott would be waiting for her, on his knee, by the cherry blossoms. Instead, an informed attendant at the basin's paddleboat station instructed her to complete her journey by heading northwest. Kimmy looked up and smiled. Of course: The *Lincoln* Memorial.

The story went that when Scott popped out of his hiding place behind one of the pillars, he took Kimmy by the hand and led her to the South Corridor, where the Gettysburg address is inscribed on the wall. There, wearing his old Nebraska jersey, Scott began to read the address, indeed on one knee, also with ring in hand. He stopped after the first four words of the second paragraph: "*Now we are engaged . . .*"

Though I was not part of the demographic that would typically be enamored by a story that reeked of Harlequin Romance, I became engrossed in this tale that I felt could parallel my own life. Ron met Amy. Yin met yang. A duality: not opposite, but complementary. She engendered the confidence I sought, and I'd like to think I did the same for her. She teased me in a way that minimized my shortcomings. She sometimes praised me, without saying a word, to make me feel incredibly important. She touched me in a way that made my heart (and my dick) nearly explode. We were innocent and naïve, and so despite her cynicism we viewed each other in a dramatically unfettered, fair and passionate light. I loved Amy for understanding me, despite my flaws.

KIMMY and Scott were wed at the Cathedral of the Risen Christ, around the corner from school. After the ceremony, a convoy of cars led them down Sheridan Boulevard on a short drive toward the reception at the Lincoln Country Club, where The Repeats were waiting. Kimmy's father was a successful real estate attorney, and no expense was spared on his only daughter's shindig. Not to be outdone by Josh Hirsch's Bar Mitzvah, the Bennett family transported springtime to late November; the normally drab ballroom was bursting in a sea of red roses imported from Columbia, and a pair of white doves were released to travel south together. In attendance was state royalty, Cornhusker head football coach Tom Osborne (tied with Johnny Carson as the world's *most* famous Nebraskan), fresh off a win the day before against archrival Oklahoma. Always the gentleman, he signed autographs and posed for photos, but made sure the attendees focused on Kimmy and Scott Campbell, and not on him.

Though I was not invited to the wedding, I was made a

roadie for the event so I could live vicariously through Scott and earn a few bucks while looking really fucking cool in the process.

After a grand entrance and a series of embarrassing toasts, the bride and groom finally spoke. Instead of talking politics or speechifying, they simply alternated reading verses from E. E. Cummings' "I Carry Your Heart with Me." It was dignified, beautiful, elegant, and captivating. Adults cried, children smiled, and I daydreamed. Not to be taken too seriously, however, Kimmy and Scott showed their sense of humor and timing, and, in dramatic fashion, had The Repeats interrupt the moved and silent partygoers with the music, appropriately enough, of The Romantics:

"What I like about you, you keep me warm at night . . ."

Benjie was in his element. From my vantage point beside the stage, I scanned the crowd and looked through his eyes. While I knew they weren't listening to his original music, it didn't matter. Beneath tuxedos and evening gowns, it honestly didn't matter. We may as well have been seeing Marley in Kingston or Elvis in Memphis. The response was visceral and universal.

I was mesmerized and couldn't stop fantasizing about my relationship with Amy and my desire to sing on stage. Fulfilling his duties as best friend, Benjie had already noticed *me*, scanned the crowed and looked through *my* eyes. He realized I was jealous even before I did, and though he craved the audience, he wanted to me to understand how it felt to be the frontman.

The first set included, among other hits, seemingly disparate yet perfectly-timed songs like Blondie's "Call Me" and Prince's "1999," and ended in a tongue-in-cheek version of

"Endless Love," with Peter as Lionel Ritchie and Benjie as Diana Ross.

The Repeats truly relished performing, but each member took his job very seriously. Peter said once, in earnest, that he needed to respect playing cover music "like I'm babysitting the original artist's child." I began to understand what he meant.

Between sets, Benjie walked off stage, directly to me. He put one sweaty arm around me, grabbed a Coke with the other, and said, "You're up." I laughed, and he responded with, "I'm serious. I talked to the guys earlier and they okay'd it. I know you know 'Abracadabra.' When set two starts, you're on."

"Dude, we're not in your house. There must be four hundred people out there!"

"Exactly. Go take a leak so you don't piss your pants when you get on stage," he said, grinning. The glow of excitement on his face could only have come from someone who had no agenda except for unconditional, lifelong friendship. I knew I had no choice. I was going to sing.

I took Benjie's advice and ran to the bathroom. Taking a leak would not suffice. Apparently an IBS attack was part of my rite of passage to "the big time."

BENJIE knew exactly what had happened. After suffering about fifteen minutes on the can, I heard a tap on the stall door. He offered a sympathetic laugh and said, "Listen, Mr. Shits, I know you can do this. Just imagine we're in my family room. No biggie. Now wipe your ass, rinse your face, and let's do this."

If I couldn't trust him, I couldn't trust anyone. Once I used up an entire roll of toilet paper tidying up, I walked up to the sink, stared at my sweaty face in the mirror, then at Benjie, and rolled my eyes, resigned. "Jesus Christ, let's get this over with."

I returned to the party and stood nervously beside the stage. Only The Repeats knew what was about to happen, and all four grinned with one collective smile. This was going to be interesting.

Benjie sauntered to the microphone, guitar in hand, face beaming. "Now, from the streets of Lincoln, Nebraska, by way of Jerusalem, my good friend and guest singer, Ron Bahar!" His outstretched hand led all eyes straight to me. This was it.

I walked gingerly on stage. Only a few feet away stood Tommy (of course, he was invited) once again with *totally-fucking-hot* Julia Turner. Tommy stared, with mouth agape. This time even Julia didn't look past me. Benjie whispered in my ear, "Just follow my lead."

The music started. I was overcome by the power of the beat, the sound, and the people. Instead of passing out, however, I felt empowered to sing Steve Miller's words:

"I heat up, I can't cool down, You got me spinning . . ."

Suddenly it felt so ridiculously natural . . . this could be addictive.

CHAPTER 11

*"Everything is possible
in the game of life"*

—SIMPLE MINDS' "PROMISED YOU A MIRACLE," FROM
THE ALBUM *NEW GOLD DREAM*, RELEASED APRIL, 1982.
IT PEAKED AT NUMBER SEVEN ON US BILLBOARD'S HOT
DANCE CLUB PLAY.

Iconic Green Bay Packers' coach, Vince Lombardi, once said, "When you get in the end zone, act like you've been there before." I attempted in vain to remember these words during the week following my "touchdown" at the Campbell wedding. I was simultaneously embarrassed and thrilled.

Leonard Nickerson, my math teacher and dead ringer for Gregory's Peck's Atticus Finch in *To Kill a Mockingbird*, was, like the character, extraordinarily reserved both in his appearance and in his mannerisms. However, when his daughter, my classmate Lendy, told her father what had transpired at the country club, Mr. Nickerson had all of the second period students greet me with applause as I entered his classroom. I blushed. He nodded. I smiled. I believe I represented to him a victory for nerds everywhere.

Tommy loved it. "Dude, some serious poontang is comin' your way. I mean, rock and fuckin' roll!" He raised a lighter high above his head, waved it just once, and paid homage to Lynyrd Skynyrd by yelling "Free Bird!" His predictable comments would not have caused me even to raise an eyebrow, except that Julia and her *only-slightly-less-hot* three-girl entourage—featuring Heather, Dana, and Jody—were standing in tow in the lunch line. I couldn't escape. There was no time for a full IBS tsunami; instead, only a little sweat and a pathetic grin. This interaction occurred despite gaining more than rudimentary experience talking to girls with my incredibly disarming girlfriend. I definitely had a way with the ladies.

Later that day, Amy trapped me in front of my locker. "Tell me, how did it feel?"

"How did *what* feel?"

"You know, being onstage with all those screaming girls going crazy over your voice."

"They weren't going crazy over my voice. Everyone was having fun and I was like a novelty . . . you know, 'Holy shit, Bahar thinks he can sing!'" I lied; I actually *did* think they went crazy.

"Oh, come on, Ron. And tell me you didn't love it."

"Love's a strong word, Amy. I said I was just having fun." I lied again. I had relived "Abracadabra" and Julia's response in my mind continuously since the moment it happened. It all gave me one giant mental hard-on.

"And you're sure it wasn't planned?"

"Positive," I answered, solemnly.

Despite my reassurances, she remained insecure. The next time we were alone, she asked me to sing to her.

I had seen *Fast Times at Ridgemont High* three times since its release in September, and I loved it. We reenacted the dugout scene (minus the dugout and, again, minus the sex) in which Stacy and the stereo salesman—also named Ron—get busy to Jackson Browne's "She Must Be Somebody's Baby."

"Well, just look at that girl with the lights comin' up in her eyes . . ."

Of course, we were actually in the Duster, this time off the road along Nebraska Highway 2, just southeast of Pine Lake. Amy interrupted my singing, not with her voice, but with her hand. She placed it on my mouth. She then smiled awkwardly, with consternation.

"Amy, what's wrong?" I asked, bewildered.

"With you? Nothing."

"So what's the problem?"

"It's just . . ."

"Just what? Is this about the 'screaming girls' again? I mean, what the fuck? Just because . . ."

"Ron, please don't swear. You know I don't like that." I did know. It was part of what made her impossibly good.

"I'm sorry. Really. Talk to me." I feared that something had gone terribly wrong.

"I'm worried. About us."

"What? Why?" I asked, incredulously.

"Just hear me out," she said. "Ron, this is so much fun, and it feels so good, but what happens tomorrow?"

"Another ride in The *'Good Times Machine!'*" I responded only half-jokingly.

"Ron, stop, I'm talking about us, the future. How is this going to work? You're Jewish. I'm Protestant. Your parents don't approve and my mom won't intervene. You're leaving next year, and I'm staying in Lincoln. Do you want me to go on?"

I was caught utterly off guard. Rather than babble in response, I remained silent.

Amy eventually tired of waiting and continued, "There's one more thing."

"What?"

"Well . . . I told my dad about . . . us . . . this."

"Amy, *why?* What were you *thinking?* My parents are gonna kill me!"

"No, they won't. Before I told my dad, I swore him to secrecy, even from my mom. He's a lot of things, but he's not a narc. He won't say a word."

"I still don't get why you told him."

"Maybe . . . maybe I wanted him to understand that he was no longer the most important man in my life."

I was astonished, but this time I was not speechless. "Amy, I'm flattered . . . and I get it . . . and you're the most important person in *my* life too . . . but if you're so worried about us, why did you go out of your way to tell your dad now?"

"Because I really want it to work . . . I love you, Ron."

"I love you, too," I answered. Neither of us had ever used those words before, but they had been implicit for a while.

She examined my face inquisitively with her probing eyes as my heart flipped. She then placed her head on my shoulder, and we drove back to the Rabbit, which was still parked at school.

BEFORE she opened her car door, I rolled down my window. "Hey, Amy," I said.

"Yes?"

"I really do love you."

"I know you do." She smiled hopefully, and we drove off in opposite directions.

CHAPTER 12

*"Don't you know by now
no one gives you anything"*

—STEVE WINWOOD'S "WHILE YOU SEE A CHANCE," FROM
THE ALBUM *ARC OF A DIVER*, RELEASED DECEMBER, 1980.
IT PEAKED AT NUMBER SEVEN ON US BILLBOARD'S HOT
100 SONGS.

A my gave me a respite; we didn't have another "relationship discussion" for several weeks. We studied and we played. I couldn't help falling more deeply in love.

In the meantime, thanks to Ms. Donovan's advice, my applications were well received. I earned four of five medical school interviews; only Northeastern Ohio apparently had no interest in singing doctors. For the interview suit, my mother and I shopped at Brandeis Department Store alone; including my father might have resulted in a plea for the return of polyester. We agreed on a conservative wool, navy blue, double-breasted number, in part because it was marked thirty percent off during the pre-Christmas sale, and in part because I refused the same brown corduroy design she loved in my Bar Mitzvah suit. However, Mom did insist on making the alterations herself. She had learned to sew by hand as a child, well before my dad surprised her with an electric Singer sewing machine after they moved to America. I must admit, she was good with the needle.

Mr. Evans had coached me for interviews by patiently guiding me through every iteration of Ms. Donovan's "tell me about yourself" question. I happily described my background (I discovered interviewers were, without exception, fascinated by the notion of an Israeli kid in the prairie), and I was eager to discuss my mentor, Dr. Rajendran, and my career goal of becoming a pediatric gastroenterologist.

However, it was not until my last interview, at the University of Wisconsin, when, surprisingly, I entered my comfort zone *during* an interview. There, my interviewer, Jorge Ramos, was a forty-something Cuban American professor of pediatric cardiology. Unlike most of the doctors I had seen that day, Dr. Ramos didn't wear a jacket. He was handsome, tall and slender, and though he had a distinguished appearance, complete with silver sideburns to garnish a jet-black quiff, his friendly smile exuded warmth.

"Ron, I just read your application and I see you like music . . . do you know about the four chambers of the human heart?" he asked.

"Yes, I do," I answered, amazed that, thanks to Mr. Dupuis, I actually understood what the hell he was talking about.

"Okay, then, come with me."

We took a walk from his office to the pediatric ward at The University of Wisconsin Hospital, situated at the west end of a beautiful lakeside campus that was frozen solid but still sparkling with a dusting of snow from the night before. Dr. Ramos stepped into a patient's room and spoke to a nurse and two sets of parents. Two children shared the room. He poked his head out the door and directed me into the room. Once inside, I saw that one boy, Michael, was dressed in street clothes, and had a small suitcase by his side. Though he moved gingerly, he had an enormous smile on his face, and it was obvious that he was about to be discharged from the hospital. The other boy, about the same age, was sitting in his bed, wearing a hospital gown. Dr. Ramos washed his hands, had me do the same, and then approached the first boy.

"Michael, I'm going to unbutton your shirt so I can have this nice young man listen to your heart." Michael was amazingly understanding and cooperative. His chest revealed a generous bandage over the sternum. Dr. Ramos placed the chest piece on Michael, and then had me take a listen with the earpieces.

"What do you hear?" he asked.

I closed my eyes and listened for about fifteen seconds. I looked up. "It sounds like: *blah blub, blah blub, blah blub, blah blub.*"

"Okay," he answered. He turned his head to the other side of the room. "Now let's do the same with young Anthony over here." Anthony was happy to oblige, and it then occurred to me that both boys had been through this exercise many times. They felt no reason to be afraid of the doctor without a jacket.

Anthony's chest looked unremarkable, but sounded different. I took another listen. "Okay, now I hear: *shhhh blub, shhhh blub, shhhh blub, shhhh blub.*"

Dr. Ramos smiled. We thanked the boys and their parents for their time, and walked back to his office. Interesting, but what was that all about?

He waited until we sat down before he spoke. "Last week, both boys' hearts looked about the same. Both had something called a ventricular septal defect, or VSD. It means there's a hole between the two lower chambers of the heart. It's not supposed to be there. The '*blah blub*' you heard in Michael represents the normal closure of the four heart valves, and the '*shhhh*' you heard in Anthony represents the noise made when blood travels through the hole between those two chambers. But don't worry, Anthony's heart will sound just like Michael's this time tomorrow."

Then Dr. Ramos reached in a drawer and retrieved . . . a pair of maracas. "Ron, do they have these in Nebraska? Because I think I introduced them to the entire Midwestern United States," he joked. He then handed me one. "Swirl it around just once," he suggested, now smiling.

I followed his instruction: "*Shhhh.*"

"Sound familiar?" he asked.

Now *I* was smiling.

"That's *my* music," he continued. "I use the maracas with my medical students and interns to help teach them about heart sounds. Once they hear it, they never forget. I thought of it once while listening to some salsa. This way I always have a piece of home with me wherever I go."

We talked about his family's emigration from Cuba to Florida, along with the Latin Sound and how it was the foundation for much of the modern music I loved. He had been obsessed with salsa star Celia Cruz since he was a teenager, and he played for me her most recent album, which she recorded with Willie Colón the year before. It was, indeed, sublime. Every immigrant has a story, but this one felt close to my heart.

A few weeks later, in early January, I came home after a brief visit with Amy. We had mixed things up a little and took the Rabbit for a bounce to Holmes Lake. Maneuvering around that subcompact was difficult, to say the least, and our best-laid plans went awry as our interlude was abbreviated when I racked myself on the stick shift. This time she had no problem when I squealed, "Fuck!" at the top of my lungs.

When I arrived home, still grimacing, my parents were waiting for me at the door. Both were smiling.

"Where *werrre* you?" my mother inquired forcefully, with arms flailing in a quintessentially Israeli expression.

"It's only five! I'm hardly ever home this early!" I answered, utterly confused.

"Look!" my father pleaded. He was pointing to the kitchen table, where a flat, square package, padded and wrapped in butcher paper, stared back at me. It had a nameless return address from Madison, Wisconsin, but not from the University.

"Well, *arrren't* you going to open it?" implored my mother.

I was perplexed. I had heard through the grapevine that acceptance letters from Wisconsin came in the form of a single page, sealed in an envelope with the familiar Bucky Badger mascot logo.

My mother could no longer contain herself:

Hebrew:	"אוי אלוהים! רוני, פתח את המעטפה!"
Transliteration:	"Oy eloheem! Ronnie, p'tach et hama'atafah!"
Literal Translation:	"Oh God! Ronnie, open the envelope!"
Intended Translation:	"Open the fucking envelope!"

I grabbed the package. I could barely hold on to it because my hands were shaking; my heart pounded relentlessly. Finally, I held my breath and opened it. Inside was a record album cover: Celia Cruz' latest, *Celia & Willie*. The seal was already broken, and I looked inside. The album was there, but so was a smaller envelope, with the not-so-menacing red, white, and black rodent Bucky staring back at me from beneath the return address.

The letter inside read: "*Dear Mr. Bahar, On behalf of the University of Wisconsin School of Medicine and Public Health, we are pleased to inform you . . .*"

At the bottom of the typed portion was a handwritten note:

Dear Ron,

Congratulations. This music should help you keep your rhythm. Hope to see you this fall.

Sincerely,
Jorge Ramos

After I finished reading the letter, I looked over at my parents, who stood in an awkward embrace, as though they didn't quite know what to do with each other. My mother was speechless, but she couldn't hide her tears. My father finally broke the silence by kissing me on the cheek and saying, "My son, the doctor."

I put the album on the turntable. The doctor without a jacket was introducing me to a new genre of incredible music and a new way of hearing it. We listened to all ten tracks, and my parents danced to the sounds with a modified Israeli folkdance step (it was all they knew). Their rare, uninhibited display of sheer joy captivated me. I eventually just sat on the couch and laughed.

It was ridiculously cold outside. However, a small piece of my mother's iceberg of resentment for spending her own adult life away from home had just melted.

THE next day, I received (a) a congratulatory dozen peanut M&M's cookies from Amy, (b) a congratulatory session with Amy in the Duster, and, once I arrived home for the evening, (c) a congratulatory acceptance letter from another medical school—The University of Missouri-Kansas City—a mere three hours by car from my home and from my girlfriend.

Despite my profound desire to remain physically close to Amy, who planned to attend college in Lincoln, I agonized over my choice. I had bonded with Dr. Ramos, with little Anthony, and with the frigid, but welcoming school by the lake. I also feared that Amy would be infuriated knowing that I would even consider moving more than twice the distance away from her in Wisconsin. I contemplated not telling her about the second letter, but Amy had a way of finding things out.

I asked Mr. Dupuis for advice. "Son, there's no question you need to go to Wisconsin. Like a rose, love needs time to germinate. If the soil, the precipitation, the temperature, and the sunlight all cooperate, there is little to stop its growth." Flowery yes, but really fucking unhelpful.

I called Iris for her opinion. "Create an algorithm that takes into account all possibilities, like bad weather, competing boys, fatigue, weekend homework, furious parents, et cetera. Then determine the sequence of events that would occur if any one of these circumstances were to occur. Finally, express it diagrammatically and decide which course yields the strongest result. Simple!" No, not so simple.

After three days, I finally built the courage to directly confront Amy . . . sort of. Instead of showing her the second letter after school, I read it to her over the phone, and I was unable to disguise my ambivalence.

"That's great, Ron," she said, hardly convincingly.

"So what do you think I should do?"

"I think you should do whatever you think is right." Fuck.

"But—"

"But *what?* You can't just write a list of pros and cons over this one, Ron. You have to do what your heart tells you to do." Ouch. She was right, chickenshit.

"But—"

"Ron, stop trying to get me to give you an answer. You're a big boy; you decide."

"Okay, you're right . . . I'm going to Wisconsin." Silence. More silence. Fuck. Fuck! "Amy?"

"What? What do you want me to say? That I'm thrilled you'll be farther away?"

"No, of course not. It's just that, well, Wisconsin just *feels* right. It has a great pediatrics program, and the hospital was amazing, and Dr. Ramos . . ."

"Ron?"

"Yes?"

"I've been thinking about it a lot—about the singing, about medicine, about Halloween—remember when you told me I could trust you?"

"Yes."

"Well, this isn't easy for me, but I'm *trying* to trust you right now. As I said, just do what your heart tells you to do."

CHAPTER 13

*"It feels so right, so warm and true,
I need to know if you feel it too"*

—FOREIGNER'S "WAITING FOR A GIRL LIKE YOU," FROM
THE ALBUM *4*, RELEASED SEPTEMBER, 1981.
IT PEAKED AT NUMBER TWO ON US BILLBOARD'S HOT
100 SONGS AND WAS BILLBOARD'S NUMBER EIGHTEEN HIT OF
1982.

I was a chameleon of sorts; though I was not at the pinnacle of any one social group, I was generally accepted in just about every crowd at school. My pedestrian (almost literally) running skills helped me garner credentials among jocks (deservedly so, as I still contend that it's the most difficult sport of all time). Iris's fearless entrance into the computer lab at a time when women almost never dared to travel through its threshold, along with her subsequent triumph in the engineering school at college, provided me with near celebrity status among the math geeks. My ability to talk Cheech and Chong movies with stoners allowed me to turn down countless bong hits at parties. Perhaps my general lack of comfort in my own skin forced me to empathize and somehow meld with those who felt "different."

As a result of these "qualifications," I decided, on a whim and a pipe dream, to run for senior class present. I assumed that my opponent, Lucy Davis, scoffed when she discovered she would *not* run unopposed. Lucy, who may have inspired both the terms "mean girl" and "ice princess," had an almost inexplicably strong following among the *big-platinum-blonde-acid-wash-jean* lemmings of Southeast High School. She was, indeed, reasonably intelligent and attractive—she did model part time for the Miller and Paine Department Store catalogue—but her scorched earth attitude toward life left teenage roadkill in its path on a routine basis.

I felt a tap on my shoulder and turned around. "Karma!" It was Mike Nemeth, benevolent math genius.

"Huh?"

"Lucy. She fuckin' laughed at me when I asked her out once." I remained confused, so he continued, frenetically.

"Am I not a nice person? Did I not tutor the shit out of the entire physics class to prep them for the AP exam?"

"Yeah, I'll never forget you for that, but dude, you lost me . . . what are you talking about?"

"I bathe regularly and I don't pick my nose . . . I mean, I'd go out with me if I were . . ."

"Jesus, Mike, just get to the point!"

"She stuffed the ballot box and she got caught! You win!" Then he smiled. "Karma!" He turned and walked away.

Lucy's concession call to me consisted of, "I'm not sure how this happened, but congratulations, I guess." Karma.

ANNE Read, our class treasurer, was independent-minded and a non-traditionalist, to say the least. She was a star mid-fielder in our regional soccer club, and broke gender barriers by trying out for the football team as a placekicker. Though she easily out-booted her competition, she was ultimately disqualified by the league rules committee for possession of a vagina.

Instead of moping, Anne channeled her efforts as editor of Lincoln Southeast's monthly publication, *The Clarion*. She was not only an outstanding athlete, but she was also a great student; she intended to embark on a career as a writer and would become a journalism major at Northwestern University beginning the next fall.

Not unexpectedly, Anne advocated for a Sadie Hawkins Dance, where the girls ask the boys out to the event. She was not intimidating to either gender. She happened to be cute, but her physical attributes were irrelevant. Boys always love a tomboy, especially a smart one, and they would certainly line up to date her; girls universally admired her as their fearless, uninhibited representative of the '80s woman, Nebraska style.

I was the lone male class officer, so Anne directed her thoughts to me. "Let me turn the tables on you, Ron," she said. "It must be stressful to always be the one to get up the nerve to do the asking." She had no idea how truer words were never spoken. "Fuck convention. We can also see how much guys will put out for a free meal. Bottom line is, it'll be fun." Anne was funny if not brutally honest. When the dance proposal came to a vote, Anne, Vice President Jill Fager, Secretary Chris Evans, and I gave it unanimous approval.

Ironically, my parents wouldn't allow me to accept an offer to the dance, so Amy and I went stag. Embarrassing.

Naturally, my thoughts went to the event's music. Of course I planned on hiring The Repeats, and I dreamt of a "repeat" on-stage display of my own. However, when my parents found out about my secular public performance, they were proud yet adamantly opposed. My dad was never known for his tact. "Ronnie, it's a slippery slope. I don't want you to get carried away thinking you're going to make a career out of this. God granted you a beautiful voice, but you were put on this Earth to be a doctor, not to swing your hips like Elvis and sing that garbage on stage. Don't let this be a distraction. Your acceptance to medical school is conditional, and it's only February. You have to do well during your last semester of high school, and you can't risk your future by wasting your time with this band bullshit."

So I did what any teenage American boy in my position would do: I went behind his back.

FOR the first time, I helped make the set list. My singing would now be premeditated, and I was slated to finish the first set. The songs were cherry-picked as a retrospective from *Billboard's* Top 100 Hits of 1982, rising from less popular to more popular:

Set One:

98. Loverboy: **"Working for the Weekend"**
82. Kool & the Gang: **"Get Down on it"**
79. The Police: **"Every Little Thing She Does Is Magic"**
65. America: **"You Can Do Magic"**
53. 38 Special: **"Caught Up in You"**
48. Rod Stewart: **"Young Turks"**
43. Stevie Wonder: **"That Girl"**
33. Earth, Wind & Fire: **"Let's Groove"**

Set Two:

30. Men at Work: **"Who Can It Be Now?"**
29. The Motels: **"Only The Lonely"**
24. Dazz Band: **"Let It Whip"**
16. Tommy Tutone: **"867-5309/Jenny"**

11. Soft Cell: **"Tainted Love"**
5. The J. Geils Band: **"Centerfold"**
3. Joan Jett and the Blackhearts: **"I Love Rock 'n Roll"**
2. Survivor: **"Eye of the Tiger"**

The boys contemplated a grand finale, featuring the number one song of the year, Olivia Newton-John's "Physical." Though Benjie and Peter were willing to entertain the notion, primarily out of jest, Jeff and Johnny conscientiously objected, citing "philosophical differences" with Ms. Newton-John; they considered its potential performance nothing less than cruel and unusual punishment. So to avoid a mutiny, the idea was scrapped.

Benjie was as self-confident as ever, with good reason; the band was busy every weekend, garnering both larger crowds and larger paychecks. He had no concerns about any stolen thunder, and, in fact, encouraged my singing the last two songs of the first set rather than just the one.

Given my inherent lack of funk, duplicating Stevie Wonder and Earth, Wind & Fire would be no small feat. I respectfully channeled Stevie by rehearsing with his early-day signature black Wayfarer sunglasses and my interview suit. Though the quality of my voice was not in question, my robotic stage presence clearly needed some work. With a great deal of practice, including one embarrassing moment when Mark Gross caught me gyrating in front of a school bathroom mirror, I began to look a little more Motown and a little less C3PO.

I had a contingency plan in case my parents discovered my subversive activities. I would simply tell them my reluctant-hero version of the story . . . about how Benjie was overloaded with learning so many new lyrics, how he didn't want to strain his vocal cords too much, how I was doing him a favor, how singing wasn't interfering with my schoolwork, how I was going to tell them but simply forgot, how . . .

I practiced with the band under the guise of studying AP chemistry. After all, music *was* chemical, wasn't it? Call me sentimental, but just as Amy, my eyes, and my boner were all interconnected, even the most banal, clichéd songs of my era could give me the chills under the right circumstances.

THANKFULLY, I was not in panic mode the night of the dance, but I *was* a bit nervous. I overdid it with my matching Old Spice deodorant and cologne and was forced to lather, rinse, and repeat to dilute my aura. I desperately wanted to strike that delicate balance between, "aw shucks" and, "I'm with the band."

The event took place at the school gym, and, despite the room's shitty acoustics, the band rocked as usual. Though the majority of the $10 cover charge went to The Repeats, the class officers made the most of what was left, with a re-spectable (spiked) punch bowl, streamers, balloons, and a poster of the original Sadie Hawkins cartoon character.

Amy was effortlessly beautiful, and I was still in awe every time our eyes met. *How on Earth did I ever get this girl to give me the time of day?*

We didn't really dance; we just sort of caressed each other and swayed. Despite her recent trepidation, Amy was still quite comfortable with my hands placed squarely on her butt. Though teachers served as chaperones, they understood the futility of attempting to separate second-semester seniors.

"Number seventy-nine! The Police," yelled Benjie.

"Though I've tried before to tell her of the feelings I have for her in my heart . . ."

The combination of Amy, the music, and the chemistry were almost too much. Boner. Chills. Boner-chills. Thank you, Sting.

I know. Pathetic.

At some point I noticed Anne and her date, none other than Sundar, in a less-familiar but equally amorous embrace. *Yes, Anne,* I thought, *he* will *put out.* Another victory for both.

As number forty-eight, "Young Turks," ended, Amy and I unglued ourselves from each other. I really didn't care who saw us or heard us. "I love you," I said.

"I love you, too."

I headed for the stage, ecstatic. I was never happier, smarter, or cooler.

Benjie roared, "Back for only his second performance outside Tifereth Israel Synagogue, Lincoln Southeast's own Ron Bahar, with number forty-three, Stevie Wonder's 'That Girl!'"

I ran up the stairs, took my place at the microphone, and looked out at the crowd. I saw before me a menagerie of blurred faces, moving lips, and wide eyes. I couldn't make out the identity of any of them, not even Amy. I could hear a wave of cheering, but in a muffled, unintelligible, Charlie-Brown's-teacher sort of way. It was surreal.

"That I love her, that I want her, that my mind, soul, and body need her . . ."

Unbelievable. Something about having only my peers as my audience made the experience even sweeter than the wedding performance. My insecurity temporarily dissolved. It was self-indulgent, but God did it feel great.

The sunglasses and suit were a hit, and thank God for

the Old Spice. I had barely started, but I sweat profusely. So, in summoning all of my newly acquired rock-star powers, I ripped off my jacket and tossed it into the crowd. Girls congregated immediately in front of the stage, and one of them grabbed it and put it on. As they were so close, I now recognized their faces. *Oh, shit.*

Lucy Davis was wearing my jacket, and, admittedly, she looked hot. She had a great rack, and, superficiality aside, the lapel unintentionally (or intentionally) accentuated her cleavage, already exposed in a low-cut, spaghetti-strap dress. My eyes were now functioning perfectly well, and I did a double take. Lucy noticed me staring at her, and she wasted no time with additional, superfluous taunting. Before I knew what was happening, she had jumped onstage and grabbed my ass with the same familiarity that I had shown Amy's.

The audience screamed with approval. I braced myself, and, remembering The Repeats' mantra, "ride the wave," let Lucy dry hump me in front of hundreds of my schoolmates while I finished "That Girl." I gave my best "aw shucks" smile, and held on for dear life.

As the song concluded, Lucy planted a big, fat, drunk kiss directly on my lips before sauntering off the stage. I had to laugh. So did everyone else in the room, except for one person. Out of the corner of my eye I saw Amy. If looks could kill, Lucy and I would have been victims of a double murder. But would it have been justifiable homicide? I was embarrassed, but I was only human.

Thankfully, Benjie interrupted my train of thought. "Number thirty-three, Earth, Wind & Fire's 'Let's Groove!'" I regained my composure as The Repeats led with a killer falsetto and the music simply took over. I turned directly to Amy, and followed suit:

"Gonna tell you what you can do with my love, Alright . . ."

We ended the set to a jubilant audience. Though Amy would not uncross her arms, she did manage a grin. Thinking I had snatched victory from the jaws of defeat, I jumped off the stage to talk to her. Before I was able to reach her, however, I was engulfed by Heather, Dana, and Jody.

"Ron, that was amazing," squealed Heather.

"A-mazing," chimed in Dana and Jody.

Not to be outdone, Lucy approached. Employing her best striptease, she slowly removed my jacket, which was now bathed with the scent of her Charlie perfume. Her breath was equally fragrant from alcohol.

"A-mazing," I heard for the fourth time, now from Lucy. She was still lucid enough to realize what she was doing when she rubbed her enticing boobs on my chest. She then slowly slid the jacket over my shoulders. "You're not who I thought you were," she whispered, all too audibly. She planted one last, painfully long kiss on my lips, turned, and stumbled to the punchbowl.

Amy witnessed everything. "You know what? She's absolutely right," she stated before turning and walking out. Karma?

CHAPTER 14

*"Please let me explain
I never meant to cause you sorrow or pain"*

—JOHN LENNON'S "WOMAN," FROM THE ALBUM *DOUBLE
FANTASY*, RELEASED JANUARY 12TH, 1981.
IT PEAKED AT NUMBER TWO ON US BILLBOARD'S HOT
100 SONGS.

The magnitude of Amy's jealousy was unchartered territory for me. So much for trusting me. By the time I realized what had happened, she was gone, and I was hopelessly short of ideas to successfully make amends with her.

Set two of the Sadie Hawkins Dance was nothing short of spectacular. The pheromonal effect of the frontman paid off again, as after the show Benjie would receive yet another blow job, this time from none other than Lucy.

So my best friend and confidant was unavailable to offer suggestions on how to remedy the situation, and I knew that the sex-crazed duet of Tommy and Sundar were unlikely to provide cogent advice on how best to defuse a potentially explosive situation with a girl. Though I was clearly not cheating, my female friends would sympathize with Amy, and a chat with my parents was obviously not an option.

I thought about calling my sisters, but I remembered

they were out for the night so I planned to sleep on it. By the time I reached home, my parents had already gone to bed. However, my grandmother Hannah, who was visiting from her adoptive home of Toronto, was still awake. For as long as I can remember, she was a night owl, and this evening was no exception. I found her sitting in the kitchen drinking tea, so I approached her to give her a kiss goodnight.

"Hey, Granny," I said sullenly. "What are you doing up so late?"

Granny sensed that something was amiss. "Sit down, *dahling*," she said. I didn't want to have this conversation, but I was not in a position to say no to her. No one was.

She put her strangely youthful hand in mine. "Ronnie, what's wrong?"

"I don't know . . . I just had a misunderstanding with . . . a friend."

"A 'friend'?" What kind of friend?"

How the hell was I going to answer this question? "You know. A *good* friend," I said finally.

My grandmother considered my answer carefully before responding. "Ronnie, life is short. Trust me, I know. You don't have time to waste *ahguing* with this girl." She paused. We smiled. "Go to my room and get me my purse. I want to show you something."

I returned a moment later, purse in hand. She took it from me and reached inside to grab a booklet. "This is a collection of poems I have written over the years," she said, displaying the simple ruby red paperback to me. "I started writing after my second husband, your grandfather, died." She looked up to the sky. "Rest his soul," she added. "Writing has helped me cope with some difficult times. Open the book and go to page ten. I want you to read it out loud."

"The Blessing of Friendship"

You argue
You fight
You explode
Then you completely clear the wreckage.
Now you start filling in with new materials:
Calmness
Guilt feeling
Regrets
And last of all forgiveness.
Then you cement all this with
Understanding.
Now you have laid a stronger foundation
With your companion
Relation or friend for which you
Should be grateful to your maker.

"Now go to the *laaast* page. Thirty-three."

"Forgiveness"

Oh, to forgive!
It is the tonic for all!
It is the cure for malice,
The cure for hatred.
It puts out the fire that might
Impair one for life.
Wine of forgiveness that rejuvenated
Every fiber of mine,
To life, to life, to life again.

"Ronnie, go to your friend. Life is precious, and so is time. God gave you both, and it's a sin to waste either. I don't care who's at fault. Is she worth the effort?"

"Absolutely," I said, grinning again.

"Then go to her and apologize."

"But, Granny . . ."

"No 'buts!' Go."

No one says "no" to Granny.

How on Earth did she understand what was going on? It would later occur to me that if one lives and suffers long enough, perspective and insight become second nature . . . especially with the right attitude. Melodramatic? Maybe. Awesome? Definitely.

I drove back to Amy's house. The sky was clear, but by then it was midnight and a bone-chilling 2 degrees Fahrenheit outside. The Duster's defroster was barely strong enough to form two tiny peepholes on the windshield, so I traveled mostly by feel and adrenaline over the icy roads. I parked one block away from Amy's house to avoid raising Carol Andrews' suspicion.

Thankfully, Amy and Carol lived in a ranch-style house, so I wouldn't have to perform the traditional *toss-the-rock-on-the-window-to-get-the-attention-of-the-girl-at-the-second-floor-bedroom*. However, I did have to worry about Diego, Amy's German Shepherd. Diego slept in Dr. Andrews' bedroom, so I would have to employ all of my marginal ninja skills to pull off a moonlit apology. I scampered across ice and reached Amy's window to find the shades halfway drawn. I could still see her through the frost of the window, and, as usual, she wore "pajamas" (grey sweats and an oversized Nebraska Cornhuskers T-shirt) while reading before going to bed. In her hands was a copy of Danielle Steel's appropriately titled *Once in A Lifetime*.

While I was concerned about (a) disappointing Granny, (b) scaring the shit out of Amy, and (c) getting my balls munched by Diego, Defender of Single Moms, my overwhelming desire to make things right with my girlfriend willed me to stay.

I tapped lightly on the window. Amy jumped. "It's me," I said in a hushed tone.

Thankfully she heard me and quickly, but reluctantly, approached the window. I was certain she was more anxious to keep Diego from barking than she was excited to see me. She stretched her shirttail and used it to defrost a small circle on the window. "What are you doing here?" she asked, exasperated.

"I need to tell you about my grandmother." I answered.

"Your grandmother? Are you drunk?"

"No, you know I don't drink . . . okay, I know the grandmother thing sounded weird, but just hear me out. Open the window, please." She turned the lock and attempted to raise the window . . . without success. The frame was frozen shut. I tried as well, in vain. Was this transparent barrier a cruel joke or just a bad metaphor? I must have looked pitiful.

Undeterred, I continued. "Amy, I'm sorry about what happened tonight . . . but I'm not like your dad and I never will be. Just try and be happy for me and my performance tonight, and stop worrying about whether or not you can trust me. All I know is that I love you, and I'll do anything to make it up to you."

"Ron, there's nothing to make up. You don't understand. You need to decide what you want: Do you want to be a doctor, or do you want to be a singer? Do you want to be with me, or do you want to play the field? I really don't know what you're thinking. Before we started dating, I told you I'd be around when you're ready for me. Well, I'm still not convinced that you are."

"Listen . . . I love medicine and I *think* I want to be a doctor. I love music and I *think* I might want to sing. But I *know* I love you. Period. Please give me another chance."

"First, I need you to understand something . . . I will never, ever let anyone get away with treating me badly again." She began to cry. *Oh God, please don't,* I thought.

Just then, Diego let out a howl. Our eyes simultaneously widened. I put my hand on the window and mouthed the words "I love you." Silence. I needed a response! Another howl.

She matched her hand with mine on the opposite side of the window. "I love you too," she echoed, voiceless and teary-eyed. Bewildered but relieved, I took off, forgetting about the slippery surface below. When I reached the sidewalk, I lost my balance, went airborne, and landed directly on my tailbone. Too scared to moan, I gathered myself and, like a tightrope walker on speed, scurried to the Duster.

I could still hear Diego barking in the distance. Mercifully, the cold ignition turned on only the second attempt, and I skidded toward home. My ass was throbbing, and my heart was pounding; I couldn't decide whether to laugh or to cry.

CHAPTER 15

"Woman you want me give me a sign
And catch my breathing even closer behind"

—DURAN DURAN'S "HUNGRY LIKE THE WOLF," FROM THE
ALBUM *RIO*, RELEASED JUNE 7TH, 1982.
IT PEAKED AT NUMBER THREE ON US BILLBOARD'S HOT
100 SONGS.

The following week, Amy left my professional aspirations alone, but she continued to question my commitment to our relationship. We spent no time together in either the Duster or the Rabbit. Instead, we reverted to a classic junior high school tactic: passing notes. There were no hearts circumscribing the name "AMY BAHAR," nor were there any "AMY + RON = LOVE" equations on perfumed paper. There was, however, unbridled teenage passion:

Amy, I love you so much, it hurts.

Do you?

Yes, don't you know by now?

Maybe. But you need to let me know where you stand.

Where I stand? Are you kidding? We've been through this a million times. I love you and only you.

You know what I mean.

No, I actually don't.

I'm not a plaything. You can't just have me when it suits you. I have feelings. I'm not asking for a long-term commitment. I'm asking for your undivided attention.

Why are you punishing me? What I did was wrong, but how many times can I say I'm sorry. AND WHAT I DID WASN'T THAT BAD!!!

I'm going to ignore the "wasn't that bad" part. I know you're sorry. I believe that. I want to know if you're really into us. Meaning you and me. Together.

Amy, you have no idea how . . .

I stopped writing. I sensed something, someone, in my space. I looked up.

"Ron, I realize it's second semester of your senior year, and that you know just about everything, but I'm sure you'll find that if you actually listen to this lesson on the mating call of the sea lion, you'll find it fascinating . . . and pertinent," said Mr. Dupuis, with a wink and a sarcastic grin. A brief chorus of giggles filled the room, then silence.

I could feel my face turning hot; certainly it was red as well. Mr. Dupuis was not the type of teacher who would take the paper from my hand. He simply let me crumple it and shove it in my pants pocket. I dared not even glance at Amy, who undoubtedly was mortified as well.

My heart was blue, but my balls were bluer. I couldn't stop thinking about Amy. She had a point. I *did* want her, all of her, and I needed to show it. While I was wracked with a Nebraskan tornado of guilt by betraying my parents' trust, I was also gripped with the primal urges that make us all human. Yes, I loved her, but fuck it, I was also horny.

———

THE following weekend, my grandmother accompanied us to Sabbath services. She was overwhelmed with excitement about reading aloud from the Torah on the temple's *bimah*, Hebrew for altar. In her traditional Iraqi and Indian cultures, Jewish women were strictly forbidden from this activity. However, Hannah Bahar's conventional mind succumbed to her progressive heart. "Your grandfather would be proud," she said confidently. Unlike me, she experienced no guilt.

Her voice was beautiful and clear. It took a center-stage performance for me to appreciate how her mystical, Sephardic, Middle-Eastern Jewish dialect distinguished itself from the Ashkenazi, Eastern-European American synagogue drone, diluted by two generations of Midwestern drawl. This week's Torah portion was *Mishpatim*, Hebrew for laws.

Though I had heard *Mishpatim* once a year since I could remember, I didn't pay much attention to it until now. In the midst of her reading, my own grandmother chanted the following verse (Exodus 21:10):

Hebrew: "אם אחרת יקח לא שארה כסותה וענתה לא יגרע."

Transliteration: "Eem acheret yicach lo she-erah kesutah v'onatah lo yigrah."

Literal Translation: "If he takes another for himself, he should not diminish her sustenance, her clothing, or her conjugal rights."

Intended Translation: "Give her what she wants, Tiger!"

My ears perked up, and a broad smile formed on my face. Being amorous, in and of itself, was not a sin. Was Granny giving me permission to have sex? She paused between each verse for dramatic effect, so when I chuckled aloud upon hearing these words, the entire congregation turned to me and offered a collective and disapproving, "Shhhhhh!"

Undaunted by a second moment of profound embarrassment in less than a week, I planned to walk home from the service on my own. I had a plan.

"I'm just going to stop by Benjie's on the way," I said.

"Okay, but don't be long. Your grandmother made us curry chicken," answered my mother.

I headed straight for the corner of 33rd Street and Pioneers Boulevard to The Swing In, the 1980s Nebraska equivalent of 7-Eleven, complete with video games, dirty magazines, and condoms.

I had forgotten that Mark Gross worked behind the counter on weekends. *Good Lord, not Mark. Anyone but Mark,* I thought to myself. I marked time by playing *Ms. Pac-Man* and *Tempest* in the video game section, as though I would Swing In for this purpose every day.

"Dude, check this out," I heard from the register. Mark beckoned me with the February 1983 *Playboy* cover photo of Kim Basinger. "She's super hot." I offered a perfunctory nod of approval. My mind was on the Trojans placed, appropriately, next to the cigarettes. I summoned all of my courage and nonchalantly grabbed a pack of Juicy Fruit, some strawberry Poprocks, and a three-pack of larges (I had briefly contemplated Magnums before recalling my experiences in the men's locker room).

"I thought your parents didn't allow you to use money on the Sabbath, Ron," I heard a voice state inquisitively from behind. This time I was not embarrassed. I was panicked, as

I could recognize Old Mrs. Goldberg's squeaky voice from anywhere.

I simultaneously threw my intended purchases behind the register and turned around. Sweat poured down my face. "Oh, hi, Mrs. Goldberg! I was just . . . uh . . . looking . . . and talking to my friend, Mark."

"I know Mark . . . he's a nice boy." She turned to him; he shoved aside the *Playboy* and offered his best *Leave-It-to-Beaver*-Eddie-Haskell smile. She continued, "Mark, did you hear Ron was going to medical school next year? And he sings so beautifully, too. The whole community is so proud of him."

"Yes, I know . . . about medical school *and* about his singing. He's a good boy *too*," he added, scarcely containing his laughter.

Mrs. Goldberg tortured me as she rummaged slowly through her change purse to find the $5.39 needed to purchase toilet paper, Pringles, and a box of tea bags. When she finally left, Mark looked at me, smiled, and said "'Just looking' . . . my ass." He picked up the three items and put away the Juicy Fruit and the Poprocks. "I'm assuming you won't be needing those. Would you like some smokes with your cock socks, big boy?" Mark was relentless. I paid for the Trojans and left.

I placed the condoms in my wallet and raced home to an Indian feast. My grandmother was still on cloud nine after the morning's triumph. "Granny, that was awesome," I declared.

"*Acha,*" she answered in Hindi with affirmation, still glowing. After a sip of Manischewitz and a slice of challah, I scarfed down the chicken curry. "Slow down *dahling,*" she said, smiling and briefly peering at my mother with a competitive glance. Mom could only roll her eyes.

By the time I had finished eating, my entire body was

permeated with curry. Though I loved the aura, I didn't want to lose my virginity smelling like a samosa. I took a quick shower and replaced the curry with Old Spice.

Thankfully, as a rule my parents spent Saturday afternoons napping (both a Bahar and a Jewish tradition), so this time was always my own. I knew Carol Andrews was out of town attending a conference, and that Amy would be working, at home alone, on a big history paper. Not surprisingly, she was writing about Israeli Independence. She told me she wanted to understand me better. She made it difficult not to love her.

I went to the basement to call her in private. She picked up on the first ring. "Hello?"

"It's me. Are you home alone?"

"Yes, but . . ."

"I'm coming over. I'll be there in, like, ten minutes."

"Ron, are you sure you want to . . ."

"Yes. I'm on my way."

I walked at a rapid pace. While my heart was pounding and my gloveless hands were freezing, I tried to convince myself that I was thinking more with my head than with my dick. Before I knew it, I was at her door. I knocked only once. She opened it quickly and shuttled me inside. She had on the same T-shirt and sweat pants she wore the night I saw her after the dance. It didn't matter what she wore; she was always hot.

"Ron, it's broad daylight. You know it's not a good idea to . . ."

Once again, I interrupted her. "I don't care. I needed to see you."

She could only stare. Those eyes. She *was* beautiful.

I continued. "Remember when you asked me if I was 'really into us'? Meaning you and me? Together?"

"Yes."

"Well, I am." She let me hold her. We kissed. Without thinking, we walked, clutching each other, into her room. We kissed some more, eventually horizontally on her bed. A hamstrung Diego barked ineffectively, as he was locked in Carol's bedroom. I could feel my heart beating in my ears. We smiled at each other. It was the most passionate moment of my life. Did I mention she was beautiful?

I paused for a moment. "And by the way, Amy, I *am* taking us seriously. I memorized every word of the note we wrote each other in class."

"Really," she said, laughing. "Prove it."

"Okay. I even have it right here in my wallet for you to verify." I opened the wallet, and before I could reach for the note, the Trojans popped out. I gasped. I prayed the condoms would be the only things that would be released prematurely. I realized there was nothing suave about me, but this performance was ridiculous. I looked nervously at Amy.

We stared at each other as I tried to think of something clever to say. No such luck. Finally, she broke the silence. "Were those part of your plan?"

I nodded.

"Ron, we're just not ready. I remember the part of the note when you told me you love me. I *do* believe you. But I don't want to do this as a reaction to pent up emotion. I want to do it when we're ready."

"Amy, I think we *are* ready."

"No, we're not. Between med school and music and me, you're all over the place. And what about what's going on in *my* head? Do you think I haven't thought about this moment almost continuously for the last four months? I just . . . I just . . ."

"Just what?" I asked, desperately.

"I just want to make sure you're committed. I know it sounds silly, but I can't stop thinking about you leaving me to go to Wisconsin. I don't know if I'll be able to take it, and I know I sound petty and jealous, but the thought of you with another girl over there makes me crazy."

"Amy, I don't know what more I can say, except I love you and I want you."

"I love you, too. I really, really, love you. But I need you to go home right now. If it's going to happen, I think we'll *both* know when we're ready."

I was in disbelief. I knew Amy well enough to understand that when she made up her mind, there was no arguing with her. Any attempt would be futile. I stood up. For a moment I thought I might die of cock block. She rose and kissed me once more. "Go," she said, smiling optimistically. She was beautiful.

CHAPTER 16

*"Use the body
Now you want my soul"*

—HALL & OATES' "I CAN'T GO FOR THAT (NO CAN
DO)," FROM THE ALBUM *PRIVATE EYES*, RELEASED DECEMBER
14TH, 1981. IT PEAKED AT NUMBER ONE ON US BILLBOARD'S
HOT 100 SONGS.

was at Benjie's house when the phone rang at dinner-time. As usual, Sheldon picked it up himself to berate the caller before taking a message. "Can you talk to Benjamin? I don't know, *can* you? Who is this, and why are you calling me 'brother,' especially during dinner?" He spoke aloud as he transcribed the caller's information: "Rex Dawson from Capitol Records for Benjamin Kushner. Area code 213- . . ."

Benjie leaped up then wrestled the receiver from his father. "Hello?" he asked, breathlessly.

Benjie and Rex spoke for several minutes as Sheldon stewed. Marcia waved him off. "Sheldon, let him be. It's important."

Rex continued, "Brother, I want to hear you in person. Mind if I stop by the show this Saturday?"

"Hell no, Mr. Dawson. Hell, no. I don't mind at all."

"Call me Rex, brother. See you Saturday."

"IF this doesn't pan out, I fucking quit!"

"Jesus, calm down, Peter," said Benjie. "I told you, if this rep is worth anything, he'll be able to understand that we play covers for the money *only*, and if he just listens to our music, he'll realize how good our original stuff is. He'll get it, I promise. We just have to be ourselves. Now that we're getting him through the door, he'll be sold."

"I just feel like a fuckin' sellout sometimes," answered Peter.

"Listen, I love most of the music we play, but it's not our own. I didn't blow all of those weekends over the years practicing the piano with my dad to be part of the second coming of The Monkees or Greg Brady as Johnny Bravo. We're The Well Endowed, and I want to play more of our own music."

"We *all* do. But it's survival. Benjie's right. Fuckin' relax, dude," Jeff interjected.

When The Repeats formed, its members feared being typecast as minimally talented musicians who appealed only to the lowest common denominator. The money was good, but was the end result worthwhile? Had this collection of accomplished players copied their way into irrelevance?

Capitol Records had sent its feelers out to Lincoln during a signing push of new Midwestern acts of the early 1980s, and The Well Endowed seemed to fit the bill. Talent scouts from their Artists and Repertoire (A & R) Division loved that the band had the ability to play original music, but at the same time understood both the monetary value of Top 40 and how to perform it.

After providing the details of his conversation with Rex to his parents and me, Benjie relayed the good news to the band. An impromptu practice session was held that night, and another was planned for the following evening, only twenty-four hours before The Well Endowed would be heard by Rex at Duffy's Tavern. Of course, I wanted to live vicariously through The Well Endowed's big break. I confabulated some excuse about calculus, physics, and Sundar to my parents, and took off to The Garage.

THE Garage was a converted four-hundred-square-foot storage unit in the working-class neighborhood of Havelock. This formerly independent small town just north of Lincoln was eventually annexed by the city. The Well Endowed utilized it for late-night jam sessions, practices, drunkfests, and occasional blowjobs. However, there would be no alcohol or fellatio this week; the band was dead serious. Rex explained to Benjie that he was hoping to hear both original and cover music to get an idea of the breadth of their repertoire. "No problem," Benjie promised Rex.

I sat silently in the corner of The Garage to take it all in. My thoughts raced through a constellation of pride, hope and envy. Yes, I was really fucking jealous. The band eventually settled on a cover set that included some of their best-received, pheromone-releasing numbers, like Rick Springfield's "Jessie's Girl" and AC/DC's "You Shook Me All Night Long," but also incorporated newly-learned hits, including Blue Oyster Cult's "Burnin' for You" and Bruce Springsteen's "Hungry Heart." Jeff wanted one more song to "shock the shit out of Rex." The banter commenced. Benjie lobbied hard for Kajagoogoo's "Too Shy." Jeff prophetically dubbed the band a *"guaran-fuckin'-teed-one-fuckin'-hit wonder,"* and instead advocated for something more "cutting edge"—"I Will Follow," from a new Irish band called U2.

Benjie refused. "U2? Are you fucking kidding me?

They're not even a *one-half-one-fuckin'-hit wonder*. They've never even had a hit in the United States. They're not even British! If you're gonna go foreign on me, gimme British Invasion, not Irish Invasion! I swear no one will remember U2 in five years. You can put that in writing."

Before youthful passion launched the pair into a fistfight, I respectfully offered my two cents, "You guys do a great 'Rock This Town.'"

An awkward silence ensued. Had I overstepped my bounds? Friend or not, there was indeed an unwritten rule about non-band members rummaging around in their business. Finally, Johnny, ultimately the diplomat of the group, diffused what could have represented an ugly end to my relationship with The Well Endowed.

"You *know* he's right," he said, shrugging his shoulders. Five sets of eyes quickly scanned the room.

"Cool," answered Benjie.

"Cool," Peter and Jeff chimed in together.

I also knew I was right (Benjie was a rockabilly prodigy and the genre was becoming mainstream), but I dared not gloat. I was already traversing through unchartered waters.

Creating their original music set was simple and required little preparation. The band collectively poured so much of themselves into what they hoped would become the nucleus of a debut album that the choice, order, and execution of songs had become as integral as the instruments they played. Though they had heard Rex's name only a few hours before, they had been preparing for this moment for months.

The following evening's practice went far more smoothly. I was admittedly nervous about returning to The Garage. Fortunately, my presence was well-received, and I was greeted with four separate, single head bobs and four nonchalant, "what's ups?"

As they felt comfortable with their original music set, the band completed a run through of all of the cover songs, concluding with Stray Cats' "Rock This Town." All seventeen and a half years of me nearly trembled with anticipation, and my enthusiasm was palpable. This could really happen.

"Well, my baby and me went out late Saturday night . . ."

Whether I was perceived by The Well Endowed as "one of the boys," or simply as a sympathetic mascot, I was accepted. Even Jeff's rough exterior softened a bit from the night before. "Benjie, let's do it again. This time let the doctor sing," he pronounced, grinning, not at Benjie, but instead directly at me.

Though my experiences of the last several months lessened my stage fright, I may have been even more intimidated by this audience of four young musicians with high aspirations and even higher standards. I could only stare at Jeff.

This time Peter broke the silence. "Well, what the fuck are you waiting for, numb nuts? Let's do it!" He always had a way with words.

I cracked a smile, but I was still concerned about disrupting what my tender ears considered perfection. *Oh, what the hell.* So I sang. *We* sounded really fucking great, and I felt really fucking great.

The chorus ensued, and an ass-kicking guitar solo followed. I had visions of The Well Endowed playing in front of a packed Yankee Stadium. But where was I in this dream? *Slow down, cowboy, and stop fantasizing; this is their gig, not yours,* I thought.

Instead of letting myself ruminate, I regained focus and decided to live for the moment. Zillie would have been proud.

The band cherished The Garage because of the deafening silence heard after the conclusion of each song. No drunk, horny women to fawn over the boys even in the event of a mundane performance. As each of The Well Endowed was more self-critical than the next, the boys would take turns judging their own individual performances, even if they felt flawless. Outwardly they considered this process cathartic, but to me it felt more like a musician's version of a confessional, where the young sinners had to fabricate indiscretions to the priest because they hadn't really behaved badly that week. "Forgive me father, for I sounded flat."

"Rock this Town" ended with the splash of snare and cymbal, but the room did not become quiet. Instead, loud clapping was heard at the sliding-door entrance. Our heads popped up. Though we had never met the clapper before, his identity was obvious.

"Rockabilly. I love it, man," said Rex.

Rex Dawson stood six feet, four inches tall and looked shockingly similar to George Hamilton. He had skinny legs and a slight paunch, purposely covered with a partially zipped royal blue Polo jacket. To complement his wardrobe, he reeked of Ralph Lauren's Chaps cologne. Though he was probably about fifty years old, his leathery tan aged him prematurely. His radioactive appearance stood out among the pale, post-winter Nebraskans.

"Rex?" inquired Benjie.

"At your service, brother. You must be Benjamin. Hope it's all right that I showed up one night early. I was working in Denver and got the last flight out. The boys at Duffy's told me you might be here."

"Happy to have you here. And call me Benjie. How long have you been here?"

"Long enough to have the shit shocked out of me," he answered, peering at Jeff and laughing with an undertone of a smoker's cough. "You boys sound great."

Jeff turned crimson.

"Hey, I thought there were only four of you. Who's the guy with the voice," Rex asked, pointing at me.

Shit. Now The Garage truly *was* quiet. I had to nip this one in the bud.

"I'm not part of the band. I'm a medical student," I answered before I had fully considered the question. What a fucking stupid answer.

"A doctor who can sing? Fantastic. Tell me more, brother."

"Well, I mean, I'm not a medical student yet, and I do sing, but only for fun. Just forget about me. I'm not the talent here." I'm not sure how my words could have flowed less smoothly. I couldn't know what The Well Endowed thought, and I couldn't look them in the eyes to try and read their expressions. Dumbass.

After one last agonizing pause, Rex declared, "Well, alright, brother. But lemme know when you'd like to step out of the operating room for some real fun."

I chuckled uncomfortably, and the moment ended, mercifully.

WORD got out about Rex, and locals came out in droves to support The Well Endowed on Saturday night. Both the cover and original sets transpired flawlessly. The audience took partial ownership of the show, as they knew the community's own musical reputation and success were also at stake. Nebraska was more than just football and corn. But the crowd's enthusiasm was not contrived. It was organic, visceral, cool, and honest, and it propelled the Well Endowed to the next level. The band concluded with what they considered their best original song, "Chameleon Man."

"The sun comes shining through
Only for a little moment or two
And still I managed to tan, I'm a chameleon man.
Then the rain comes pouring down
And it floods this little town . . ."[1]

I sat in the back to let the moment marinate. My eyes welled with tears. I wasn't sure why. As the crowd begged for an encore, I felt a breathtaking slap on the back. It was Rex, balancing both a Marlboro Light and scotch on the rocks with his other hand. I played off my emotions and dried my eyes while pretending to wipe away sweat from my forehead.

"Helluva show, doc. Helluva show." He then looked at me in earnest. "Listen, these guys have a future, but so could you. And I'm not talking about saving lives. There's something about your voice that resonates."

A smile crept over my face. "Thanks, Rex, but I've already gotten in to medical school, and I don't even play an instrument."

"Tell that to Mic Jagger."

"Good point."

"And don't bullshit a bullshitter. I know what you're thinking. Mom and Dad have big dreams for their baby boy, and you don't want to disappoint them. I don't now what kind of doctor you're gonna be, but you sing like a fuckin' bird."

I figured out why I had been crying.

"Doc, do you believe in destiny?"

"I'm not sure. Why?"

"Sometimes, when you least expect it, something or *someone* comes along and changes your life. I see it all the time. Call me when you're ready."

CHAPTER 17

"Hold me tight, babe, don't leave me by myself tonight
'Cause I don't think I can make it through the night"

—EDDIE MONEY'S "THINK I'M IN LOVE," FROM THE
ALBUM *NO CONTROL*, RELEASED JUNE 11TH, 1982.
IT PEAKED AT NUMBER SIXTEEN ON US BILLBOARD'S HOT
100 SONGS.

The Passover Festival was my mother's Christmas. I'm not talking about presents or caroling, and I'm certainly not talking about ham. Passover meant coming home. Zillie and Iris flew in on Friday, were paraded at synagogue along with my grandmother on Saturday, and, following family tradition, slept in until noon on Sunday. In 1983 the Seder was Monday night, March 28th.

A Seder, which literally means "order" in Hebrew, is the ritual feast marking the first night of Passover. The event commemorates the freedom from slavery and exodus of Jews from Egypt.

Always the teacher and bible scholar, my mother loved inviting non-Jewish friends to our home for the event so she could describe to them in detail the story of Moses and his struggle with both God and the Jews to bring his people to The Promised Land. I generally listened intently but did not participate much, so that I could stuff my face with matzah ball soup and brisket.

The story of Passover is chronicled in a short book called *The Haggadah*. Our *Haggadot* (plural) were not hardbound, red velvet-covered, dog-eared, underline-filled heirlooms, but instead were mass-produced, royal blue, 1965 copyright, sixty-four-page, "Deluxe Edition" paper-bound booklets distributed (even in Nebraska) for free in supermarkets, compliments of Maxwell House Coffee and The General Foods Corporation. I loved them. I loved their unintentionally comical cartoon depiction of the ten plagues. I loved their wine and gravy stains. I loved that they made my mother happy.[1]

Guests tended to alternate between university colleagues and family friends. The dean of engineering came in 1981, and in 1982 we entertained Sundar and his family. Perhaps in a brilliant attempt to combine both types of visitors, or perhaps simply to placate my disappointment in their refusal to allow me to date Amy, this year my parents decided to invite the entire Andrews family, including Steven, who was visiting from Michigan.

Let my people go.

I had updated Zillie and Iris with the basic truth about my deepening relationship with Amy. Though no two people on the planet understood my plight better than my sisters, I feared that, as usual, they would be relentless in their taunting. "I'm begging you guys to take it easy on me," I implored.

Invoking a line from the *Haggadah*, Iris turned to our sister and asked, sarcastically, "Zillie, why is this night different from all other nights?"

"I don't know, Iris, why *is* this night different from all other nights?" she herself questioned, giggling.

"Because on all other nights, we eat and drink either sitting or reclining, but on this night, we *all* recline as we watch Ronnie sweat profusely while he simultaneously tries to impress his clingy girlfriend, his suspicious future in-laws, and his overbearing parents."

"Seriously, shut up," I begged. I knew my words fell on deaf ears. This night could be very painful.

My mother had spent the better part of the previous week "kosherizing" our home for Passover. No housekeeper or child could be trusted to complete her version of spring cleaning, in which she would singlehandedly scrub down the kitchen so it would be free of *chametz*, Hebrew for leavening agents, like yeast. To complete the task, she would place all non-perishable items in the garage, throw out the perishable ones, and replace them all with rabbinically-certified Kosher-for-Passover foods. The end result was an immaculate kitchen, bottle upon bottle of Manischewitz wine, box upon box of matzah, and drunk, constipated parents.

IN an attempt at civility, Steven and Carol Andrews arrived together with Amy, a prompt half an hour before sunset. My mother could never quite understand Gentile punctuality and would genuinely be surprised whenever guests arrived on time. When the doorbell rang, she was always still knee deep in chicken broth, so she'd send my dad to entertain the guests.

The Andrews were, of course, well read on the Passover story and practices, so they knew better than to bring a bottle of Inglenook or Carol's famous homemade Black Forest Cake. Instead, they brought roses.

"Carol, Steven, come in. And thank you for the flowers," said my father, smiling. He gave both a warm hug. When he saw Amy, he said nothing, leaned in twice for a hug, retracted, and then gave her an awkward handshake, as if to say, "I'm not sure what the hell to do with you, but I do care about you, so just get inside."

Though Amy so thoroughly resented her father, and had no illusions about a reconciliation between her parents, she was noticeably eager to portray Carol and Steven's relationship as amicable. "Mom, Dad, why don't you sit together," she stated more than asked.

Perhaps the best thing about Passover is that, whether the Seder is experienced in Jerusalem, Buenos Aires, or Lincoln, its tales and rituals are the same and have been for centuries. Despite our deserved reputation for wandering, we Jews are linked by the event. I know that anywhere in the world where Jews live, Moses's frightening and uplifting story will be lovingly told, and I know that the participants in any Seder are obligated to drink four full cups of wine.

Yes, four full cups.

In the spirit of "when in Rome," the Andrews agreed that Amy should be allowed to immerse herself in the novel cultural experience and partake in all aspects of the Seder.

Yes, four full cups.

An extra leaf was inserted in the table to accommodate all nine participants. My grandmother liked her elbow room, so she sat at one end of the table. My parents were situated on either side of her. The professors Andrews, guests of honor, were located at the center of the table, with Carol by my mother and Steven by my father. Iris and Zillie sat opposite each other next to the professors, so Amy and I were placed next to each other at the other end of the table. I'm right-handed, so I sat on the right; Amy is left-handed so she sat to my left. My mother liked to make sure there were no dominant limbs colliding.

The Seder progressed in a shockingly smooth fashion. My grandmother charmed the guests with tales of her childhood in Baghdad. *Page 6, drink the first cup of wine.* The Andrews and the Bahars exchanged faculty war stories, and

Amy and I listened intently as Zillie and Iris gave advice on prerequisite classes, kosher-style fast food, and the best boom box choices for dorm rooms. *Page 27, drink the second cup of wine.* According to custom, I reclined and my outstretched legs slid under the table. As Amy drank, or perhaps as she was emboldened by the new power she felt she wielded over her parents, she abandoned her inhibition and began to rub my thigh with her non-dominant hand. Zillie and Iris both gave me "the look." I think they knew what was happening. I didn't care.

I too abandoned by inhibition, and yes, I had a woody during the Seder.

Page 30-37, grace after the meal. Upon its conclusion, a third cup of wine is poured for everyone in anticipation for the arrival of Elijah the prophet, forerunner of the Messiah. A child, representing the future, is asked to open the door at an eastern entrance, in the direction of Jerusalem.

"*Dahling*, would you open the door for Elijah?" Granny asked me.

Oh God, Granny, no, not yet, I thought. I didn't need to look down to know that I was pitching a tent with my boner. Standing up would cause instant humiliation, acrimony, and the end to my love life as I knew it. I froze. I dared not look at my sisters; I didn't want to know what was going through their heads.

Amy sensed my fear and immediately understood my predicament. Always a quick thinker, and despite her inebriation, she immediately sprung into action. She turned to Granny. "Mrs. Bahar, would you first explain why we open the door for Elijah?"

Granny smiled; she knew full well that Amy was the "good friend" we had discussed weeks before. She proudly started, "Amy, *dahling*, each of the four glasses of wine represents one of the promises . . ."

Just then Amy pinched my thigh—hard.

As part of physiology class, Mr. Dupuis taught Amy that the autonomic, or unconscious, nervous system is divided into parasympathetic (feed and breed) and sympathetic (fight or flight) segments. The former is responsible for erections, and the latter is responsible for ending them.

After nearly flying out of my seat, I collected myself then gave Amy an incredulous look. In a flash, she looked quickly at my crotch then looked up again, smiling.

Boner gone. Life saved. I sauntered to the east-facing door and opened it. Welcome, Elijah. Thank you, Amy. Thank you, Mr. Dupuis.

My father and I cleared the table and carried the dishes to the kitchen. The cracked matzah created a disaster on the dinner table, so my mother followed behind to retrieve the crumb brush. A bit tipsy herself, she turned to my father; she was no longer able to contain herself:

Hebrew: "חבל שהיא לא יהודיה. היא כלכך יפה, חכמה, ונחמדה."

Transliteration:	"Chaval sh'hee lo yehudiah. Hee kolcach yafah, chachamah, venechmadah."
Literal Translation:	"It's too bad she's not Jewish. She's so pretty, smart, and nice."
Intended Translation:	"I can see why Ronnie likes her, but if your son so much as kisses her, I'll kill him."

CHAPTER 18

"We,
So tired of all the darkness in our lives"

—JOE JACKSON'S "STEPPIN' OUT," FROM THE ALBUM
NIGHT AND DAY, RELEASED IN JUNE, 1982.
IT PEAKED AT NUMBER SIX ON US BILLBOARD'S HOT
100 SONGS.

In 1983, if you didn't have a prom date, you didn't go to prom. I literally begged my parents to allow me to escort my "good friend and study partner" Amy, who had no date. I played the, "I just want to be like everyone else" card with every ounce of persuasion my adolescent body could muster. After several conversations between my mother and Carol Andrews, and after endless pledges that the relationship would remain platonic, my parents caved.

My father made an *"I'm-not-fucking-around,"* declaration with his Mr. Spock, single eyebrow raise and a wagging index finger, "Ronnie, remember what I said about playing with fire. Respect Amy, and when this prom thing is over, that's it."

"Dad, I swear."

"We don't swear in this house." Really?

"Okay, I promise."

My mother sat silently. She stared at me almost with pity and pretended to adjust her glasses while she subtly dried a tear from her eye. She couldn't fool me. I had learned from the best. As upset as I was that I had to grovel for something that seemed like my inalienable right as an American teenager, I knew she understood my plight, if only just a little.

THE Well Endowed signed a record deal with Capitol Records. Though the contract heavily favored the label, with its relatively small take for the band, a clause for exclusivity, and no release commitment, Capitol essentially "owned" The Well Endowed. But it was a contract nonetheless.

Capitol would allow the band to reach its tentacles farther across the Midwest and to larger, more lucrative venues. Outside of school dances and weddings, The Well Endowed had previously measured its audiences in the dozens. With a behemoth organization promoting them, however, they could take the next step and fill hundreds of seats in locales such as The Ogden Theater in Denver and The Park West in Chicago, so that their original sound could grow.

Before the deal was inked, the band members, all Southeast High School alumni, had already agreed, both for old times' sake and as a favor to me, to play one last prom. To be frank, the band knew it was phasing out performing cover music, and thought it would be fun to dip into the archives (if two years could constitute archives) and combine them with a few new hits. In addition, this time Benjie actually coaxed the band into granting me a "mini set" as lead vocalist. I still think they must have been drunk for Benjie to have convinced them, but I was willing to ignore my lack of self-confidence and ride their coattails.

Round two of sparring with my dad involved my attempt to persuade him that I *needed* to perform at the prom. This time my angle would be . . . oh fuck it . . . this time my angle would be that I was a senior in high school and I was at the top of my class and I was going to medical school and I wanted to celebrate in a manner commensurate with my achievements. And, goddammit, I had a great voice and I wanted to sing in front of an audience and have some fun!

"Dad, I need this."

"What you *need* is an education."

"I need *both* dad," I pleaded. "Haven't I proven enough?"

The Old and New Worlds collided; what the hell did singing pop music at prom mean to him, anyway? You study, you work, you provide. If you need to leave your homeland as a teenager and move to a foreign country alone to get ahead, so be it. I trembled. I didn't want to cry. The mere thought of doing so humiliated me, especially if it were to occur in front of my father. I would rather have bawled in front of every guy I had ever met and be ridiculed until the end of time. Fuck. It's not that my dad somehow sought to exploit my weakness and make me feel like shit. This was the same man who gave me a kiss on the cheek every morning before I left for school. I knew he loved me. He just didn't understand, and I didn't want to disappoint him.

I held it in. A stare down began, and though it probably lasted only a moment, it felt as though it took centuries. I was afraid that if I spoke, the waterworks would ensue. He finally broke the silence. "Fine," he said, exasperated. "But keep your priorities in order."

LATER that night, I called Amy. "Yes!" she exclaimed. "How did you get your parents to agree to both me *and* the singing?"

"I don't know. Maybe it was because I loosened them up by doing tequila shots with them."

"No, really!"

"Honestly, I don't know. I feel like their default answer is always 'no' because maybe they think they're protecting me. But I know what I want, and I don't want to be protected anymore."

"I know." Amy paused before continuing. "Ron?"

"Yes?"

"I *do* want to be protected."

CHAPTER 19

*"Aren't we the same two people who live
Through the years in the dark?"*

—THE EAGLES' "I CAN'T TELL YOU WHY," FROM THE
ALBUM *THE LONG RUN*, RELEASED FEBRUARY 8TH, 1980.
IT PEAKED AT NUMBER EIGHT ON US BILLBOARD'S HOT
100 SONGS.

Dude, have you ever hooked up with a girl?" asked Jeff, seemingly just to make conversation.

"No," I answered, laughing. "Virgin Jew."

"What? How long you been going out with that girl Amy?"

"About seven months?"

"Seven months? Are you fucking kidding me? What the hell are you waiting for? She's hot!"

"I agree. She *is* hot. And I'd be lying to you if I told you we haven't talked about it. She's just not ready."

"What do you mean she's not ready? Dude, Big Dick and The Twins need to practice before you go off to med school and try and conquer all those cute dairy farm girls in Wisconsin. I bet most of them have never done it with a circumcised guy before."

"But I . . . I mean she . . . I'm not going to . . ."

"Ron, I'm going to stop you right there . . . hey guys!" he

yelled at the other end of The Garage, where the rest of the band was practicing "Too Shy." Jeff had promised Benjie that if the band signed a record deal, Kajagoogoo would be front and center on subsequent set lists.

"We got a penile emergency here!" Jeff added. Like Peter, he did have a way with words, and he himself was certainly not "too shy." Laughter and ridicule ensued. I couldn't allow the mockery to get the best of me. In their own twisted way, I knew they meant well.

The band then made me sit alone at the opposite end of The Garage while they had a private conference. It lasted about five minutes. For the most part they whispered, but every few moments I would hear iterations of, "No that's not gonna' work," "Yes!" "I think he's ready," or, "that is fucking *genius*." Of course there was the intervening guffaw.

When the meeting adjourned, all four Well-Endowed Repeats called me back to their jerry-rigged conference table, which consisted of a cardboard box and what was left of a large Godfather's Classic Combo pizza, circumscribed by four cans of Coke.

"Ron, what's the theme of this year's prom?" asked Jeff.

"All Knight Long. Spelled K-N-I-G-H-T, not N-I-G-H-T. Get it? Like The Lincoln Southeast *Knights*? It was my idea."

"Okay, two things. First, I wouldn't admit to anyone that it was your idea. Second, that theme is for everyone else. The five of us are going to have a different theme."

"Okay," I answered," smirking. "What is it?"

"'Music to get laid by.' Dude, it's perfect. Do you have any idea of the power of the love ballad?"

At this point I could barely contain my amusement. "No. Please, go on."

"So we've already explained to you how a bunch of

average-looking shmucks like us get so many women, right?"

"Average looking? Speak for yourself, ya fuckin' ogre," Benjie interjected, chuckling.

"Don't interrupt me, Kushner, I'm on a roll." He continued, "Well, if we really want to seal the deal and actually screw, we pull out all the stops . . . we go straight to the love ballad."

"I love it," I said, grinning.

"You think we're kidding? Here's the new set list. The last one is yours." He handed me a sheet of paper. I grabbed it and read it.

"Holy shit. This is amazing. You're really *not* kidding."

I practiced my mini (three-song) set list with the band almost nightly for the two weeks leading up to prom. While the voice came naturally, I continued to require extensive body-language training. Benjie attempted, initially in vain, to help me perfect a dramatic *grab-microphone-clench-fist-shut-eyes-in-anguish* combo. "The key is to make it look effortless and spontaneous," he instructed. *Good luck with that,* I thought.

He went on to explain the almost magical effect of the *point-finger-at-the-hot-girl* maneuver, how it had to coincide precisely with the appropriate lyrics, and, in his case, that hand and finger movements needed to be timed perfectly between guitar strumming. Though use of the love ballad helped, it was not necessary with his level of expertise. He then demonstrated his wizardry with "Too Shy" by grabbing the microphone during the first verse, squeezing his eyes shut and clenching his fist in anguish during the second, and sealing the deal by pointing at a hot girl during the chorus:

"Modern medicine falls short of your complaints . . ."
(grab microphone).

I understood why he longed to use that song. He had honed his craft, and Kajagoogoo would get him laid. If I wanted to follow suit, I had a lot of work to do.

I rented a paisley tuxedo jacket and wingtip shoes for the event. Though I may have been overcompensating for my otherwise lackluster appearance, I thought at the time that I looked pretty damn good. Amy was generally modest and would never admit that she wanted to look beautiful. She never really had to try; without sounding trite, it was natural for her. She ordinarily didn't spend much time shopping either, but on this occasion she dragged her mother through Nebraska's department store circuit until she found the perfect burgundy tiered puffy-sleeved sequin number at Dillard's department store in Omaha. The color matched my paisley perfectly. I had never seen her in heels before and, despite the panty hose, her legs were tantalizing. We would rock. And maybe, just maybe, I would get lucky.

Sundar continued to go out with Anne after their very successful shared Sadie Hawkins conquest. We double dated in the Duster and arrived at the ballroom of The University of Nebraska's Student Union early so I could help set up. I was, in the end, still a glorified roadie. Though they knew I would be singing, I refused to tell them what songs we would be performing, admittedly in part to maximize the surprising aphrodisiac effect of the love ballad set.

Before entering the Student Union, Amy took me aside. "Listen, babe. I want you to know that I *am* happy for *you*, I promise. I saw how thrilled you were the last time you performed, and regardless of what you do with your life, you should be able to enjoy yourself. Just be good to me." She smiled brightly at me and kissed me quickly but delicately on the lips. Her statement required no response; of course I would be good to her.

Jeff lay in wait as we arrived. He gave Amy a once-over with his eyes, and then turned to me. I received a knowing smile, followed by a head nod. I had to look the other way to avoid cracking up.

The pomp and circumstance of the prom royalty presentation was met primarily with cheers, but when Queen Holly Goodwin and King Chris Taylor were introduced, a contingent of hecklers made themselves heard. Though we pre-dated the anti-prom, or "morp" (prom spelled backward) era of the 1990s, there was some dissention from a limited but vocal nonconformist wing of the student body. I couldn't help but think that a small part of me was one of them. Though the "royal court" represented nothing more than a post-pubertal popularity contest, I found solace in my own hot date, and in my temporary role as the frontman.

So I got over it.

BENJIE was masterful. In addition to playing the guitar, he played the audience. I felt I was in the presence of an emerging star when I heard his heart-tugging acoustic rendition of "Let My Love Open The Door."

"I have the only key to your heart . . ." (grab microphone)

Girls were putty in his hands. The set ended, and I was up next. How the hell was I supposed to compete with that? I wasn't even that nervous. No debilitating IBS attack. I was simply resigned to my comparative mediocrity. I figured I might as well try and have fun.

"Ladies and gentlemen, back for his second and final tour stop before embarking on a fabulous career saving lives, special guest singer Ron Bahar!"

I ran onstage and thanked Benjie for his flattering introduction with an awkward and undeveloped '80s version of the bro-hug. I then looked down at Amy, who made her way to the front row. She looked extraordinarily sexy, and she knew I felt that way when we made eye contact. She blushed, and I could feel myself doing the same. I finally stopped staring and looked back at my band members. Jeff motioned me back to his drum set. I complied with his request.

"Dude, this is it," he whispered to me. "Take full advantage of the love ballad . . . and if Amy doesn't feel it, just assume there's something wrong with her and move on to the next chick." He winked. I nodded, but his words bothered me. This was Amy he was talking about. There was no "next chick."

I froze for a moment, but regained my composure when the band began to play The Alan Parsons Project's "Time":

"Time, flowing like a river . . ." (grab microphone)

The fans' response was electric, and clearly dominated by female voices. Amy just smiled at me. We blushed . . . again. I caught myself staring . . . again. Styx's "The Best of Times" began to play:

"Tonight's the night we'll make history . . ." (grab microphone)

The crowd noise was overwhelming, as the girls began to

chant: "Ron! Ron! Ron!" I looked around the stage at all of The Repeats. In unison, Benjie, Jeff, Peter, and Johnny all gave me their own *finger-point-at-the-new-kid-on-the-block*. I had never felt more universally accepted.

"Rock and fuckin' roll!"

I instantly recognized Tommy's voice and mantra. I turned back to the audience to find him and *totally-fucking-hot* Julia Turner also pointing at me. They were standing next to Amy, who blew me a kiss. Holy shit! Was this really happing?

If my final song, Journey's "Faithfully" didn't get me in bed with Amy, nothing would:

"And being apart ain't easy on this love affair . . ." (grab microphone)

When "Faithfully" ended, the entire audience spontane-ously pointed at me. I raised my right arm and gave a peace sign to the crowd. "Thank you!" I yelled. My voice was barely audible over the screaming throng of girls.

I jumped off the stage directly in front of Amy. I hugged her tightly, and whispered in her ear. "I want you. Let's do it tonight."

"Do *what?*" Amy replied, confused.

"You know . . . *it*. Amy, I think we're ready. I love you and I'm pretty sure you love me, and we've been going out a long time now, and . . ."

"Ron, I do love you, but I'm not ready. And I'll never let myself rush into anything, not even with you."

"But, Amy, seven months is not rushing it!"

"Ron, come on, we've already been through this. Tonight has been so special so far. Let's not ruin it by arguing." She then kissed me almost dismissively on the cheek.

Her response sucked the air right out of my lungs. She

was so beautiful, we were meant for each other, and we were deeply in love. So what was the problem? Apparently, Amy found my performance simultaneously exciting, skillful, and humorous, but clearly not sexy.

I continued to hold her in my arms, as though fearing that if I ever let go, our relationship would become hopelessly platonic. We eventually looked at each other. Her hazel eyes still sparkled. I wanted her badly. After a long pause, I finally mustered the energy to say, "Okay, Amy."

And so the luster of the love ballad was tarnished.

CHAPTER 20

"Alarmed by the seduction
I wish that it would stop"

—SQUEEZE'S "TEMPTED," FROM THE ALBUM *EAST SIDE STORY*, RELEASED MAY 15TH, 1981. IT PEAKED AT NUMBER FORTY-NINE ON US BILLBOARD'S HOT 100 SONGS.

Amy, Sundar, and Anne wandered around campus to inspect Amy's prospective dorms for the following school year while I helped the band pack up their equipment. I worked slowly and silently, as I was trying to figure out what I would say next to Amy. What was there to talk about, really? I was hurt, but did I have a right to be? We were only seventeen, and Amy had already made her position perfectly clear. Perhaps I was just embarrassed about being rebuffed so steadfastly. And then there was Jeff.

"So you ready for the old, 'in-out-in-out' with Amy?" he asked, slyly. "Fuckin' love ballads work every time. She's primed dude."

"We'll see," I answered, awkwardly.

"Trust me, man, she's good to go."

"Who's good to go?" asked Amy, surprising us from behind.

"This drum set," interjected Jeff, answering for me. He

smiled and offered me another wink. "You lovebirds go. We'll finish up."

"No, no, I want to help."

"You've helped enough. We're almost done here and I know you guys have an after-prom to go to. You definitely don't want to miss any of that."

Amy was surprisingly oblivious about what had transpired. Was I missing something, or was she really just "not ready?" Worse yet, was I wrong about her feelings toward me? I suddenly felt ashamed and wanted to leave.

"Okay, let's go." I looked past Amy, toward Sundar and Anne, and started walking back to the Duster.

"Ron, remember Cindy Patterson? She graduated from Southeast last year. Anyway, she let us into Abel Hall, you know, the giant dorm on 17th Street. It's absolutely huge, and they had a lot of really cool people there. I think I'm going to try and live there this fall. I'm glad I dragged Sundar along since he's staying in Nebraska. He hasn't decided on a dorm yet either, and I think he liked it too."

"That's great, Amy," I answered sardonically. She looked bewildered. "Sunny, why don't you ride shotgun this time?" I asked Sundar as we approached the car.

Finally Amy understood something was amiss. The passenger side of the Duster's front row had essentially become her property over the course of the school year. "Ron, what's wrong?" she asked as she climbed in the back seat behind me.

"Absolutely nothing." Sundar and Anne were fondling each other just outside the car. I tapped lightly on the horn. They both jumped and laughed.

"Sorry, dude," said Sundar as he opened the passenger door. Anne slid in back next to Amy, and Sundar took her place beside me. My single-minded and obviously disappointed friend gave me the *"why-the-fuck-can't-I-sit-next-to-my-date-and-have-her-put-her-hand-where-it-doesn't-belong?"* look. I knew my pouting was immature, but I couldn't help myself. The band had created an image of me that I had started to believe.

I drove silently to the after-prom, which, of course, was at Tommy's house, the only one that could contain the anticipated crowd. The twenty-minute drive seemed to take forever. Tommy's street was teeming with cars, so we were forced to park a couple of blocks away and walk.

Sundar and Anne hopped out and held hands as they walked toward the house. I looked down and shoved my hands in my pockets to avoid having to look at or touch Amy. She grabbed my arm. I turned to her, albeit grudgingly.

"Ron, I get it. You're upset because I turned you down. But there's something you don't understand. I don't need some contrived event like the prom to lose my virginity. That's not the way I want it to happen. I want it to happen *spontaneously*—not after you've sung to all of those girls and put a spell on them with that voice—I want it to be our moment, not theirs."

"Amy, I don't understand. Are you jealous?"

"No . . . well . . . maybe."

"That's crazy. I love *you*. I admit that I love the attention, too, but I don't really care about those girls. I just think we're ready to take the next step."

She pulled me close. "Ron, I *do* think it's going to happen, but not tonight. Just be patient. We'll know when the time's right." Pine Lake had no streetlights, but the moon was bright and it illuminated her with enough light that I could see every detail of her ethereal face. I was powerless in her presence, and holding her and looking into those eyes wasn't making me less amorous.

WE caught up with Sundar and Anne, and, by the time we reached Tommy's house, we, too, were holding hands. Given the noise emanating from inside, knocking would be pointless, so we walked in. Citing his desire to "preserve their angelic image of the class of 1983," Tommy managed to persuade his parents to leave town for the event. With an additional stroke of genius, he had Tommy's neighbors, Judge White and his wife Roberta, travel with them. Unreal.

"I'm forever yours, faithfully!" Tommy screamed, playfully mocking both Journey and me from the across the room.

I flipped him off with a smile on my face.

"Dude that was *awesome*," said Tommy.

"I *loved* it," added Julia, looking *totally-fucking-hotter-than-usual* in a black form-fitting bustier-topped sleeveless number. It was impossible not to gawk at her, and it was almost as difficult to prevent Amy from knowing that I did. Julia was already drunk, the kind of uninhibited but not yet word-slurring or nauseated drunk most prom-goers dream to achieve. She hugged me tight and whispered in my ear: "Meet me upstairs . . . alone."

Holy shit.

Again, I stared at Julia, but only for a moment. Tommy grabbed me. I was startled, and half expected him to punch me in the face, even for unintentionally using the power of the love ballad on his girlfriend. There was a lull in the music, so when Tommy yelled, "Rosanna!" in the same ear Julia used to proposition me just seconds before, I felt something similar to a warning bell pounding that side of my head.

In 1983, in Lincoln and across America, Toto's own love

ballad, "Rosanna," was wildly popular. The song, inspired by actress Rosanna Arquette, had become the subject of a trendy drinking game among high school and college students alike. Whenever Rosanna's name was uttered, merrymakers were obligated to take not just a sip, but instead a giant-ass gulp of beer. The word "Rosanna" is sung twenty-one times in the song, which lasts five minutes and thirty-two seconds. Those numbers translate to one slug every 15.8 seconds. Results ranged from laughter to vomit to unconsciousness, depending on the size of said student and giant-ass gulp.

Tommy was nothing if not persuasive. "Listen, rock star . . . tonight you're drinking. I don't give a flying fuck about your grades or your reputation. You've got nothing left to prove in high school. Live it up, doctor. You've earned it!"

He made some good points. And my mind was spinning. I wanted a drink. Or two. Or three. But what would Amy think? She was still standing next to me, and I turned to her and gave her a look as though I were asking my mommy permission to reenter the pool less than thirty minutes after eating.

Amy may have been jealous, but she remained entirely nonjudgmental. "You go ahead," she said, smiling. "I'll pass."

"Are you sure?" I inquired.

"Of course. Besides, you're a big boy and you don't need *my* permission to do anything."

"Rosanna" began. Tommy had exactly twenty-two seconds before the first Rosanna and the first obligatory shot. He grabbed me again. I had no time to think.

A keg of Pabst Blue Ribbon, or PBR as it was affectionately known, sat proudly on the kitchen island. Plastic cups had already been poured for everyone. I was literally trapped between the keg on one side, and Tommy, Mark, Sundar, and Christine on the other. There was no turning back:

"All I want to do when I wake up in the morning is see your eyes . . . Rosanna, Rosanna . . ."

We all began to chug, refill, and chug. Five down, sixteen to go. I mean it's not as though I had never drunk alcohol before. In fact, I was well acquainted with the warm feeling that ascends over one's face even with the first sip of red wine. Beer was different. It was cold and bitter, and there was no subsequent warmth, or fuzziness for that matter, especially when consumed in this fashion.

Thirteen down, eight to go. Already buzzed and uninhibited, I looked at my friends. Their proximity and their silly, intoxicated grins appeared to be linked together like a string of pearls, especially with the effect of the PBR. I was no longer worried about who was going to drive the Duster home. Instead, through the fog, I was somehow able focus on my spectacular performance, my even more spectacular rejection, and on Julia. Yes, Julia. Just behind Tommy, she was staring . . . at me. Despite my inebriation, it was at this point that I understood that Julia's solicitation was real . . .

Twenty-one. Good God, was I drunk. I had no idea where Amy was and, at that point, I really didn't care. Tommy jumped on the island to grab everyone's attention. "For the first time, thanks to 'Rosanna,' the doctor of rock and roll is officially wasted!" The room exploded with a combination of cheering and laughter. Tommy then hopped down and put his arm around me before offering me some fatherly advice. "Ron . . . you're *the man* right now . . . make the most of it." He then launched a loud, smelly, and protracted belch in my face before walking away. Thanks, Dad.

Julia wasted no time. From across the kitchen, she tilted her head to motion me upstairs. She was excruciatingly hot, and I was exceedingly shit-faced, so I followed. The house was exceptionally crowded, so I kept a small distance and about twenty people between us so no one would notice. I had been to the Hanson's house many times, and I knew the layout well. Just ahead, I could see her entering Tommy's sister Susan's bedroom. After about thirty seconds, I walked in. Julia had already removed her dress, and lay on the bed wearing nothing but panties and a bra. I was shocked; she smiled. She was magnificent, and she knew it. "Do you have any protection?" she asked. She was horny and drunk, but she wasn't stupid. "No glove, no love," she added, matter-of-factly.

If someone had asked me the prior fall if I would be in the position where I could decide to forgo waiting to lose my virginity to my beautiful, intelligent, charming, and loving girlfriend, and instead blow my wad with some crazy-hot temptress who was attracted by my transient rock-star qualities, I'm fairly certain I would have said "no." Was it my animal magnetism or was it dumb luck? If I succumbed to the seductress, would I be a legend (in my own mind) or just an asshole? Was I out of my mind?

I had never discarded the Trojans I purchased from Mark at The Swing In a few months before, and, in fact, had fully intended to use them that same night with Amy. "Yup," I answered, sheepishly. I was nervous, but very, very excited.

"Then put it on, rock star," she said, smiling. She sat up, grabbed me by the belt, and pulled me toward her. She touched my crotch and looked up at me. "I don't really have much work to do here, do I?" I blushed. She undid my belt and pulled down my pants and underwear in a single move of wizardry.

I proceeded to fumble hopelessly with the Trojan wrapper. After what seemed like an eternity, she grabbed it. She used a combination of fingernails and teeth to tear it open immediately and handed it back to me, now chuckling. I was still wearing my jacket, and I was sweating profusely.

Suddenly I was overwhelmed with guilt. "Julia, I can't . . ."

"Can't what? Get it up?" "Looks pretty 'up' to me."

"No, I just can't. It's not right."

"Are you kidding? Do you realize what you're saying? To me?"

"Yes. I'm really sorry, it's just . . ."

Just then the door opened. There stood Amy and Tommy. I had literally gotten caught with my pants down . . . and my dick up. Had I really forgotten to lock the door? Was I really so arrogant that I thought I had earned the right to lose my virginity to one of my best friend's girlfriend? And that punch in the face that I had worried would happen before? Well, it happened.

Then everything went blank.

CHAPTER 21

*"It was fun for a while
There was no way of knowing"*

—ROXY MUSIC'S "MORE THAN THIS," FROM THE ALBUM
AVALON. IT WAS RELEASED APRIL, 1982, BUT DIDN'T REACH
US BILLBOARD'S HOT 100 SONGS UNTIL COVERED BY
10,000 MANIACS IN 1997, AT WHICH TIME IT REACHED
NUMBER TWENTY-FIVE.

My head hurt.

I would've been happy that I was unconscious for what was apparently about fifteen minutes, since amnesia seemed a good alternative to recalling what had occurred during those moments. However, Sundar was more than happy to offer me the humiliating blow-by-blow (or single blow, in this case) account.

"Dude, you were out like a fucking light. Amy was pretty upset. She ran out of the house and Chris drove her home in Mark's car. Tommy called Julia 'a fucking slut.' Then he said 'get *the fuck* out of my house' and pointed to the door. She put on her dress really fast and took off with her underwear in one hand and her high heels in the other. I have no idea where she went . . . she has a *great* body, by the way."

Thanks for the reminder, I thought.

He went on. "I basically had to scrape you off the carpet and drag you downstairs with this awesome fireman's carry."

I declined his offer of a dramatic reenactment.

He wasn't finished. "I threw you in the back seat of your car. I was in no shape to drive and I know Jim Burton doesn't drink, so I asked him to take us to my house. You *really* fucked up."

Thanks, again.

"By the way, you need to take a look at your face. It's a mess," added Sundar. He returned moments later with a hand mirror. I removed the ice pack that had been placed over my eye and caught a glimpse. Oh God.

"You're going to have to tell your parents, Ron." I looked up. The act of craning my neck already exacerbated the throbbing sensation around my left eye, but seeing Dr. Rajendran's troubled expression nearly caused my entire head to detonate. I could tell that my mentor was not angry with me. It was worse; he was disappointed. He touched my brow. I winced. "There's nothing broken, no orbital fracture. It's just a shiner, but it's going to take a while to heal, and it's going to look a lot uglier before it resolves."

"Sorry, man, I tell my dad everything," explained Sundar.

"But—"

"Please, Ron," interrupted the doctor. "It's time to face the music, son. Lying to your parents will only make things worse. I'm not a religious person, so I'm not going to pretend and preach that I think it's the righteous thing to do. But I am a man of science, and I'd like to think I'm a man of honor. Consider how hiding the truth about what happened tonight will gnaw at your conscience . . . *and* your intestines. You already know how the mind and gut interact. With your IBS, if you don't come clean, you're going to create a tempest in you body. The honor part goes without saying. You've made some decisions that you probably regret right now. You can never undo them, but you can certainly own up to them and show that these indiscretions shouldn't brand you for the rest of your life. I don't think it's a good idea to fabricate a story about your eye. Do you understand what I'm trying to tell you?"

"I think so."

Sundar's brother, Babu, had been listening to the entire conversation. Like Sundar, he essentially had no filter. "She . . . is . . . *hot*, dude! How *was* she, really?" he asked, genuinely interested. "Was it worth it?" Sundar could barely contain his laughter.

"Babu, please! Not now," said Dr. Rajendran, as sternly as his mild-mannered personality could muster.

I was utterly humiliated. And sad. And lonely. What the hell had I been thinking?

I had no idea what to do next, so I stayed at the Rajdendran's house and lay awake in Sundar's basement. My parents had already understood that I wouldn't be coming home that night, so I had a little time to figure out what I was going to tell them. Or not tell them.

The light from a nearly full moon shone through the basement window. It was then that I began to appreciate the profound quiet that suffused Lincoln neighborhoods at night. The crickets were not yet in season, so the silence was deafening. The alcohol and fist-induced fog had cleared, and I began to concentrate on the light, my own pulse, and the rise and fall of my chest. My mind started to spin. I thought about Amy, and the first time we held hands; I thought of how goose bumps and Peanut M&M's turned to kissing and fondling . . . and love. I thought about Anthony, the little boy from Madison with the hole in his heart. His had certainly been fixed, but I had made a concerted effort in creating another, deeper, wider one inside Amy. The moonlight eventually reached my face. With it, I felt a wave of shame engulf me. I wasn't dreaming. I didn't deserve Amy, and I didn't deserve to become a doctor. What a complete shithead.

It was 3:00 a.m. I got dressed and left. I ran toward Amy's house.

CHAPTER 22

"And he's gonna break her heart to pieces
But she don't wanna know"

—TOM PETTY AND THE HEARTBREAKERS' "WOMAN IN
LOVE (IT'S NOT ME)," FROM THE ALBUM *HARD PROMISES*,
RELEASED JUNE 29TH, 1981. IT PEAKED AT NUMBER
TWENTY-SEVEN ON US BILLBOARD'S HOT 100 SONGS.

had no idea what I would tell Amy, but I was terrified of losing her, so I kept moving. I must have looked ridiculous tearing through the streets of Lincoln in the middle of the night with a black eye and a paisley tuxedo. Worse yet, I couldn't borrow running shoes from Sundar since his feet were significantly smaller than mine. I was, therefore, forced to run in wingtips with no socks; I couldn't find them in my rush to leave the Rajendran's house.

Let's just say tuxedo shoes aren't conducive to sprinting. Though adrenaline led me quickly to Amy's neighborhood, my feet hurt like hell. I had the bright idea of discarding the offending footwear and running barefoot for the last half mile. Bad move, Cornhusker; Amy's front yard greeted my right foot with a fresh pile of dog shit, compliments of Diego.

Okay, I deserved that.

I took the final steps toward Amy's uncovered window while rubbing my excrement-laced foot in the cold, dewy grass. Her bedroom was dimly it, so I laid the shoes at the foot of the window and peered inside. To my horror, I saw Amy . . . with Tommy.

If they were having sex, Amy and I would have been even. What I witnessed may have been worse: they were having "a moment." Their bodies, still fully clothed, were nearly silhouetted by Amy's reading lamp, but there was no mistaking Tommy in a deeply emotional embrace with my girlfriend. *My* girlfriend. She lay there, receptive to his careful advances. Having heard me lament my virginity more than once, Tommy knew better than to try and add her immediately to his long list of conquests. Instead, after wiping away one of her tears, he leaned in, caressed her hair, and kissed her softly on the lips. Goddammit, that was *my* move!

I felt sick. I had assumed Amy was incapable of succumbing to the spell of any man, even Tommy. Not so much. I was well acquainted with Tommy's *technique*, and I saw Amy falling for him before my eyes. She was savvy, but she was also vulnerable; he was obvious, but he was also Tommy. It took me five fucking years to gather the courage to kiss Amy. It probably took Tommy five fucking seconds, and it all came so naturally to him. I imagined Amy hearing a nonchalant tap on the window before seeing his handsome fucking face appear out of fucking nowhere. She would then open the window and allow him to leap effortlessly into her room and into her life.

Between passionate kisses, they smiled with pure satisfaction. Oh God, no. Perhaps he was falling for her, too. At this point, I felt like a lowly voyeur. I scampered to some nearby bushes, dropped to my knees, and puked.

In an attempt to regain my composure, I took a deep breath and looked up. There, directly in front of me, stood

Tommy's Beemer, shining in the moonlight like a James Bond-mobile. I truly wanted to kill him.

In a few fleeting moments, I had squandered all of the integrity and machismo I had worked so diligently to garner over the course of the school year. My insecurities came flooding back. I hated myself.

Barefoot, malodorous, nauseated, lonely, and despondent, I ran home.

CHAPTER 23

"Darling, I confess, yes I've ruined three lives
Did not care 'til I found out that one of them was mine"

—THE ENGLISH BEAT'S "I CONFESS," FROM THE ALBUM
SPECIAL BEAT SERVICE, RELEASED SEPTEMBER 21ST, 1982.
IT PEAKED AT NUMBER THIRTY-FOUR ON US BILLBOARD'S
HOT DANCE CLUB PLAY.

couldn't study, run, or sing my way out of this one. Zillie wasn't there to bail me out, and Carol Andrews was too smart not to question my sudden absence, Tommy's sudden presence, and the shiner that everyone would talk about. By the time I reached my house, it was four thirty in the morning. I bought a few more hours alone in my room. Of course, I couldn't sleep, so in my head I wrote a speech to my parents.

Before taking the plunge, I waited until I heard two teaspoons tinkling in coffee cups in the kitchen so I could bolt in an unfettered fashion to the bathroom to inspect my face. Once inside, I locked the door, closed my eyes, and turned toward the mirror. Holy shit, I was hideous. It now made sense why my field of vision had decreased so drastically, as my left eye was nearly swollen shut. And "black eye" was a misnomer; it was a kaleidoscopic mess.

My mom's concealer was not exactly an option, so I took a shower and skulked back to my room with a towel draped over my face. I wasn't sure if the pain in my head was from my injury or from the headache created by my own folly.

"Ronnie, are you awake?" asked my dad from the kitchen. "Come tell us about that silly dance. And where is your car? It's not in the driveway."

Fuck. I forgot about the Duster. "It's at Tommy's house," I called back. "Sundar took me home because . . . because I was running low on gas and I was worried that the station on Highway 2 would be closed. I didn't want to take any chances. I'll get it today. Sorry. I'll be there in a minute. Just let me get dressed." Great. I was already lying.

Panic set in as I vacillated between the factual and fictional versions of my tale, and sweat poured down my face as I removed the towel and dressed. Though during my seventeen years I had perfected the art of procrastination, I knew that on this occasion—this debacle, this fucking fiasco—I could no longer stall. Forget the IBS that Dr. Rajendran promised would manifest itself if my deceit continued; I was now on the verge of a fully-fledged panic attack. As the adrenaline once again flowed freely within my body, I felt the thud of my pulse in my ears and, for the first time in my life, I experienced *real* tunnel vision. I sat down on my bed with my head in my hands, trembling with fear. I closed my eyes and concentrated on my breathing to prevent myself from hyperventilating. I began to encounter chest pain, and tried to intellectualize to myself that I was not, indeed, having a heart attack. I was too young. Or was I? I was too healthy. Or was I? Fuck. I really thought I might die.

Breathe. So what was really going to happen if I went out there, prostrated myself and divulged my sins? Would they forgive me? Would they disown me? Would my dad turn biblical on me and stone me? Zillie's words of advice—"fucking *carpe diem*," and "don't be a coward"—eventually echoed enough to prevail and willed me to stand.

I walked out of my room and, with dread, headed toward the kitchen. I was exhausted, not just from lack of sleep, but also from the myriad emotions that had depleted me over the previous thirty-six hours. A profound sense of immaturity overwhelmed me. I had failed miserably as a boyfriend and as a son; how could I handle the responsibility of becoming a doctor, let alone a singer?

I crossed the threshold of the kitchen with my head hung low. Then I looked up.

"Ronnie, what happened?" my mother yelled as she stared at me in horror.

"Everything," I answered, solemnly.

"What the hell is going on?" my father demanded.

"I made some mistakes. Actually, a lot of mistakes."

"Who did that to you?" my mother implored.

"Tommy."

"I'll kill him!" roared my father.

"No, it was my fault," I argued. "I deserved it. And I'll be fine. Dr. Rajendran already took a look at my face and told me there was no fracture . . . but there are some things I have to tell you. You're not going to be happy with me, but try and understand . . ."

"Ronnie, you're scaring me. What did you do?" my mother asked. She grabbed ice from the freezer, wrapped it in a dishtowel, and hurriedly applied it to my face. She began to sob. Fantastic. This was going really well so far.

Surprisingly, instead of collapsing with the weight of my embarrassment, it was at that moment that I became consumed with the desire to grab my parents by the collar of their JC Penney his and hers terrycloth bathrobes and make them understand that I could not possibly live up to their unrealistic expectations of a seventeen year old Jewish kid from Lincoln, Nebraska. I got it; they were protecting me . . . but couldn't they comprehend my desire for assimilation and companionship? How much were their sacrifices worth if neither they nor I could be happy as a result?

"Look!" I howled. "I've been dating Amy since last Halloween. She's my girlfriend. Or she *was* my girlfriend. I wanted to have sex with her, but she wasn't ready. I got really drunk last night, and ended up naked with Tommy's girlfriend instead. Tommy caught us, punched me in the face, and knocked me out. There! That's it!"

A horrible silence ensued. What probably lasted all of ten seconds felt like eons. Then my eyes began to dart, alternating between views of my parents. Tears poured down my mother's face. I had rendered her speechless. Finally, my father pursed his lips. His face became flush with rage, and I braced myself for an eruption of volcanic proportions.

Instead, my father suddenly clutched his chest, grimaced, turned pale, and collapsed.

CHAPTER 24

"You're running around, I can't stand it
You're fooling around with my heart"

—ERIC CLAPTON'S "I CAN'T STAND IT," FROM THE
ALBUM *ANOTHER TICKET*, RELEASED FEBRUARY 11TH, 1981.
IT PEAKED AT NUMBER TEN ON US BILLBOARD'S HOT
100 SONGS.

My father regained consciousness within seconds, but intense chest pain persisted. My mother turned to me and yelled, "Get on the phone and call an ambulance right now! It has to be his heart!" I watched, astonished, as, for the first time in my life, this relentlessly proud, strong, and fearless man appeared frightened to me. My mother held his hand, as though attempting to transfer these superpowers to herself so that she could now rise to the occasion. She turned and glanced at me, just long enough so that I knew she felt I was utterly reckless, selfish, and inept.

"911 dispatcher, what is your emergency?"

"Uh . . . I think my father's had a heart attack."

"Is he conscious?"

"Yes, but he's in a lot of pain and he's short of breath."

One good thing about living in a city the size and density of Lincoln is that emergency vehicles can reach any house within three minutes. I heard a siren almost immediately, and paramedics from Lincoln Fire Station #6 arrived just moments later.

My mother knelt at my father's side while I greeted two burly, uniformed men at the door. The blond, crew cut, corn-fed pair, who undoubtedly played football in former lives, nearly tossed me aside like a ragdoll while positioning a gurney next to my father.

"Step aside, please," the larger of the two announced quickly and firmly. The name GARNER was boldly embroidered in gold above his navy chest pocket.

I watched in amazement as Garner and his partner, Jameson, seamlessly, if not compassionately, tag-teamed both verbal and physical duties.

"What's your name, sir?" asked Garner.

"Ezekiel."

"What's wrong, Ezekiel?" asked Jameson.

"I don't know. My chest feels like an elephant is stepping on it. And my left arm is killing me."

"Okay, Ezekiel, we think you're having a heart attack," answered Garner.

"What are you talking about? I'm not having a heart attack. I'm just upset because my son is an idiot."

Undeterred, Jameson interjected. "Ezekiel, we *really* think you're having a heart attack, and we don't have time to quibble with you. Here's some aspirin. I want you to chew on it. It's going to help with the clot in your heart. Then I want you to stick this nitroglycerin tablet under your tongue. It'll help relieve the pain. Then I'm going to place an oxygen mask over your face to increase the amount of oxygen that goes to your heart."

My father resisted by placing a hand over his face. "Wait! Nitroglycerin? Isn't that for dynamite? I'll explode! I don't want it."

Garner and Jameson couldn't help but grin at each other after hearing my father's unintended comic relief. "You're not going to explode, Ezekiel. I promise. We're professionally trained to treat this kind of problem. We're going to take you to the hospital right away so the doctors and nurses can take care of your heart. Every second counts, so take the medications, let us put the mask on your face, and let's go," said Jameson, matter-of-factly. Jameson and Garner gave my dad one second and one combined look that rendered any opposition to their instructions futile. My father then dutifully chewed, dissolved, and masked his way to the hospital.

"Don't tail the ambulance . . . it's not safe," stated Garner. "We're going to Lincoln General, so meet us in there in the emergency room."

Before being loaded into the ambulance, my father gave one last forlorn look to my mother. Though she kept it together, seeing him in a sickly, vulnerable, and defeated position was too much for me to bear. He left. She drove. I cried.

I was officially the world's worst person.

My already-conservative mother took her instructions very seriously; the eight-minute, normally pleasant, sloped, grassy, flower-dotted 2.7-mile drive from South 39th Street —past Benjie's house, Maude Rousseau Elementary School, and the Lincoln Country Club—to Lincoln General Hospital, took exactly eight excruciating minutes. "Please go faster," I pleaded.

"No. I don't want to compound one mistake with another." It was a fun ride.

THE emergency room was simultaneously antiseptic and stale; it smelled of rubbing alcohol and pus. The charge nurse first escorted us past both an elderly man moaning about bedsores and a freckle-faced teenage girl huffing and puffing staccato breaths during an asthma treatment. Then we reached my father. Instead of exploding from the nitroglycerin, he was having an animated conversation with a doctor, as though the two of them were talking politics. Dumbfounded, my mother and I rushed to his side.

"Dad, are you okay?" I asked while propping the pillow under his head. I had no idea what else to do.

"Yes, I'm fine. Stop fussing over me."

"What do you mean, you're fine?"

"I mean you still make me want to pull my hair out, but I no longer feel as though I'm being hugged by grizzly bear."

IV tubing dangled from his right arm, and a cluster of wires was attached to twelve "leads" spread over his body. We had clearly interrupted my father and the emergency room physician, Dr. Driver. In reality, the two of them were having a heated discussion about my father's EKG, which appeared to have confirmed a heart attack.

"Ronnie, leave your father alone," interjected my mother, with both fear and exasperation. Let's find out what the doctor has to say."

Dr. Larry Driver was a ruddy-faced, middle-aged, rotund man with a red but balding crown of hair and a red but greying beard. I could have sworn I was looking at Santa Claus's son. He had a jolly disposition to match, and a challenging patient such as my father appeared to pose no obstacle to his ability to care for his patients.

"Mr. Bahar, the EKG shows that you've experienced a disruption in blood flow in your right coronary artery . . ."

"That's *Doctor* Bahar, and explain to me exactly what you're talking about. I'm an electrical engineering professor. I'll understand."

"Okay, but only for a moment. Every . . ."

". . . second counts. Yes, I know. That's what the paramedic said. But I'm not doing anything without understanding what's happening to me."

"Okay, here goes . . . but this is going to be the quick and dirty version, Dr. Bahar." He turned and pointed to the EKG. "These are tracings that reflect the electrical activity of the heart from the electrodes we put on your body. Part of these tracings is called the ST segment. When this segment is elevated in these three tracings as it is in yours, it means you have a clot in your right coronary artery, and it's blocking the flow of blood to the backside of your heart. That's the heart attack right there, and that's why you're having pain, or 'angina,' as we call it. It's not the worst kind of heart attack, but it's a heart attack nonetheless. Now, there's a new IV medication we're giving called streptokinase. It's an enzyme that comes from bacteria, and it helps the body jumpstart its ability to break up clots. It's a relatively new drug and we know it works, but we need your consent to use it."

"Well, what are the risks?" asked my father.

"Bleeding, abnormal heart rhythms, and low blood pressure."

"Could it kill me?"

"Yes it could, but you're much more likely to die from an untreated heart attack than you are from the streptokinase. The potential benefits of the medication clearly outweigh the risks, and I strongly recommend giving it to you without further delay."

My father stared at the EKG and was obviously fascinated by the upward and downward deflections of the tracings that literally put in black and white his clearly defined predicament. However, his normally left-sided analytical brain occasionally succumbed to irrationality.

"Can't I just go on a crash diet?" he inquired. Again, my father offered some poorly timed inadvertent humor.

"No, Doctor, you can't. Please sign this consent form so we can go ahead and give the medication," he said with a sympathetic smile.

My father looked at the paper and then at my mother, and said, "I don't think I should do it. It sounds too risky."

My mother, who could no longer contain herself, intervened:

Hebrew:	"יחזקאל, חתום כאן!"
Transliteration:	"Yehezkel, chatom kann!"
Literal Translation:	"Ezekiel, sign here!"
Intended Translation:	"Listen, since we've been together I've let you make all of the important family decisions, including moving me away from my home. But this is a matter of life and death, and if you think I'm going to sit idly by while you meditate, you're wrong. So take that fucking pen, sign that fucking paper, and do what the doctor says, do you understand?"

My father signed the paper, took his medicine, and lived. And I was a total fuckhead.

CHAPTER 25

"Since you're gone
Well, nothing's makin' any sense"

—THE CARS' "SINCE YOU'RE GONE," FROM THE ALBUM
SHAKE IT UP, RELEASED MARCH 8TH, 1982.
IT PEAKED AT NUMBER FORTY-ONE ON US BILLBOARD'S
HOT 100 SONGS.

A sshole."

I turned my head as I shut my locker. It was Christine, Amy's best friend and my strongest and hopefully most sympathetic remaining link with my newly ex-girlfriend. My friendship with Chris sprouted when she moved to my neighborhood in ninth grade; we immediately bonded through the torture of Mr. Horvath's orchestra class. He was mean, and I sucked. Not a great combination. Chris played the violin, and I attempted to play the French horn. It's difficult to imagine anything less sexy than an already awkward fourteen-year-old boy, badly in need of a shave and some acne cream, playing that instrument, and she was only too happy to remind me of my shortcomings whenever the opportunity arose. Chris was not only smart, but she was also funny. She had a way of making me laugh at myself despite the merciless ridicule.

Though she had a heart of gold, Chris came from three generations of no-nonsense Nebraska cattle ranchers, and, like her forefathers, she never minced words. Oddly, she looked like Mary Anne from *Gilligan's Island* (unfortunately, without the red and white checked halter top). So, despite her wholesome exterior, she had to be taken seriously.

If I had escaped Tommy's house without being "exposed," of course I would have felt differently. As I was not much of an athlete, I had hoped that my academic and sexual conquests would represent my victory lap as I headed toward my graduation from Lincoln Southeast High School. Inevitably, my stupidity and hubris cost me dearly; my anticipated triumph had become nothing more than a joke. I had broken essentially every unwritten rule of decorum, and I had stripped myself from my self-imagined status as perhaps the school's greatest Renaissance Man. Chris was not going to let me off easy.

"Chris, what can I tell you? I fucked up."

"Yes, you did fuck up . . . royally. But before I tell you what a dick you are, tell me how your dad's doing."

I could scarcely look her in the eye. "It's only been a few days, but he's already a lot better. Thanks for asking. He's going to be in cardiac rehab for about two months, and he has to take a lot of medicine and change the way he eats and exercises, but the doctors say he should be okay."

"Thank God," she said, obviously relieved. "You know I've always had a soft spot for him . . . Okay, back to you: what the hell were you thinking?"

"Chris, don't rub it in. She was absolutely perfect, and I blew it—"

"Wait!" she interrupted. "What do you mean 'perfect?' Amy's a lot of things—she's my best friend and I love that girl—but she's certainly not perfect. Stop putting her on an unrealistic pedestal, dipshit, and put your actions in perspective. She really loved you and thought you were different. She thought you were nice. And smart. And romantic. And honest. So it turned out you were most of those things, but you weren't honest. So deal with it."

"How?"

"I'm not sure. She's *really* pissed right now. And I think you should know something—and you can't tell anyone or I'll kick you in the nuts—Tommy paid Amy a visit after his party. She hasn't told anyone else, but *I'm* telling you because I care about you, even if you *are* a jackass."

I swallowed hard. I had to feign ignorance, and at the same time I wanted desperately to understand exactly what happened and exactly how Amy felt about Tommy . . . and about me. I suppressed the urge to spill my guts to Christine. I hadn't even told Sundar what events ensued after I had left his house. "Oh God," was all I could manage in response.

"Well, I think she might be into him. And Tommy usually gets what he wants." *Thanks for reminding me, Chris.*

"Did they . . ."

"I don't know," she said earnestly. "Listen, Amy and I are close and she and I have talked a lot about you for a long time, *way* before you ever started going out with her. She knew how you felt about her, but she knew that you were shy around girls. She loved that about you and she knew that she had to push you along, so she did. She loved that you cared about her when her parents split up. She loved you for who *you* were, and yes, you fucked up. So I know what's going on in your head. I know you worked really hard the last three years and you've been imagining yourself as a perfect student with a perfect voice and a perfect girlfriend and a perfect future as a perfect doctor. You were going to show the world that it didn't matter that that you were a little different than everyone else, that you were an underdog. You were going to be a hero. Well, it didn't work out that way, because you didn't love her for who *she* was. So don't tell me you think she's perfect; if she were you wouldn't have done what you did. Now you're just wallowing in self-pity. But guess what? You're not perfect either."

The truth rendered me speechless.

She stared at my swollen face and paused briefly before speaking. "You look like shit, you know? I just don't want either of you to get hurt any more than you already have been." She shook her head. "Give your dad a kiss for me," she said, and walked away.

THAT evening, after dinner, the doorbell rang. I grudgingly arose from the family room couch and turned my eyes away from the television. I didn't want to miss the end of *Family Ties*, but I thought it would be a bad idea to give my parents the impression that I was both stupid *and* lazy. I searched through the peephole and saw Amy. I could feel my pulse accelerate. Holy shit, was she really going to forgive me? I quickly fumbled for the knob and opened the door.

"Hi," I said nervously.

She dressed casually in a Supertramp T-shirt, Levi's, and Keds, and her tousled hair covered her right eye. I adored that look, all of it. With both arms she held a grocery bag, and I instinctively reached out over it to remove the irresistible lock from her face. She responded with a limbo maneuver and an upward blow from the corner of her mouth to dodge me and to clear her view. The bag then seemed strategically placed as a buffer from me. "I'm here to see your dad," she said plainly and walked directly past me into the kitchen. She knew, from spending those many evenings at my house, that my parents would be there at 7:30 drinking tea and reading the paper.

Amy placed the grocery bag on the table, and my parents stood and greeted her with authentic but pained smiles and silent embraces. There was little to say, but to observe the moment was more excruciating than to participate in it. Amy finally spoke. "Dr. Bahar, why don't you see what's in the bag?"

My convalescent dad tentatively reached inside and retrieved three Tupperware containers. As he opened them, one by one, his anguish disappeared. "Why did you decide to do this, and how did you know how to make all of it?" he asked.

"Well, I figured that since you love Indian food, and since you have to watch what you eat now, I'd try and make you some vegetarian dishes. So I went to Mrs. Rajendran's house this afternoon, and we cooked some things I thought you'd like." She turned to my mom. "I hope you don't mind. I really love your food and I didn't want to overstep any bounds, but—"

"Don't be silly, Amy . . . I think it's great." Of course, my mother wiped away tears. I stood idly by and watched like an idiot, *persona non grata* in my own home.

"This one is mango dal. Here's ginger, split pea, and vegetable curry, I think they call it *Subzi dalcha*."

"Yes, yes, yes!" confirmed my father, excitedly.

"And that last one's cauliflower stew."

"Amy, I don't know what to say . . . I *do* love it . . . but you didn't need to do this," added my father, who was clearly and genuinely touched.

"I know I didn't. I just wanted to. You both have been so good to me over the years . . . it was the least I could do."

"Will you come over tomorrow evening and eat it with us for dinner?" asked my mother.

"I don't think that would be a good idea," she responded, now looking downward. "I think I should go." She then hugged my parents briefly once more and headed straight for the front door while avoiding eye contact with me. She let herself out. My uncomfortable mother quietly placed the Tupperware in the refrigerator as my dad refocused his attention on the newspaper.

I couldn't possibly have felt smaller.

CHAPTER 26

*"I keep forgettin' things will never be the same again
I keep forgettin' how you made that so clear"*

—MICHAEL McDONALD'S "I KEEP FORGETTIN' (EVERY
TIME YOU'RE NEAR)," FROM THE ALBUM *IF THAT'S WHAT IT
TAKES*, RELEASED AUGUST, 1982. IT PEAKED AT NUMBER
FOUR ON US BILLBOARD'S HOT 100 SONGS.

I spent the remaining weeks of the school year keeping to myself. I was utterly defeated; the ubiquitous staring and snickering chipped away at my dying soul like a vulture. The subtle, insidious, but continuous volley of contempt from classmates, teachers, hall monitors, and janitors alike proved almost too much to bear.

In contrast to the discrete sounds of giggling, a visit to the men's room provided an unregulated backdrop for a dramatic re-creation of my after-prom debacle. In his typically cheeky manner, Mark Gross broke the two unwritten public restroom rules that (a) a guy doesn't use the urinal directly next to another guy if other urinals are available, and (b) a guy never, *ever* looks at another guy's penis when the first guy is taking a piss. With Sundar and Andy Weigel witnessing, Mark stared directly at my unit and declared, "Dude, nice cock! Too bad you never had a chance to give Julia a ride with that crotch rocket!" With his own drawers dropped, he grabbed his own dick and thrusted. "Oh, Julia, take me home!" he wailed. He contorted his face, pretended to climax, and immediately fell asleep, still standing, in narcoleptic fashion. Then, just as suddenly, he awakened, rearranged his furniture, zipped up, and walked out. I wanted to laugh with, cry with, and kill Mark all at once.

Demoralized, I looked up at Sundar and Andy. Sundar shrugged and explained, "Dude, you gotta admit . . . he's fuckin' hilarious."

Andy was perhaps the politest person on the planet. Even so, he chuckled, shook his head, and added, "Ron, I'm . . . I'm sorry. You made your bed, you lie in it."

Despite the unintended attention, I felt utterly alone.

EVEN Mr. Dupuis couldn't help. Gossip regarding the weekend's events reached the teachers' lounge almost immediately, and my subsequent encounter with my mentor and idol was quite uncomfortable. We never discussed what transpired; there was no need, as his disillusioned eyes said everything. He immediately accommodated Amy's request to switch seats with Matt Decker, who had perhaps the world's worst body odor. I then felt I had suffered enough. Though he continued to lecture with a smile, I couldn't really pay attention to what would otherwise have been a scintillating discussion of vitamin K and its role in blood clotting. Paranoia replaced humiliation, and I sensed thirty pairs of eyes burning a hole in the back of my head.

After class, I approached Amy's new desk with no distinct plan in mind. I simply wanted to communicate with her, as every attempt since my misadventure had been snubbed. "Amy," I said with trepidation. She turned and stared blankly at me. "I understand that you won't return my phone calls . . . I actually don't know if your mom ever gave you the messages I left, but—"

"She *did* give me the messages," she interrupted, "but I had no desire to call you back. I *really* have nothing to say to you. I think you should leave me alone."

"But I'm—"

"You're what? Sorry? I don't want to hear about it," she answered sharply. She slung her backpack over her shoulder and exited in disgust.

I grabbed my notebook and headed for the door to follow her.

"Let her go, Ron. Just give her space." It was Mr. Dupuis, who tried to stop me from across the room. "I don't know if you'll ever get her back, but if you want that chance, you have to be patient."

We stared at each other for a moment. "Okay," I answered meekly, and left.

The embarrassment and the subsequent wound were deep. I thought Frank Dupuis envisioned me as his protégé, and was, therefore, mortified at my depravity. I knew he was still rooting for me, but I would rather he slug me in my remaining good eye than be embarrassed by me. I didn't need anyone to pity me, and I knew I deserved the treatment I had already received, but good God, how long was this indignity going to last?

MY dad appeared gaunt and exhausted as he arrived at my high school graduation ceremony surrounded by my mother, Zillie, and Iris; despite the rehabilitation process, the heart attack had taken its toll on his body. However, with the support of his family, he remained surprisingly upbeat.

"Ronnie, I'm very proud of you," he said, smiling. My visiting sisters, who flanked and locked arms with him on both sides, simply rolled their eyes.

Though my mother was still nervous about my father's every move, she, too, was happy. She did, after all, wear her best pantsuit and derby hat for the event. She hugged me and said, "You've made it," whatever that meant.

Though my parents did not openly blame me for inducing my father's heart attack, I remained wracked with guilt. Yes, he ate too much. Yes, he was sedentary. Yes, he had a family history of heart disease. But I was still a jackass.

I think my mother was so delighted that my father survived such a traumatic event and that I was leaving for medical school in a few months that she left the "Amy issue" alone. My parents must have also (correctly) assumed that Amy and I were not on speaking terms. Indeed, since my father's homecoming, Steven Andrews had called him several times to wish him a speedy recovery. Though I didn't know exactly what else was discussed, my father's strangely placid behavior suggested he understood Amy's antipathy towards me.

For the graduation ceremony, boys were paired with girls in a walk down the aisle at downtown Lincoln's Pershing Auditorium. Besides its façade's giant cartoon mural of the sporting events it presented, the 4526-seat multipurpose arena was perhaps best known for its annual hosting of the National Roller Skating Championships.

According to tradition, a graduating girl asks a graduating boy to the walk. Though the pairing was strategized, it was not to be misconstrued as romantic; the invitation was entirely platonic. Nevertheless, those who went unasked were extremely disappointed, as the absence of a partner would trigger a random pairing from the vice-principal: a jock with a nerd, a stoner with a cheerleader. The chameleon in me didn't care about her social status; I just needed a friend. Somehow Christine had mercy on me and decided it would be a good idea for us to take the stroll together.

"Ron, you've got to get over yourself. I'm doing this for you *and* for Amy," she explained. "She doesn't know we're walking together. She's going to be pissed at me for this, but it's going to make you look a little more human. I've known you for a long time now, and I know that deep down, you're not a total shithead. Maybe just ninety percent," she said, grinning.

I mustered a smile in return.

THE graduation ceremony itself was, well, unceremonious. For the event, I was adorned with some stupid fucking gold medal and some stupid fucking gold sash for finishing school with straight fucking As. Who fucking cared?

Of all of the 483 graduates seated at the floor of the arena, Chris and I sat directly behind Amy . . . and Tommy. Platonic, my ass. What demonic vice-principal planned this arrangement?

Rather than listen to the mind-numbing speeches about ambition, regret, and the world being my oyster, I stared at the back of Amy's head for seventy-four minutes. The slight wave of her mane of hair cascaded flirtatiously from the space between her cap and gown and shined spectacularly under the spotlights. When she adjusted her hair, her head tilted to the right in such a way that was both inquisitive and sexy. In doing so, her left earlobe was revealed. Even *it* was sultry; it shimmered from the diamond hoop earring she had received from her parents for graduation. She was imbued with Ralph Lauren's Lauren, a scent I associated with those amorous moments with Amy in the Duster, and eventually I found myself leaning forward, closing my eyes, and taking a whiff. In my defense, if she wasn't perfect, she was pretty goddamn close.

Suddenly, I felt Chris punching me in the shoulder. She did her best to suppress screaming at me, and instead whispered, "What the hell are you doing, freak show? You think being a stalker will help get her back?"

Though I regained my composure, Tommy put his arm around Amy's shoulder as if to say, "Fuck you, Ron." As he did so, Amy's head tilted just a bit more in his direction. Her hair shined a little more brightly, her earlobe dangled a little more seductively, and her scent emanated a little more robustly. "Fuck you again, Ron," added Amy, without saying a word.

I seethed as I considered the most practical way of amputating Tommy's arm. Then I remembered that I had no one to blame but myself. Chris pulled me back into my chair, and I continued to smolder. Once again I closed my eyes, this time in an attempt to transport myself to last October and Tommy's backyard and the fog and seeing Amy and her silhouette in the black cat costume and being nervous but drunk with desire and kissing her for the first time and . . .

"Ron, what is *wrong* with you?" implored Chris, this time with a stronger punch and a louder whisper. I opened my eyes, somewhat disoriented. "Get up, whack job! We're getting our diplomas!"

Just ahead in the aisle walked Amy and Tommy. They were holding hands; Tommy sauntered and Amy turned to him, if only for a moment, to offer him a smile. They looked so comfortable I nearly vomited, again.

Sensing both my anguish and my nausea, Chris had had enough. "Listen, dumbshit, this is *my* graduation too, so don't try to ruin it for both of us by feeling sorry for yourself. Now hold my hand like a real companion and let's go."

I did as I was told. Through each step I was reminded of the difference between those with an agenda and those who provide true friendship. As we approached the stage, Chris offered *me* a smile. I answered with a grin, but I felt petty as I was summoned to receive my diploma after Chris.

"Ron. Jonathan. Bahar," barked Principal Wesley Lauterbach from his podium. I walked across the stage mechanically, barely looking up to take the certificate in its folder from none other than Mr. Dupuis. Our eyes met. I said nothing. What was there to say? Mark Gross was naked under his gown. Sundar high-fived the principal. Anne Read wore a Goldilocks wig. I did and said nothing. Three fucking years and I did and said nothing.

Mr. Dupuis shook my hand and pleaded, "Ron, lighten up, it's graduation day. I told you, be patient."

As Chris and I returned to our seats, Amy's eyes met mine. She quickly panned toward Chris and back to me before pursing her lips. She wasn't flustered. She was fuming. Once seated, Chris leaned toward me and whispered one final time, "I'll deal with her later, but you owe me."

When all of the names were called, a final benediction was given, and Principal Lauterbach bestowed a hearty "Congratulations, Class of 1983!" to all of us. Caps and tassels flew skyward with a simultaneous cheer. The anticlimax was profound.

Now what?

CHAPTER 27

"I walk along the city streets you used to walk along with me
And every step I take reminds me of just how we used to be"

— "ALWAYS SOMETHING THERE TO REMIND ME," WRITTEN
BY BURT BACHARACH AND HAL DAVID, RECORDED BY THE
BAND NAKED EYES FOR THEIR ALBUM *BURNING BRIDGES*,
RELEASED JANUARY, 1983. IT PEAKED AT NUMBER EIGHT ON
US BILLBOARD'S HOT 100 SONGS.

With my Bar Mitzvah money, I purchased two items; the first of which was a royal blue Schwinn ten-speed bike. I had to argue with my parents in order to buy the men's model. They were concerned that, with the bike's horizontal crossbar, the family jewels would be crushed with just one merciless thump over just the wrong crack created by asphalt, which would buckle under just the right amount of pressure created by a combination of syca-more roots and the sweltering Midwestern summer sun. I could only imagine the mockery I would experience while riding around my neighborhood with the dreaded women's diagonal crossbar. Perhaps the last thing a teenager is ca-pable of doing is *not* succumbing to peer pressure, so my pleas for avoiding such a fate were indeed passionate. My eventual victory represented a small, but important moment in my ascent to manhood.

The second acquisition was a Minolta XG-7 single lens reflex camera with a 50 mm f/1.4 lens. Its silver and black exterior was beautiful, and I treated it like the prized possession that it was. Despite the fact that it was always stored in its case, I followed my parents' cocooning advice and created a special supplemental protective padded nest for it in the outer pocket of my otherwise overflowing backpack. With it, at a moment's notice I was able to chronicle, often inadvertently, myriad moments that made me feel different from my peers, such as Christmas caroling, public displays of affection, or any demonstration of athletic prowess.

Once Amy and I started dating, I took photographs of her at every opportunity. Though she had disdain for the limelight, she grudgingly obliged. In these images, which cataloged everyday moments—from mediocre finishes at cross country meets to fast food runs at The Runza Hut to performances of The Repeats—she was strategically placed so that, while she would not be the center of attention, her unintentionally irresistible grin always stood out. I was, therefore, able to post these pictures neatly on my bedroom wall without arousing my parents' curiosity.

I kept only one photograph of the two of us in my wallet. It was a simple snapshot taken by Chris the prior November at the high school parking lot in front of the Duster. I loved it because it wasn't pretentious. There was no posing involved; there was just the two of us leaning against the car holding hands while smiling, not at the camera, but at each other. We were deeply in love.

AFTER graduation, I worked as a non-kosher sandwich maker at our local Wendy's for about one month before following the money north, up 48th Street, to work with Sundar selling cameras at Target. In the process, my pay rose from $3.35 per hour to $3.40 per hour.

Initially Sundar offered to make plans with me, to play tennis (John McEnroe had just won his third Wimbledon title), to go to a movie (*Return of the Jedi* was in full swing in theaters), or to meet up with Anne to reminisce or divulge our intentions of conquering Planet Earth. I routinely declined; it just didn't feel right. An outsider would likely accuse me of irrationality, but I felt lost, that my future was meaningless without Amy. Both Sundar's patience with me and his invitations eventually waned.

After one such feeble, "No thank you," from me, instead of responding with his usual, "Suit yourself," Sundar finally expressed his frustration. "Come on, dude. Remember what I told you a long time ago? It's all in the attitude. There *will* be other Amys. She's a great girl, but you gotta move on."

BENJIE was irreverent and even less patient, so his attempt to interrupt my reclusive existence began with a knock on my bedroom door, followed by an imitation of yours truly.

"Amy, it's me, Ron! Open up!"

"Shut up!" I answered, irritated, but still somewhat amused. I opened the door and offered a smile, but tried to remain pathetic. "My parents will hear."

"Who cares?" He responded as he walked in my room. "I can't possibly do any more damage than you've already done."

"Good point," I answered, nodding.

"Jesus, who died in here? Open your fuckin' window, man. Your room smells like an armpit . . . do you ever leave it?"

"Only to go to work," I responded. I honored his request. Upon pulling the shades, my dimly lit room burst with the light and color of life. I then opened the window. The room was instantly permeated by the scent of our rose bushes mixed with fresh-cut grass from the neighbor's lawn. I was practically tipsy from the aroma. I felt like a newly blind man who, because of his disability, learned to compensate by concentrating on his remaining senses. I had become an expert in taking what I had for granted.

"Well, what the hell do you do here all day?"

"I don't know. I think."

"About what?"

I simply stared back. I didn't need to answer for him to understand.

"Okay, I get it," he continued. "Listen, Ron. I'm covering a new song, and I want you to hear it."

"Okay, hit me. What is it?"

"We've mostly been working on original songs for Rex and Capitol Records before we go out on the road, but I couldn't resist this one. I just love it. It's actually *a cover of a cover* of an old Elvis song. Came out this year. It's country, and I know that's not your genre, but just hang with me for a minute. Let's go to your piano. I need a keyboard, not a guitar."

I scanned my limited memory of the Elvis library, but I couldn't think of the tune I was about to hear.

We entered the living room and he took a seat at the piano bench. After an exaggerated throat clearing, and with his best Willie Nelson twang, he began:

"Maybe I didn't love you
Quite as good as I could have . . ."

Oh God, I thought, as I began to realize what I was hearing. "You're an asshole," I said, chuckling. "I'm going to fucking kill you." Of course I was not going to fucking kill him. Upon finishing "Always On My Mind," Benjie erupted with a belly laugh. I joined; it felt good.

"Okay, that was awesome and I deserved it." I said.

"One last thing," he added. "Do me a favor and stop taking yourself so seriously."

"I like your trout, Mrs. Bahar . . . but I *really* miss your brisket," announced Benjie at dinner.

"Me, too," she admitted longingly. "I miss my chocolate cake also but we all have to adapt to my husband's new diet." She turned to me and sighed. Oh, Jesus.

Benjie was oblivious to my mother's reaction, and instead focused the rest of the evening on extricating me from my funk. One nearly too successful attempt at lighting his unrelenting farts barely got a rise out me, but did result in scorched denim and a red ass. Like Sundar, he eventually tired of my moping. "Well, I think I'd better go. I have band practice tonight. Thanks so much for dinner, Mrs. Bahar." He shook my father's hand and then he pointed at me. "Maybe next time you can get this bum to come over to *my* house. He should get out more often. It's the middle of the summer and he's pale as a ghost."

I washed the dishes and, naturally, returned to my room to stare at my photos. After a few minutes, I heard another knock on my door. My parents didn't wait for a response; the door opened and they entered together.

"Ronnie, it's time to go."

CHAPTER 28

"And while I'm away
Dust out the demons inside"

—ELTON JOHN'S "I GUESS THAT'S WHY THEY CALL IT
THE BLUES," FROM THE ALBUM *TOO LOW FOR ZERO*, RELEASED
MAY 23RD, 1983. IT PEAKED AT NUMBER FOUR ON US
BILLBOARD'S HOT 100 SONGS.

gazed out the airplane portside and marveled at the beauty of the Mediterranean Sea and sunrise at the beach in Tel Aviv. A few minutes later and some fifteen miles southeast, per tradition, the passengers applauded as the wheels touched down at Ben Gurion Airport in the town of Lod. I had participated in this custom four times before, and it never seemed contrived. It was always organic, as were the tears that ran down the faces of many onboard.

As a child I memorized the map of Israel, even when its borders changed over time. My mother cried when, in 1982, Dan Rather reported on Israel's withdrawal from her namesake settlement Ophira, which was subsequently renamed Sharm el-Shekh by the Egyptians. The moment was bittersweet; the change also represented hope, which was already challenged by the assassination of Egypt's prime minister Anwar Sadat the year before. "Maybe something good will come from all this mess," she said, hopefully.

Perhaps my parents had the same thought when they

compelled me to visit my grandfather, potentially for the last
time.

Hebrew:	"רוני, אתה צריך לבקר את הסבא שלך בישראל."
Transliteration:	"Ronnie, ata t'sareech levaker et hasabah shelcha b'yisrael."
Literal Translation:	"Ronnie, you have to go to Israel to visit your grandfather. He has a lifetime of knowledge to share, and it's possible you may never see him again."
Intended Translation:	"Ronnie, get your ass over to Israel to see Grandpa. Stop feeling sorry for yourself and listen to a man who had every reason to despair but never did. Perhaps he can knock some sense into you so you can get over Amy and leave for medical school with a clear head."

I didn't actually need much convincing to go to Israel. Zalman Rodov would turn eighty-six in the fall of 1983, and though he had slowed dramatically and could no longer live alone without assistance, his mind was sharp as a tack. I idolized him as the Clark Kent of Israeli Independence: a humble man who, when called to duty, rose to the occasion, but when his mission of helping create a country was accomplished, he returned to his job as a land surveyor as though nothing had ever happened. Don't fuck with Zalman.

I had last visited Israel two years prior, when I attended

Chetz V'keshet, Hebrew for bow and arrow. The ten-week program catered to children of American and Canadian expatriates, who traveled the country alongside Israeli soldiers and youth. This was no ordinary teen tour; it was the Boy Scouts and Girl Scouts on steroids. Though we roamed the Old City in Jerusalem, rode camels with Bedouins, and ate falafel like most North American visitors, we also learned to fire M16 rifles by day and hiked in formation silently for hours by night under the moonlit sky.

On a salacious and much lighter note, for many, camp was synonymous with sex. Some, like me, traded only saliva, whereas the more adventurous ones knocked the proverbial army boots. The male scouts also loved spending time with women in uniform, though nothing particularly inappropriate occurred between the two groups. There is definitely something ridiculously sexy about a female soldier in army fatigues with a machine gun strapped around her shoulder. Years later, *Lara Croft: Tomb Raider* would have nothing on them.

My grandfather lived in my parents' old apartment on International Street in Haifa in the foothills of Mount Carmel—thought to be the home of Elijah the Prophet, who defended the worship of God over that of an idol. The distance from Lod, past Tel Aviv, up the Mediterranean coast by the juxtaposed modern high-rise city of Netanya and the ancient deep-sea harbor village of Caesarea, was only seventy-five miles. However, with traffic on two lane highways, along with a transfer at Haifa's central bus station, the trek lasted about four hours. Though I was exhausted from my inability to sleep on the plane, upright and cramped next to the world's loudest snorer (a rotund orthodox man with a penchant for leaning heavily, drooling, and poking his voluminous beard in my ear), I was energized by the sight of the sand and the water and the smell of pine and eucalyptus trees.

Haifa is often compared to San Francisco for its hilly topography and its spectacular ocean views. However, as the bus climbed the mountain, I could no longer concentrate on the sights because of an overwhelming sensation of sadness that Amy was not with me. Though I missed her terribly, it was not so much that I needed a companion. I honestly just wanted her to see Israel and my grandfather. I reflected on the experiences of my senior year of high school. It was my own fault that Amy would not even speak to me; I was, indeed, an idiot. Had she traveled with me, it would be her head on my shoulder as she slept on the plane. We would hold hands on the bus, and I wouldn't need to explain anything to her about Israel. She would already have read every detail and viewed every map regarding what we were about to experience. I knew she would have loved it. My girlfriend. My religion. My foolishness. My mess.

IT was late morning, and my grandfather answered the door. He stood all of 5 feet, 4 inches tall and used a cane to reach me, but to me he retained a towering, regal presence. He wore his signature wardrobe: khaki-colored slacks and black loafers, with a kerchief tucked perfectly in his pressed shirt pocket. He maintained a full head of hair, crowned by a silver swath that shamed any man's comb-over. He looked me up and down with his steely blue eyes, smiled, hugged me and proclaimed in Hebrew with a thick Russian accent, "Welcome home, Ronnie, your breakfast is ready."

I walked into the apartment and was relieved that essentially nothing had changed. It was a small and incredibly simple, but perfectly kept two-bedroom, third-story abode (I'm not sure how my grandfather was able to continue climbing its stairs). As a child, I was fascinated by two of its features, including the overhead tank with the pull-chain flush system on its only toilet and the small but beautiful stone-tiled balcony with a view of Fichman Elementary School and the hills and trees behind it. *Suck it, Tommy,* I thought. *Even your mansion doesn't have a vintage toilet, a biblical view, and a badass hero of a grandfather.* I stood at the railings, closed my eyes, and listened to the children in the playground of the school I had attended the summer after first grade. I smelled the aroma of the forest mixed with my grandfather's Turkish coffee.

My mother's sister, my aunt Shlomit, had gone to the local market to purchase food for breakfast, but my grandfather insisted on meticulously preparing the meal. Though a cheese omelet and fresh baked bread with butter would certainly qualify as comfort food to most Nebraskans, chances are that the accompanying Israeli cucumber and tomato salad would not. It worked for *me,* however. I nostalgically plowed through my feast, though I stood clear of the diesel-powered, unfiltered java.

I spent the next two hours bringing my grandfather and Shlomit up to speed on my life. I left out the part about getting shit-faced on prom night, attempting to lose my virginity at lightning speed to Julia the Siren before getting knocked out by Tommy, her jealous boyfriend, and ruining the relationship I had with my secret, non-Jewish girlfriend in the process. I instead concentrated on Zillie, Iris, high-school graduation, my father's health, and my future as a medical student in Wisconsin. As I spoke, they both smiled, and my grandfather would repeatedly interrupt, "If only your grandmother could have lived long enough to see our grandchildren." Shlomit could only wipe away tears. She was, of course, my mother's sister.

By mid-afternoon, jet lag set in. My grandfather routinely napped at this time of day, so Shlomit left and I crashed on the living room couch. About two hours later, I awakened to the sound of a whistling teakettle. My grandfather called me to the kitchen. "Ronnie, we need to talk."

I entered the room a bit dazed from the depth of sleep from which I was awakened. I smiled when I saw that my grandfather had prepared afternoon tea and toast, Israeli style: black tea in giant coffee mugs, toasted French bread, and a tub of Nutella. Goddammit, he really did love me.

"Sit down and eat," he said, and continued as I complied. "I'm glad to hear you have a bright future ahead of you in medicine, but your mother tells me you're not *really* happy. She didn't tell me why. She simply told me that she and your father were sending you here because they wanted you to see me, and they thought the trip would cheer you up . . . I want to know what's wrong."

"Well, I wouldn't exactly say I'm not happy . . ."

"Ronnie, I'm an old man. Don't waste my time; I don't have much left." He grinned, but I knew he was serious . . . and persistent. Any attempt to deceive him would be pointless. I lathered my toast with Nutella and dove in.

"Okay, it has to do with a girl."

"Tell me about her," he said, now with an impassioned look on his face. He then placed a sugar cube between his front teeth (dentures, actually . . . he had performed this maneuver for decades) to sweeten the tea as he sipped it.

I paused a moment before answering, then took one deep breath before spilling my guts. "Saba, I fell in love with a non-Jewish girl. Her name is Amy. I didn't tell my parents about her, and they discovered we had a serious relationship only after I tried to cheat on her. It was an absolute disaster, and it was all my fault. My parents were furious with me, and now Amy doesn't want to have anything to do with me."

My grandfather nodded slowly for what seemed like a century. His sugar cube had dissolved, and he finally spoke. "Do you still love her?"

"Yes."

This time he answered without hesitation. "Ronnie, I have seen a lot of pain, suffering and regret in my life . . . enough for one hundred lifetimes. What you did was stupid, but falling in love was not." He went on. "Risking my life to come to Israel was only the second most courageous thing I ever did. I think perhaps the *most* courageous thing I ever did was to pursue your grandmother."

"What do you mean?"

"Unfortunately you never met her and you've only seen pictures of her. She's pretty in them, but she was much more beautiful in real life, I'm telling you. I literally couldn't speak around her. She left me tongue-tied."

"Now *that* I understand," I said, laughing. "So how did you finally do it?"

"I threw up."

"You what?"

"You heard me right. I was so nervous every time I saw her that not only did I become speechless, but I also became sick."

I had a difficult time visualizing a vulnerable Zalman Rodov puking. "So what happened?"

"Well, I finally became so tired of my predicament that I decided not to hide from it anymore. So, you see, the meaning of 'courage' depends on one's perspective. Of course, courage can be defined by one's willingness to wear a uniform, carry a gun and go to battle. But sometimes, courage is simply the ability to listen to your heart. So, after vomiting, I told her I was in love with her.

"And what did she say?" I asked, still barely able to wrap my head around the all-too-familiar barf tale.

"She said she already knew."

We both laughed. "But Saba, this is different. She's not Jewish."

"Love transcends all religions, Ronnie. If you love her, try and get her back."

I couldn't believe what I had just heard.

CHAPTER 29

"Nobody's ever loved me like you do
Nobody's broken through"

—Santana's "Hold On," from the album *Shango,*
released August, 1982. It peaked at number fifteen on
US Billboard's Hot 100 Songs.

I spent the next three days escorting my grandfather around Haifa. It seemed inappropriate and borderline dangerous for an elderly man with a cane to try and negotiate the city's slopes. He, however, insisted, and who was I to argue? When I was a child, he held my hand while we visited the best the city had to offer: The Baha'i Temple, the cable car, the Druze village at Daliat El Carmel, Elijah's cave, and, of course, the beach. We had now come full-circle.

We had an unspoken and mutual understanding that these days likely represented his swan song as a tour guide. By the same token, we never discussed Amy again. At the end of our third afternoon, we took the bus for an overnight stay in Shlomit's west-side neighborhood, The French Carmel, which overlooked the Mediterranean. Before we entered her home, my grandfather turned to me and said, "Ronnie, take a seat with me at this park bench."

Though the sun was setting, the balmy, humid, salty air blanketed us with warmth. We sat silently for several minutes, watching the sky change its jeweler's display of sapphire, gold, ruby, and emerald. I remembered Frank Dupuis's lecture on color during sunset: "When the sun is at its peak, the short-wavelength visible blue lights are scattered more than the longer-wavelength lights to reach your eyes from all directions. That's why the sky looks blue in the middle of a sunny day. As the sun descends in the horizon, the light passes through more and more air and thus more and more air *molecules*. When that path is long enough, the blue light is completely scattered and gives way to longer-wavelength yellow, orange, and red lights, and even a flash of green light." I then tried to ignore his words and instead live in the moment. Two gulls and a catamaran crossed our view of the sun in a manner that would have made Ansel Adams convert to color photography. The scene was spectacular.

As dusk settled on the horizon, my grandfather finally broke our silence. "Ronnie, I think your parents have told you about what I did after World War II to help European refugees secretly enter this country from Cyprus."

"You mean helping them ashore on lifeboats? Yes, of course."

"It was from these same beaches."

"Yes, I know."

"I'm proud of what I did, but I'm not mentioning it to boast," he explained. "I brought you here because I want you to think about those people . . . what they went through . . . what they sacrificed . . . what they dreamt about Israel."

"I can't even imagine."

"I think you *can* imagine," he answered kindly, and continued. "I think they were incredibly brave and proud of being Jews and keeping their faith. The look on their tired faces, at the point they reached the shore and kissed the sand before running to shelter in one of our houses, is something I've never forgotten."

I considered the relative triviality of my predicament as he went on. "And though what they did was courageous, they would tell you they had no choice. Once they were here, however, they became part of the country and the society that saved them. They *chose* to become farmers or bus drivers or teachers or electrical engineers. They even chose to become doctors or singers." He paused and smiled. I smiled back. God, he *was* good. "And they fell in love, just as they do in Europe or Africa or South America . . . or Nebraska."

He had one subject remaining on his agenda. "Now, Ronnie, I haven't heard you sing since I came to your Bar Mitzvah almost five years ago. You know I don't like it when those horrible electric guitars play that *cat music.*" (The term "cat music" was actually spoken in English to emphasize his disgust for what he considered a bastardized version of the acoustic guitar he had played decades before). "But your mother tells me you have developed a very special voice, and that you sing the words to some of this cat music on stage. Apparently you have quite a reputation . . . so, let's hear something."

I burst out laughing. "But you just said you hate cat music!"

"I'm waiting," he answered. Then he stared at me. He was serious. This was going to be a command performance.

I contemplated his request. I reminded myself that, besides the words "cat" and "music," he understood only a handful of English words. *Okay,* I thought, *he asked for it. And Lord, forgive me for what I'm about to do. But who doesn't love Marvin Gaye?*

"Oh, baby now let's get down tonight . . ."

Yes, I sang "Sexual Healing" to Zalman Rodov. He ate up my performance with the glowing pride that only a grandparent could display. In my nearly eighteen years, I had never seen him unfold that meticulously placed kerchief of his . . . until that moment. After wiping away tears of joy, he responded only with this brief colloquialism:

Hebrew: "‫כל הכבוד‬!"

Transliteration: "Kol hakavod!"

Literal Translation: "All of the respect!"

Intended   "Hell, yes!"
Translation:

To this day, I believe it was my all-time best performance.

SHLOMIT made the best schnitzel outside of Europe, and the scent of this Austrian-style pan-fried chicken would have led me to her home from the other side of town. Shlomit's husband, my uncle Haim, answered the door and offered me a bear hug before leading my grandfather and me to the living room. He looked paradoxically like Vladimir Lenin, complete with receding hairline and goatee, but the comparison between the two ended with their appearance. Haim spoke his mind, but he had a heart of gold and doted over his family.

Shlomit and Haim Pesso had three daughters: Sigal, Rakefet, and Yael. Sigal, the oldest, was my age. Unlike many of her American counterparts, she would complete her obligatory two years of service in the Israeli Army before starting college. After a short summer break, new soldiers would participate in basic training. One advantage of living in a country the size of New Jersey, with the unity of a single (if often dysfunctional) family, is that, when given leave, enlistees could hitchhike home for the weekend. Sigal was stationed in Northern Israel, near Nahariya, a seaside town about six miles from the Lebanese border and less than one hour by car from Haifa. It was, therefore, easy for her to arrive on time for Sabbath dinner. Depending on their proximity to home, recruits would often invite other soldiers for the weekend, away from the grind of army life.

Like my aunt and uncle, my three cousins were very effusive and quick with warm embraces. "Sit down, Ronnie!" demanded Rakefet in Hebrew. Not quite fifteen, she was already the most assertive of the sisters and would later show her leadership skills as a colonel in the Israeli Air Force. "We have a surprise for you," she added. She turned to the kitchen and yelled, "Dalia, get off the phone and come in here!"

During the 1970s, Dalia Klein lived three doors down from the Pesso family. Her mother moved to Israel from the Gulf of Aden in 1950 as part of "Operation Magic Carpet," in which 49,000 Jews were airlifted from Yemen, Djibouti, and Eretria to escape anti-Semitism. Her father's parents immigrated to Palestine from Germany in 1939 while the Nazi government still encouraged Jews to leave the country. Through disparate routes, families like Dalia's helped form Israel's melting pot.

I had last seen Dalia five years earlier. I seem to remember a shy, gangly girl with a mouthful of braces, who clung nervously to Sigal. You could imagine my reaction, then, when Dalia entered from the kitchen. I saw before me a genetic cocktail that successfully merged supermodels Christie Brinkley with Iman. Her seemingly endless legs, copper skin, indigo eyes, wavy, honey-brown hair, and perfect teeth successfully combined to create nothing less than a miracle of circumstance, nature, and dentistry. One could also imagine the *magnitude* of my reaction, given that she was still wearing her uniform.

"Hi, Ronnie," said Dalia, excitedly. "Remember me?" She kissed me on both cheeks and grabbed my hands for just a moment before letting go. Holy shit she was hot. And not shy.

I stammered before answering. "Uh, *shalom!*" I finally responded clumsily with an unintentionally exaggerated American accent. So smooth.

"She's beautiful, isn't she?" interjected Haim. So subtle.

Dalia simply smiled as Shlomit took over. "Dalia's family moved down to Tel Aviv last year, so she thought about coming to Haifa to spend the weekend. When she heard you were coming, she was happy to say yes to our invitation."

I performed the "extended versions" of the Sabbath blessings per the request of the entire unabashed Pesso family. After my dog and pony show, I guzzled Carmel wine (Israeli Manischewitz) to calm my nerves. Dalia was strategically placed next to me, perhaps specifically to fuck with my head.

"Doesn't he have a beautiful voice?" asked Shlomit, directly at Dalia.

"He really does," answered Dalia. I was incredibly uncomfortable, but I was equally horny. I busily consumed a pile of Persian rice and schnitzel while stealing glances at her.

Between bites, we made small talk about life in America. I could barely concentrate on her questions regarding Michael Jackson, Miami Beach, and leggings. Leggings? What the hell did I know about fashion, and who gives a fuck? I literally couldn't listen to her, as I was entirely too focused on her sun-bronzed breasts, which peeked alluringly around her partially unbuttoned shirt, as if to say, "What are you waiting for, anyway?"

My head continued to spin as dinner finally came to a merciful end. After we shared dish-drying duties, Dalia turned to me. "I haven't been to Carmel Beach since I moved from Haifa," she said. "Will you take me down there?"

"Now?" I asked, enthralled.

"Yes, silly. How often are you in Israel, and how often does a girl ask you to take a walk on the beach?" At this point, I had no idea what the hell was happening or what the hell she saw in me.

THE circuitous route from the bluff to the beach involved several switchbacks. As this surprisingly long walk with Dalia progressed, we held hands, and I became increasingly skittish. I vacillated between thoughts of sex—did I still have the Trojans?—to irritable bowel syndrome—would I fart?—to Amy—what did my heart tell me *now?*

After a near-death experience with a tour bus while crossing the coastal highway, we arrived at Carmel Beach. Once there, we sat barefoot, side-by-side, silently facing the water, which was minimally illuminated by the sky above and the neighborhood behind. I pretended to be calm; my heart pounded. Thankfully, the din of the waves muffled the sound of the storm brewing in my belly.

"What are you thinking about?" she asked.

"You really want to know?"

"No, not really," she answered, giggling.

"Okay. Just tell me something . . . I'm guessing you don't have any problems meeting men . . . so why did you want to spend time alone with *me?*"

"Do *you* really want to know?"

"Yes, actually, I do."

"Alright . . . I asked you down here for the novelty."

"The *novelty?*"

"Yes, the novelty. I've never been with an American boy before."

I laughed. "You know I'm also Israeli."

"No, you're not!" She smirked. "Just shut up and kiss me."

I didn't argue; our lips met. A grope fest ensued, and I quickly found myself on top of a shirtless, pantless, exotic, sizzling Israeli soldier. She smiled as I grabbed for my wallet to retrieve a Trojan. "Hurry up, American boy!"

American boy? Novelty?

I felt a plastic condom wrapper and wrestled it free from the inner confines of the billfold. As I did so, out popped the photo of Amy and me holding hands by the Duster. Though in this lighting the image would not be discernible to Dalia, what now was only a pair of silhouettes was more than enough to taunt me. It had traveled with me across eight time zones as a memento, not just of our relationship, but of my giant clusterfuck . . . and my ability to perpetuate it. I quickly shoved the photo back into the billfold, and Dalia appeared not to notice. However, I began to perseverate, as flashbacks of prom night collided with those of me on top of Amy in the Duster. I had betrayed her so easily before, and I desperately needed her back. So what the fuck was I doing? Regardless of whether or not I would have sex with Dalia, I was engulfed with an overwhelming sense of remorse.

I looked down. I had gone flaccid. It was indeed dark outside, but it wasn't too dark that Dalia couldn't recognize what had happened to my confused penis. She looked at me in disbelief. I was, again, humiliated.

CHAPTER 30

"I found a picture of you, oh oh oh oh
Those were the happiest days of my life"

—The Pretenders' "Back on the Chain Gang," which
was released as a single in October, 1982, and later
on the album *Learning to Crawl* in January, 1984.
It peaked at number five on US Billboard's Hot
100 Songs.

D alia had promised never to divulge to anyone what had transpired at the beach. However, she left the following morning before I awoke, and the dumbfounded look in the collective eyes of the Pesso family made it clear that, with some combination of a literal and figurative game of Telephone, my parents would hear of my misadventure before I returned to Nebraska.

Three days later, and after a tearful good-bye at what would be the last time I would see my grandfather, I stepped on a bus and roamed Israel alone for a week. I tried desperately to collect my thoughts, as I was still emotionally numb. I felt robbed of the sense of invincibility I thought I had earned as an Israeli-American exiled to Nebraska, destined to triumph as some sort of superhero with a cape, a stethoscope and a microphone. Instead, I was relegated to the role of the tourist with his tail and his floppy dick between his legs. I would sit silently, smelling the diesel exhaust while in my mind and with my camera I chronicled faces, roads, trees, monuments, and the withering Levantine sun. It didn't help that in the 1983, most Israeli buses still had no air conditioning.

Thanks to about thirty gallons of Coca-Cola, I managed to avoid evaporating while traversing the country from north to south to visit my interpretation of Israel's Greatest Hits: the artists colony and center of Jewish mysticism in Tzfat, the Sea of Galilee, the Tower of David in Jerusalem, and the waterfall of the verdant oasis at Ein Gedi. Despite its inherent conflicts, Israel still had a way of vanquishing all of the cynicism I had developed over the previous few months. My numbness had resolved. I was, in the end, hopelessly nationalistic and romantic.

Time and loneliness reminded me of what my grandfather had asked me about my heart, what made it tick. I again envisioned Amy traveling with me. Only Amy. While in Jerusalem, a solicitor for a local synagogue handed me a pamphlet containing the Song of Solomon, the biblical story of two lovers' desire for each other. In it the Tower of David is referenced: *"Thy neck is like the Tower of David built with turrets, whereon there hang a thousand shields, all the armor of the mighty men . . ."*

But here come the good parts: *"Behold, you are beautiful, my love; behold, you are beautiful; your eyes are as doves . . . Thy two breasts are like two fawns that are twins of a gazelle, which feed among the lilies . . ."*

Your eyes are as doves? Twins of a gazelle? Who said the bible can't be sexy? The Song of Solomon is commonly read during Passover as an allegory of the love between God and his people. I preferred to take its poetry literally. Clearly *Penthouse Forum* did not invent erotica. Of course, it was sappy, but I didn't care. I was in love.

The approval I sought from others seemed meaningless in comparison to what I desired from Amy. I never planned on falling for her, but I did, and she had become an integral part of my life. I was rudderless without her. She understood me better than I understood myself, and I had lost her trust. I simply clung precariously to the hope that I had not lost her love as well.

THE day I left Israel, I stopped by an airport shop to purchase a postcard. On a particularly beautiful one was an aerial shot of the Old City. Its caption, written in Hebrew, English, and Arabic, read, "Holy City to Jews, Christians, and Muslims alike."

"*Weeech waaan arrre you?*"

I looked up. The voice came from a middle-aged vendor, speaking English with an exceedingly thick Israeli accent that made the listener understand the meaning of the guttural "R." He sported slightly offensive smoker's breath, tarnished teeth, sooty fingers, rumpled hair, and an equally rumpled short-sleeve oxford shirt with a pocketful of Israeli Noblesse cigarettes.

"I'm sorry, I don't understand what you're talking about," I answered in Hebrew.

"*De postcard!*" he responded, excitedly. "*Weeech waaan arrre you? Jeweeesh, Chreeestian, or Moooslem?*"

I thought for a moment, and then answered with a question:

Hebrew:	"מה אתה חושב?"
Transliteration:	"Mah atah choshev?"
Literal Translation:	"What do you think?"
Intended Translation:	"Who the fuck are *you*, shit breath?"

Grinning, he responded, again in English: *"If you Jeweeesh, why you not live herrre?"*

First Dalia, and then this guy . . . why the fuck were people questioning my nationality *and* my religion? Remembering that any unusual behavior would spark a rush of security officers in the international airport of this rightfully paranoid country, I decided not to get into an argument with Mr. Self-Righteous. Instead, I quietly paid for the postcard and a stamp with an image of the Israeli flag and left for my gate.

I borrowed a pen from the gate attendant and thought long and hard about what to write Amy. There were so many things I wanted to tell her: words of love, contrition, shame, adventure, and optimism. I came up with the following:

I miss us.

I dropped the postcard in a mailbox and boarded my plane home.

THE trip had been simultaneously energizing and exhausting. I trudged down the aisle and found my window seat. I again reached for my wallet and extracted the photo of Amy and me. I stared intently at her eyes. Those hazel eyes. I remember trying to review in my mind the physiology of love, of pheromones and testosterone, and the evolutionary advantages of choosing a mate for life in order to propagate my own DNA. I then contemplated my ability to overcome the principles of human genetics; I just needed to *will* myself to get past Amy.

"Behold, you are beautiful, my love; behold, you are beautiful; your eyes are as doves . . ."

I was such a pain in the ass, even to myself.

I fell asleep.

Tel Aviv to New York, New York to Chicago, Chicago to Lincoln. My parents met me at the airport, not knowing how to approach me.

"How was the trip?" my father asked, as both of my parents hugged me optimistically.

"Beautiful and very hot," I answered. "I'll get my photos developed this week. You'll love them. But it was also a little sad. Saba is an amazing man, but he's really slowing down."

My mother hated the fact that she lived so far away from her elderly father, and she was quick to change the subject. "We heard that Dalia was at Shlomit's house, and that she grew up to become a beautiful young woman."

She's kidding by bringing up that subject, right? I thought. "Yup," I replied curtly.

A penetrating silence engulfed the ride home in my parents' very quiet new Pontiac Bonneville. My mother gave it another shot. "Ronnie, are you looking forward to leaving for Wisconsin? It's only a few weeks away."

I hated small talk, even if it was with my own parents. It made me feel especially lonely, but I put up a brave front. "Very much so . . . I just think it's going to be weird without my friends."

"Well, you'll come back over Thanksgiving break, and I'm sure you'll be so busy there with school and new friends that you won't even really think about it."

I gave up. I had no answer. Again, silence. I knew I frustrated my parents, but I honestly didn't know what to say to them. I knew they meant well. I wasn't angry. I wasn't bitter. I was just empty.

Once home, I walked down to the basement to call Benjie. He had never visited Israel before. I lived semi-vicariously through his many musical exploits, and my trips to the Middle

East were the only subject for which he lived vicariously through me. "I wanna hear about the trip," he said. "But first let me tell you what's going on with the band. Things are really happening. Capitol Records is releasing an EP with 'Chameleon Man,' plus two new songs we just recorded: 'Ready As I'll Never Be' and 'Land of the Free.'"

"Holy shit! That's awesome. I can't wait to come to The Garage to hear them."

"Cool . . . and another thing . . . you've absolutely seen the last of The Repeats. In order to be taken seriously as artists, we gotta stop covering music. Oh, and Rex also convinced us to change the name The Well Endowed. Said it was just too suggestive to give us wide audience appeal."

"What? Seriously?"

"Seriously."

"Then what's the new name?"

"Ready?"

"Ready."

"Guava."

"You realize that's a fruit?"

"Yes, thank you for telling me, genius. Of course I realize it's a fruit."

"So is there a meaning behind calling the band Guava?"

"Nope. It's catchy. No other reason. You think there's some deep meaning behind every band's name? R.E.M. was randomly found in the dictionary . . . sounded good. Rush got its name because the band was in hurry to come up with one . . . sounded good. KISS and The Who had absolutely no reason behind their names . . . just sounded good."

"You don't have to convince me. I like it."

"Sounds good." We both laughed.

I told Benjie everything: my grandfather, Dalia and my dick, my tour alone, my callous attempt at lechery, my remorse, and my longing for Amy. I'd like to think he understood, and he did, for the most part. He too was a young Jewish man living in Nebraska. And of course I was responsible for this mess. But there was something about being a first-generationer that added another layer to the complexity of my situation: that feeling of utter solitude, that perpetual state of awkwardness. If somehow I were able to harness Sundar's ability to shed this layer with total disdain, perhaps I would feel comfortable in my own skin.

"Dude, Dalia sounds fucking *hot!* What the hell is wrong with you?"

Yeah. He didn't quite get it.

"Ron, I got one more thing to tell you about Rex," added Benjie.

"What?"

"He hasn't forgotten about you. He keeps asking about 'the doctor with the voice.'"

"Bullshit."

"I'm not bullshitting, man. My band knows exactly what it wants to do. You don't. I just don't ever want you to regret any more decisions you make. Just think about it."

As I hung up the phone, I heard my mother walking down the stairs. I didn't know whether or not she had heard any of my conversation with Benjie.

"Ronnie, I know *you'rrre* mad—"

"I'm not mad."

"Okay, if *you'rrre* not mad, then *you'rrre* upset." As again I didn't respond, she continued. "I think you need to know something about your parents . . . we moved to this country twenty-one years ago with *everrry* intention of moving back to Israel when dad finished graduate school. But things didn't turn out that way."

I had no idea where this conversation was going, but I assumed it would end with my mother crying.

She went on. "*Everrry* night before we fall asleep, we lay in bed talking about what we did right and what we did wrong. Should we ever have come to America? Did we pick the right place to raise children? Did we make the right decision trying to keep our kids from dating non-Jews?"

I raised my eyebrows.

"Don't be so *surrrprised*," she said. "There's no textbook on how to become the only Israeli family in Lincoln, Nebraska. And we had no parents here to offer any advice or help. We were on our own, and we're not perfect. How do you think it feels to be 'the woman with the funny accent,' to be a minority *within* a minority? How do you think it feels to be uprooted from the place you love and the place your parents helped build? I understand—"

"No you don't!"

"Let me finish . . . *I understand* you still have feelings for Amy."

Oh God, I thought. *Here it comes.*

"You think your father and I are totally blind? You think we have no feelings ourselves? We love *both* of you. You think we feel no guilt about the predicament we helped put you in?"

No tears. No hysteria. Just the truth.

I finally answered, again with a question. "Mom, do you believe in free will?"

"You know we Jews are responsible for our own actions. It's part of what makes us Jews."

"Okay, I accept that. But do you believe in fate?"

My mother thought for a moment before replying. "I just don't know, Ronnie."

"Well, I do. I know I'm not exactly a victim of circumstance. I know I made some big mistakes. But I think I was meant to be with Amy."

"I know you do."

TEN days later, my mother handed me a letter. It was addressed to me but it had no return address. We both knew who sent it. I left the kitchen and walked in to my room to read it alone. Inside the envelope was a postcard with a photograph of The Greg Kihn Band performing "The Breakup Song" at The Nebraska State Fair on September 10th, 1982.

Ron, the truth is I miss us too, but I don't know if I'll ever be able to forgive you for what you did. I trusted you, and you knew exactly how important that trust was to me. Yet you broke my heart. I would have given you everything, but you were too selfish to wait for me to be ready. I don't think you know what you want, and I don't know if you ever will. I've moved on, and I think it's best if you do the same.

Good luck,

Amy

CHAPTER 31

"And you may say yourself,
'My God! . . . What have I done?'"

—THE TALKING HEADS' "ONCE IN A LIFETIME," FROM THE
ALBUM *REMAIN IN LIGHT*, RELEASED FEBRUARY 2ND, 1982.
IT PEAKED AT NUMBER NINETY-ONE ON US BILLBOARD'S
HOT 100 SONGS.

'm fairly certain the phrase "dropping like flies" was not derived in reference to the short lifespan of insects, but instead to the intolerable, unrelenting, and wilting heat and humidity of August in Nebraska. There was something both maddening and debilitating about taking a shower, walking outside, even at night, and soaking in sweat within seconds. It was in the midst of those dog days that I spent the majority of my remaining time in Lincoln working at Target and keeping to myself at home, running in and out of air conditioned spaces.

Unfortunately, the un-air conditioned Duster was not one of those spaces. It was just a cruel and sweltering indictment of my partially fucked up American Dream. Despite the weather, I found myself, on several occasions, sitting in the driver's seat with the windows rolled down, boiling, staring into space, longing for Amy. I swear, if I tried hard enough, I could still smell her hair.

I would have given you everything, but you were too self-ish to wait for me to be ready.

I literally had no argument against that statement.

I don't think you know what you want, and I don't know if you ever will.

Or that one.

Two nights before I would leave for Madison, Andy Weigel hosted a going away party of sorts for classmates, many of whom were leaving town for college. Andy's home, tucked neatly in the woods of Calvert Place, was one of only a few in town with a pool, and would, therefore, provide a much needed and picturesque respite from the weather. Before stepping out of the Duster, I was having another one of my trance-like moments when I felt something, or someone, reach through the open car window to tap on my head.

"Hey, stranger!" It was Tommy. He carried a half-empty can of beer in his hand, with the other half of its contents and then some on his breath.

Startled, and with a raised brow, I finally answered, "Hey Tommy . . ."

"Don't worry, bro, I'm not going to punch you this time." He chuckled. "Dude, we're good . . . water under the bridge. I was getting kinda tired of Julia anyway." *Asshole.*

I grimaced ever so slightly, perhaps as my own little manifestation of post-traumatic stress. I prayed he didn't notice and tried to regroup quickly. "How's—"

"How's Amy?" he said, attempting to finish my question.

"Well, I was going to say 'How's it goin'?' But yeah, how's Amy?" I was lying, of course, and he knew it. *Asshole.*

He offered an exaggerated expression of contemplation before answering, knowing I hung on his every word. "She's . . . good," he said, smirking again. I thought it was impossible, but I sweat just a little bit more. *Asshole.*

"Cool," I answered. *No, not cool.*

"She talks about you sometimes. Don't get me wrong,

she's still pissed as hell at you, but it's like . . . it's like she's worried about you."

"Worried?"

"Yeah, *worried*. She thinks you're a complete dick and everything, but then she acts like she's your guardian angel or something."

I was puzzled but obviously intrigued. "I don't get it."

"She thinks you're a lost soul."

"Well, maybe she's right . . . but how's she my 'guardian angel?' It's not like she's watching over me or anything. And she hasn't spoken to me for months."

"Dude, if your guardian angel talks to someone, it doesn't have to be *you*. And she doesn't *want* to talk to you anyway."

"I *still* don't get it."

"She's been talking to your parents, dumbshit!"

"What?" I felt three consecutive tidal waves of embarrassment, love, and anger.

"Yeah, bro. Whose idea do you think it was to send you to Israel, anyway?" He flashed a self-satisfied, shit-eating grin. "She knows you're going off to study medicine in Wisconsin, but she doesn't think your heart's in it."

The truth continued to hurt. It hurt even more when it came, if only indirectly, from Amy. "If she's thinks I still want to sing for a living, she's wrong," I said with righteous indignation. "I've been talking about going to medical school almost my whole life. How could my heart *not* be in it?"

"Relax, cowboy!" he answered. "Look, I know you still have a thing for her. I'm not worried about that on so many different levels." I tried to protest, but I couldn't. *Asshole.* I continued to listen. "I'm just telling you what she said . . . doesn't matter . . . You know, I really like her and everything, but she's kind of a head case." I couldn't let him leave it at that. I tried to respond with an understanding bro nod. My gesture was undoubtedly weak. "*You* know, she's just . . . *insecure*. It's not exactly that she's worried about what people think about her . . . it's that she's worried about being *abandoned*."

Okay, now I'm the asshole, I thought.

"Listen, I just want to have fun. You know me. But she keeps talking to me about 'our future,' or 'will you still be around?' And I'm like, 'I'm just turning eighteen, babe. Slow the fuck down.' Ya know what I mean?"

"I think so." *Fuck, what the hell did I do to her?*

He polished off his Budweiser and continued. "And one more thing. Well, you know . . . she doesn't exactly put out. And don't you dare tell anyone I told you that, especially Amy, or I *will* kick your ass."

At that point, I would have preferred if he'd punched me both in the face *and* the nuts. I still wasn't sure if they'd had sex, and I no longer wanted to find out, especially from him. He was, by now, too drunk to understand the awkward turn our conversation had taken. Though I desperately wanted to talk to Amy before I left Lincoln, I was relieved to have heard from Christine earlier in the day that neither of them was likely to come. Tommy tossed the Budweiser into the bushes, I exited the car, and we entered the party together.

As Tommy and I walked into Andy's house, about twenty heads turned simultaneously toward us. Mark, wearing a leopard-skin Speedo with matching bandana (and nothing else), seized the opportunity by standing alone at the fireplace mantle and breaking into his best Michael Jackson:

"*Because the doggone girl is mine . . .*"

Despite Mark's hideous voice and equally hideous outfit, the audience roared with approval. Then Tommy began to grind with Mark. I couldn't help but laugh. I mean, c'mon, it was funny. Mark soon turned to me and yelled, "Next verse is yours, Bahar!"

The sentimental crowd began to chant, "Ron, Ron, Ron, Ron, Ron!" The moment definitely fell under the category of *fuck it, I'm leaving for school in two days.* Tommy and I then sandwiched Mark in a three-man grind. Though I wasn't also adorned in Speedos, only years later would I realize that the hairy-upper-thigh-exposing OP shorts both Tommy and I wore were nearly as inappropriate. I then *became* Paul McCartney:

"I love you more than he . . ."

The room erupted with laughter. The comic relief was wholly therapeutic. That night and only that night, I forgave Paul McCartney and Michael Jackson for recording "The Girl Is Mine," and I forgave myself for being an asshole.

Andy stood, right up front, hands crossed, nodding, with a smile of both nostalgia and satisfaction on his face; he was leaving for Pepperdine in the morning. "Encore!" he yelled.

Mark and Tommy looked at each other in amusement. "I don't know about you, Mark, but I think I'm out of Ron's league," declared Tommy.

"Ditto," added Mark.

Tommy then turned to me. "You know I don't sing, man. She's all yours."

"She?" I asked, confused.

"Yeah, the gig . . . she's all yours, bro . . . wait, you didn't think I was talking about—"

"No, no, no," I protested, praying I had successfully hidden another lie, not to mention my sheer embarrassment.

Mark interrupted by tugging on Tommy's shirt. "Hey, let the man sing, it's his grand finale." The two of them laughed, pointing to me as they left the fireplace. *God bless Mark.*

For weeks, I had listened over and over on my Walkman to an INXS song that I felt had been so emblematic of my relationship with the world. I had never considered that it could be performed *a cappella*, but I had also never stood before a mostly drunk collection of vulnerable, emotional wrecks until that moment. I slowed the original tempo to *adagio*, and began:

> *"I'm standing here on the ground, The sky above won't fall down . . ."*

I momentarily scanned the room to get what I assumed would be my one last miniature taste of rock stardom. Behind the smiling faces, in the far corner of the room, stood Amy—that hair, those eyes, denim shorts, and bikini top. Goddammit, she was beautiful. Our eyes met. She forced an ever-so-slight grin. I didn't give a shit if Tommy understood I was singing only to her.

One would have thought that the entire class of 1983 was headed off to war. Upon finishing, I was enveloped by a spontaneous co-ed cluster of appendages and tears. We eventually untangled, and my eyes searched the room for Amy.

She was gone.

My voice was soon replaced by a boom box and dueling mix tapes. What seemed like half of my graduating class then headed for the pool to dive, cannonball, and belly flop their way into a collective baptism of college life.

Tommy and I never discussed Amy again that night. It wasn't necessary. We both knew that he didn't love her, and I knew, deep down, she couldn't really love him either.

Two days later, I left for Wisconsin without saying goodbye to Amy.

CHAPTER 32

"Did you stand by me
No, not at all"

—THE CLASH'S "TRAIN IN VAIN," FROM THE ALBUM
LONDON CALLING, RELEASED FEBRUARY 12TH, 1980.
IT PEAKED AT NUMBER TWENTY-THREE ON US
BILLBOARD'S HOT 100 SONGS.

I always found it fascinating that my parents, who had nearly eighteen years of photo ops with me, found it necessary to wait until we were rushing to airport terminal gates to demand that we pose together for the camera. Fortunately, one of the advantages of living in Nebraska was the size and accessibility of the Lincoln Municipal Airport; it contained just four gates for two airlines (United and Frontier), and had plenty of curbside ten-minute parking spots that were easily transformed into sixty-minute parking spots due to the lack, or apathy, of attendants. My family typically reached the airport about ten minutes prior to departure times, when we would burst out of the car and assault the building as though in a scene out of a private eye show. Though not as glamorous as *Charlie's Angels*, we were at least as efficient, completing a run by the counter, up the escalator and through the checkpoint, leaving us approximately five precious minutes for a hug, a kiss, and a photo (taken by other passengers or security officers, many of whom, over the years, recognized us and our routine). Even if terror watch lists and racial profiling existed then, our swarthy appearance and our equally swarthy surname frightened no one.

The morning I left for Madison, my still fragile father bypassed the counter and sauntered to the escalator, but our overall family performance remained masterful: one college freshman with two overstuffed suitcases checked in . . . in only four minutes. As we neared the Jetway, the flight attendant announced the final boarding for my flight to Chicago, and my mother handed her Polaroid to an innocent bystander. To defray the inevitable maternal river of tears, my father evoked the same sarcastic line he had used one hundred times before. "Let's pretend we love each other," he joked while cheesing it up for the camera. It was early and I was too tired for a courtesy laugh, but I did manage a smile. My mother's sense of obligation, or perhaps guilt, helped create a collage of family lineup photos at Gate 3. So many missed opportunities to immortalize even mundane family life—Sabbath dinners, family trips, visits from grandparents, cross country wins (wait, that never happened)—were replaced by meaningless group mug shots.

"Be careful," pleaded my mother as I entered the Jetway.

THE Towers Residence Hall sat in the isthmus between Lake Mendota and Lake Monona, adjacent to the campus of the University of Wisconsin-Madison. Given that Wisconsin residents were given preference to live in the university-owned dorms, the privately owned Towers was very popular among out-of-staters like me. Each of the top eight floors of its two buildings housed twenty dorm rooms. The floors were co-ed and ungoverned by the university. At the time, the drinking age in the state was eighteen (or nonexistent with a college ID), so the stage was set for a gargantuan, cross-country release of hormones, alcohol, and bodily fluids.

The bus from O'Hare to Madison was full of future residents of The Towers, including my future roommate, Eric Freedman, from South Bend, Indiana, home of The University of Notre Dame. He and I planned a rendezvous in Chicago to reach school together. We had corresponded by phone via the medical school's roommate finding service; we would both start the six-year program that fall. No doubt my parents were excited at the prospect of their son rooming with another Jewish kid from a Midwestern college town. "You can go to synagogue together," suggested my mother.

Eric had other goals in mind. He was bright, gregarious, handsome, and horny. He planned a career as a hand surgeon, but operating on the upper extremity was not the only hand job he sought. And though his parents had no restrictions on dating "within the faith" while he attended a high school with a predominantly non-Jewish student body, they did want him to "settle down with a nice Jewish girl." He therefore approached The University of Wisconsin and its over two thousand Jewish female scholars as a kid in one fucking colossal candy store.

We found each other at the Van Galder bus stop at O'Hare. "Eric?" I asked after seeing my self-described "short but not too short" roommate. "Nice to finally meet you!" I said, enthusiastically, if not awkwardly, at the prospect of our nine-month blind date. We shook hands uncomfortably, but by the end of the three-hour trip from Chicago to Madison, we had become fast friends. We did, after all, have much in common.

REGISTRATION Week, fondly referred to as "Reg Week," took place just before classes commenced each fall. Daytime consisted of a visit to the School of Agriculture's Stock Pavilion, where a cattle call of undergrads who were hierarchically assigned a specific time of day and date raced on foot, bike, and moped between campus buildings to reserve a spot in their courses of choice. Most students, however, considered it not only a rite of passage, but also an excuse to experience seven days of overindulgence before the reality of schoolwork settled in.

Langdon Street, home of the university's tree-lined "Fraternity Row," was located just behind The Towers, and extended several blocks both east and west. Though not exact replicas from the movie *Animal House,* Langdon's stately turn-of-the-century mansions—by the 1980s in significant disrepair—bared a striking resemblance to the film's Delta House, complete with ramshackle siding and toga parties. As a bonus, their indoor beer gardens offered as much brew as Oktoberfest in Munich.

The early '80s was a time of significant expansion for the Greek System in Wisconsin. For those who were interested, a brief walk east of The Towers along Langdon offered the promise of hazing-free pledgehood, sorority sisters, and free inebriation from a handful of start-up fraternities. It was only the first night of Reg Week, and, while I had no intention of pledging, in my lonely state, the idea of an escape from reality and sobriety was quite appealing. By the time we reached the Edgewater Hotel some six blocks later, Eric and I had made a significant dent in more than one keg, had "danced" (gyrated) with dozens of random girls on crowded "dance floors" ('50s-era beer-sticky linoleum), and, upon reaching the hotel parking lot, had simultaneously vomited the evening's plunder.

"Don't worry," said Eric, confidently. "My dad's a doctor and he told me that the best treatment for being too drunk is puking . . . I feel better already." We laughed it off like brothers in arms and headed back to The Towers to brush our teeth before heading to the bars. Interesting what goes through one's head when one is drunk.

"So did you have a girlfriend back home?" asked Eric.

"*Had* is the best way to describe it."

"What happened?"

"You got about two hours?"

"If the story is good enough, hell yes!"

We barhopped west on Langdon, first to The Kollege Klub, better known as The KK, and then to Der Rathskeller, better known as The Rat, the German pub of The Student Union. During Beer 101, I told Eric everything: Amy, medicine, music, family, prom, hearts, Dalia, and postcards. Though I didn't take two hours to finish my tale, I omitted few details. Eric nodded, smiled, raised eyebrows, and several times stared, mouth agape. But for the most part he sat motionless. When I finally finished, he asked, "Is that it?"

Dumfounded, I answered, "*Yes*, that's it! What more did you want?"

"Nothing. It's a great fuckin' story. But did you see that girl over there?"

"What?"

He pointed behind me. "That girl by the bartender."

I turned around. I recognized her from 6 West, our floor at The Towers. "What's her name?"

"I don't know yet, but I'm going to find out."

They made eye contact and smiled at each other. The Human League's "Don't You Want Me" played overhead. She twirled her Star of David necklace as if to say, "I think you're Jewish and so am I. I'm drunk. I'm a good girl, but I'm very likely to do things I wouldn't do while sober. I too am horny, attractive, and short, but not too short. My parents also want me to meet other Jewish kids at school, so if you're interested, let's kiss, take a walk up Bascom Hill, and have sex by the campus observatory. It's beautiful there. No one will see. Oh, and I hope you have a condom."

He walked directly past me, beer in hand, and sallied up to Debbie Lipson from Cleveland. I knew better than to become a third wheel, so I walked back to The Towers alone. Eric and Debbie Lipson from Cleveland did kiss, take a walk up Bascom Hill, and have sex by the campus observatory. Oh, and Eric did have a condom.

The west elevator of The Towers opened. There stood several still-unfamiliar boys and girls impersonating adults, and I was nearly overwhelmed by the stench of the whisky breath that emanated from within. "Ron from Nebraska, right?" asked one of my dorm mates as I squeezed inside with trepidation.

"Right. What's your name again?"

"Aaron from Fort Lauderdale . . . this is Judy from Minneapolis."

"Hey," said Judy sheepishly. The two of them sported remarkably similar silly grins and uniforms (Chicago Cubs caps, Bucky Badger T-shirts, and untied Reebok high tops), and leaned against each other to prevent a fall.

"Hey," I responded, and added a late head nod with a complimentary wave. Goddammit was I uncool. I continued to feel obligated to make awkward conversation. "You two look like you've been friends for a long time, considering how far away you live from each other."

"No, we just met," answered Aaron, now chuckling. He

looked at Judy, and then at me. "This place fuckin' *rules*, right?"

"Yeah, it *does* rule."

"Hey, you wanna come upstairs and play quarters?" asked Judy. Thankfully, the elevator had just opened to the sixth floor.

"Thanks, but I think I'm gonna pass. I'm not very good, and I've already barfed once tonight. Can I take a rain check?"

"Sure. We'll be up in 812 if you change your mind," added Aaron, as the door finally closed.

Once in my room, I picked up the phone and dialed all but the last digit of Amy's number sixteen times before finally giving up. *So much for listening to my heart. Sorry, Saba.*

And so, I began my college career with a great roommate in a quintessential college town at a prestigious university. Still I sought to sabotage living life to its fullest by spending most of my time shuttling between class, The Helen C. White Library, and my dorm room. I memorized some of Frank Netter's famous medical illustrations, including "Prenatal Circulation," but I failed to understand their significance.

"This vascular organization is instrumental in providing heart and brain with blood of higher oxygen content . . ."[1]

Once again, school was a means to an end.

CHAPTER 33

"Be with me, seems you're never here with me
Ooh, I've been tryin' to get over there"

—GENESIS' "NO REPLY AT ALL," FROM THE ALBUM
ABACAB, RELEASED SEPTEMBER 9TH, 1981.
IT PEAKED AT NUMBER TWENTY-NINE ON US BILLBOARD'S
HOT 100 SONGS.

Given that we spent almost every waking moment to-gether, Eric and I got along exceedingly well. It's not to say that he didn't tire of watching *Late Night with David Letterman*, my primary form of entertainment, after hours of studying anatomy and physiology at the library. There were apparently only so many of the show's "stupid pet tricks" Eric could tolerate. In addition to having to hear me opine about wasting my skills as a singer, the poor guy also had to endure the Shrine to Amy—a travel-size version of the photomontage on my home bedroom wall, now trans-posed in my dorm room and dedicated entirely to my ex-girlfriend. I understood full well through Christine that Amy and Tommy remained a serious item, but I continued to hold out what most would consider irrational hope.

"Dude, can we please stop talking about the singing? I get it; you're good. But let's get real. What's the chance that if you gave up on med school, you could make it big in the music world? You're going to be a *doctor!* Stop whining! And these pictures . . . they're a little creepy, don't you think?" suggested Eric.

"But—"

"I'm telling you, man. It's creepy. Why can't you have a Bob Marley poster or, better yet, a Farrah Fawcett poster like most guys? Plus, with that 'masterpiece' up there on the wall, how do you think you're going to bring girls back to your room? It basically says, 'Either I'm engaged, or I'm a fucking stalker.' Live a little, man!"

I laughed. He did have a point, but I'm not sure I cared. Eric eventually convinced me that all work and no play made Ron a dull boy, so I did acquiesce and we made the rounds up and down Langdon each Friday and Saturday night (sometimes Thursdays, depending on homework, test schedules, and drink specials at The KK). During these outings, Eric made me adhere to the following rules, under penalty of death:

A. Never leave a party without talking to a new girl.

B. Never discuss Amy with other girls.

C. Hide the Shrine to Amy before going out in case girls would return to the room. To this end, we covered it with a makeshift, side-by-side combo poster of Bob Marley taped to Farrah Fawcett. The fortunate juxtaposition gave the appearance that Bob was about to pass a joint to Farrah.

To my credit, or perhaps to Eric's credit, I did manage to make out with Barbara, accounting major from Westchester County, and Rachel, poli-sci major from Northbrook, Illinois: both Jewish, both cute, both smart, and both funny. Under normal circumstances, the anticipation of each event would provoke my intestines to explode, but they remained unusually quiet, heralding the enormous anticlimax I would later feel.

As an added bonus, on my eighteenth birthday in October, Eric threw a post-library, Towers 6th Floor West party featuring kamikazes (a popular '80s college cocktail made of equal parts vodka, triple sec, and lime juice) and a cake constructed from donuts purchased at Dunk or Dine (made fresh twenty-four hours). Three kamikazes in, I blew out the candles and had my face shoved in said cake. The flavorful fusion of sugar and alcohol made for an interesting night. Though I did eventually puke, it was not until after fondling Missy, history major from New Jersey.

On an even brighter side, my relative indifference did breed a sense of fearlessness and imagination with girls, and I had become possibly the greatest storyteller and teammate of all time. One November evening while frat hopping, I had no problem striking up a conversation and dancing to Men Without Hats' "The Safety Dance" with Jessica from Chevy Chase, while Eric swooped in to charm roommate Allison from Minneapolis. Later, Allison, Eric, Jessica, and Ron would head to the *un-shrined* dorm room, only to have Ron conveniently leave for a walk with Jessica so that Allison and Eric could have wild freshman sex under the approving and now bloodshot eyes of Bob and Farrah. Though our actions may have been interpreted as sexist or callous, they were, in reality, a means of compensating for our own insecurities with safety in numbers. In my case they were also a reflection of my loneliness.

Meanwhile, I would weave a tall tale of my many exploits to Jessica, of the lucrative record contract I had turned down, of myriad girls I had rebuffed as lead singer of the hottest band in Nebraska, and of all of those cross country races I had won. "But I couldn't stay with the band. I had to go to medical school . . . I really had no choice," I explained to Jessica. "The admissions committee members were amazed at my research on irritable bowel syndrome, and they offered me a full scholarship during my interview!"

I continued the charade with my legitimate voice. "Sing me something," pleaded Jessica, as we stood in line to enter The KK. She was clearly excited and still buzzed from fraternity Kool-Aid.

"Like what?" I asked. She was drunken-eyed. Her pretty face was framed by long brown hair and a red cashmere beret purchased earlier in the day at the Benetton around the corner on State Street. Her kissable cheeks were rendered rosey and even more kissable by the chilly November air and the biting wind sweeping off of Lake Mendota just a block to the north. I had no final destination, and it didn't really matter. My lack of concern about the outcome of our unplanned outing was simultaneously liberating and pathetic.

"I don't know . . . *you're* supposedly the one with the voice . . . what have you been listening to lately?"

I paused for just a moment. I realized how good it felt to *just fucking relax*, if only temporarily. I felt a smile forming on my face, as I channeled Bob Marley:

"Could you be loved and be loved . . ."

Jessica was amazed. "Holy shit, you weren't kidding about your voice."

I chuckled. No pressure, no farting, no diarrhea. My mind wandered as she held me close under the pretense of a cold night. The moment was clearly different from the catastrophe on the beach with Dalia. On paper, Wisconsin, this school, this night, and this girl, were "perfect." I was still the same wide-eyed kid from Nebraska, but my heart, and my gut were absent.

Once inside The KK, Jessica told me her life story. She described in detail her close-knit suburban Maryland conservative Jewish family, complete with realtor mother, attorney father, and two "adorable" younger sisters, Jacqueline and Natalie. She loved her parents dearly but hoped to escape from their "boring" and typical upwardly mobile professions. Instead, she fantasized about moving to Los Angeles to become a screenwriter.

"We have a lot in common," she said, confidently. We held hands spontaneously.

"Why do you say that?"

"Well, I'm not talking about all the *Jewy* stuff. I'm talking about our dreams . . . we both know what we're *supposed* to do, but it's not really what we *want* to do. You don't *really* like medicine, do you?"

I was puzzled by her question and gathered my thoughts before answering. "Actually, I do. I love it. I love physiology, knowing how the body works . . . like singing . . . the way the brain plays with the diaphragm, the lungs, and the vocal cords to make music. I love understanding why, if I get nervous, or sad, or angry, or excited, my brain makes my body do all kinds of crazy shit. I love that there's part of that crazy shit that I can't control, but there's also part of that crazy shit that I *can* control. It's a goddamn miracle." I stared at her for a moment and went on, now remembering the conversation I had with my mother after I had returned from Israel, "I'm not very religious, but it's *kinda* what I love about being Jewish. You know, that a lot of what happens to us is out of our hands, but that we also have free will to *help* determine what happens next."

We sipped on Long Island Iced Teas poured in plastic cups and philosophized knowingly as teenagers do until we were fairly certain that Eric and Allison had already finished doing the nasty. "Just do me a favor," she said as we left. "Find your passion, find your priorities, and embrace them, no matter what."

"Wow, that sounds like a line from an *ABC Afterschool Special*! Did you write it yourself?" I ribbed.

We walked out of The KK, now with arms interlaced and her head leaning on my shoulder. Admittedly, it felt good to be wanted again by a girl.

Midway between The KK and The Towers, we stopped for a kiss. I closed my eyes, but I was unable to lose myself in the moment. I couldn't stop thinking about how I had finally articulated what I had felt all along about my relationship with medicine, music, and religion; each was integral to my perception of the world. Why would I sacrifice one for another? It was at that moment that my jealousy of Benjie dissolved.

I opened my eyes and looked up. In front of me stood the Hillel House, home of the Foundation for Jewish Campus Life, where Jewish students would gather for meals, services, and other *Jewy* stuff. The coincidence would have been comical if it weren't so absurd. My parents would have been thrilled. Though I felt no guilt, the moment was bittersweet.

My eyes turned to Jessica. I inadvertently stared at her a bit too long. There was absolutely nothing about her I didn't like. I just felt as though I wasn't being true to myself.

"What's wrong? Are you not into this?" she asked, rightfully so.

"No, no! I'm totally into it," I protested. "It's just . . ."

"Oh God. Is this the part where you tell me you have a girlfriend back home?"

"What are you talking about? I *don't* have a girlfriend back home." Technically, I was right.

"Well, I think I'm pretty good at reading cues . . . I like you, and I'm pretty sure you like me, too. And we're a little drunk and we've been touching each other in public for the last hour. And then you froze. So, I figure, either you're gay or you're carrying a torch for a girl in Nebraska." Fortunately she didn't think I was a stalker.

"Jessica, stop thinking like a screenwriter and just kiss me." She obliged, and I walked her back to her room at The Towers, Room 418 East. We opened the door, only to find Allison snoozing on the bottom bunk. I imagined that in my own room Bob and Farrah had tucked Eric in bed before sharing a post-coital cigarette. I knew my evening with Jessica was essentially over.

"I had a great time tonight," said Jessica.

"So did I. And you're right . . . I *do* like you." Again I was telling the truth.

"You know, you seem like a really good guy." For the first time in a very long while, I agreed.

That night I lay awake for hours. My mind spun as I tried to connect the pieces of my life. I continued to circle back to Jessica's saccharine but profound statement. *Find your passion, find your priorities, and embrace them, no matter what.*

She was absolutely right.

THE next morning, I called Benjie.

"Hey," I said. "I need your help."

CHAPTER 34

"Say – you don't want to chance it
You've been hurt so before"

—YES'S "OWNER OF A LONELY HEART," FROM THE ALBUM
90125, RELEASED OCTOBER 8TH, 1983.
IT PEAKED AT NUMBER ONE ON US BILLBOARD'S HOT
100 SONGS.

The Wednesday before Thanksgiving of freshman year marks the mass exodus over the river and through the woods for college students to decompress, come home to Mom, justify college choices, and share war stories with old friends. I had a slightly different agenda.

Eric and I retraced our steps together back to Chicago. We both assumed we were a bit wiser, but a semester of experience doesn't define maturity. Though we were just a little older, we were every bit as naïve. On the other hand, there's something to be said for a youthful, brazen sense of invincibility.

Once at O'Hare and still somewhat insecure in our own manhood in front of strangers, Eric and I left each other with a head nod and a handshake, not with a hug. I then managed to meet Zillie and Iris for the final leg home. With an hour's wait in the airport, and another in the air, we would have plenty of time to catch up before landing. We made small talk at the gate; I saved the good stuff for the flight. Though I loathed the middle seat on airplanes, I found myself swaddled and claustrophobic between the two of them to avoid explaining myself twice.

"I need to talk to both of you about—"

"Jesus, is this about a Amy again?" asked Zillie. "Can we just have one weekend together without your drama?" I thought she might spit her half-chewed airplane peanuts in my face.

"It's not what you think!" I answered.

"I can tell you right now it's *exactly* what I think. Let me guess . . . you called Amy a hundred times and you think she's finally caved and has agreed to take you back on condition you renounce your religion *and* your balls."

"Oh, shut up," I answered.

"Okay, tell me I'm completely wrong."

"You're *mostly* wrong."

"*Listen* to me. I'm about to finish college and I have no interest in a serious relationship with any one guy before starting grad school. You're so young! Why do you have to be in such a goddamn hurry? You won't really be mature until you're at least nineteen. I want to have fun just as much as everyone else, and with whomever I want, but I don't want to miss out on life in the process. Stop and smell the roses, dumbass!"

Iris piled on. "She's right, Ronnie . . . haven't you met any girls in Wisconsin yet?"

"Well, yeah, but—"

"There's no 'but!'" The barrage of interruptions continued. Just like old times. "I didn't meet Mitchell until a couple of months ago, and *I'm* almost twenty. "Can't you just play the field while you grow up a little?"

"You haven't even heard me out yet. Why do you both keep insisting I don't know what I'm doing?" I asked, exasperated.

"Because you don't!" they yelled as one.

The verbal onslaught lasted the duration of the flight. I assumed that once we landed, the torture would end peacefully. Unfortunately, it was just beginning.

THE crowded plane caused a longer-than usual, eleven-minute wait to claim our bags. My parents seemed unusually happy (and punctual) when they greeted us; even the competition for ten-minute parking spots, which forced them to leave the car in thirty-minute parking and walk two full minutes to the terminal, didn't appear to bother them in the least.

The day was long, but I was excited to sleep in my quiet, roommate-less room, to wake up without an alarm or the sound and smell of someone vomiting beer outside my door, and to eat a mountain of turkey and pumpkin pie. I slid into the back seat and closed my eyes, but only for a moment.

"Kids, we have a special guest waiting for us at home," announced my mother. My eyes reopened; my parents looked at each other with cagey grins.

"Who?" asked Iris.

"I'm not sure if you or Zillie remember her, but Ronnie will," responded my father. "He just saw her this past summer."

My heart raced. Of all the well-intended but diabolical schemes, the one I was about to hear was almost too much to bear.

"Do you remember Dalia, Shlomit and Haim's old neighbor?" asked my mother.

"Yeah, the skinny little girl with the buckteeth and the uncombed hair," answered Iris.

"Well, that skinny little girl is now a gorgeous Israeli soldier."

I was immediately bathed in a cold sweat. I couldn't speak. That night in Haifa had shaken my confidence in such a thoroughly emasculating manner that I had only recently stopped experiencing a recurring dream. In it I stood alone, in broad daylight on an Israeli beach, naked, hiding my limp, prepubescent package in front of a fucking battalion of hot female soldiers on leave. The women were heavily armed with bikinis, machine guns, and laughter. The images were so vivid that, upon wakening, I would hyperventilate. This weekend promised to do wonders for my self-esteem.

Infuriated and humiliated, I finally mustered the strength to speak. *"What is she doing here?"* I demanded.

"Ronnie, calm down," pleaded my mother. "I could sense you were still having a hard time getting over Amy—every time we spoke with you on the phone. Call it mother's intuition, but I could just tell."

"What did you do? Tell me!" I had just studied brain aneurysms in pathology class and thought one was about to burst in my head.

My father remained unfazed. "Listen, if I had the opportunity that you're about to have, I'd be thanking my lucky stars. Shlomit and Haim kept telling us about the girl . . . that the two of you had some sort of 'chemistry.' I don't know exactly what happened last summer, but she's been very interested in seeing you again since you became reacquainted. So we contacted her and helped her get permission to come to America during a scheduled army leave. We even bought her the ticket. We got a great deal."

"What?" I was seething.

"What's wrong with you, Ronnie?" he responded, this time a bit sternly. "You've got to stop bullshitting around. This girl's not only pretty, she's also smart. She wants to be an accountant, for God's sake! Your mother and I decided we couldn't let you screw things up . . . again. If you're given the opportunity, you take it . . . end of story."

By now I was apoplectic. "You can't do this! This is *my* life. If I want to 'screw things up,' I'll do it, and on my own terms, not yours!"

Zillie and Iris could only close their eyes and shake their heads in exasperation. As much as his words pained me, I did, in fact, see a different opportunity, and I did intend to take it. We arrived at home with Dalia sleeping soundly in Iris' room after a long journey. Iris claimed my room, so I was relegated to the couch. I did dream that night, but not about my questionable manhood.

"WAKE up, *Amerrrican* boy!"

I opened my eyes. It was Dalia, hovering over me, un-jetlagged and undeterred. Despite the time of year, her skin was rendered a golden brown from a week of hiking in Israel's sunny and still warm Negev Desert. Her hair sparkled with solar highlights. The '80s were the "golden" age of tanning beds; the world was only starting to take notice of the dangers of its weakening ozone and the harmful effects of the sun's ultraviolet rays on human skin. But good God, she was sexy.

This wasn't going be easy.

I smiled awkwardly. "I'm surprised you wanted to see me," I responded in Hebrew.

"Why are you surprised? Don't you remember?" She leaned in to kiss me as she now spoke in her native language. I made sure to turn my head so she would plant one firmly on my cheek, thereby avoiding killing her with my morning breath.

"What, you mean, 'the novelty?' That you've never been with an American boy before?"

"I just figured we had some unfinished business to attend to." She smiled. I couldn't help but return the gesture. Of course I was flattered that she would come half way across the world to see me, even if I was being used. Somehow her absurdly hot appearance numbed the sting of exploitation.

She twirled her hair tauntingly with an index finger. We stared at each other. She was wearing a tight, low-cut white cashmere sweater, which only accentuated her glowing skin (and excellent rack). She styled some equally tight jeans and cowboy boots, both purchased the day before at The Fort, Lincoln's finest Western apparel store. She looked quite comfortable playing the part. Finally she spoke:

Hebrew:	"תראה לי את נברסקה!"
Transliteration:	"Tar-eh lee et Nebraska!"
Literal Translation:	"Show me Nebraska!"
Intended Translation:	"Let me fuck with your head all over again!"

She broke the silence, but in reality I flinched first. So did my dick. Nice to see it was still working. And off we went.

I proudly escorted Dalia through Lincoln's important landmarks: the Capitol Building, the university's Memorial Stadium, Pioneers Park, the Runza Hut, Holmes Lake, and Lincoln Southeast High School. I had intended only a drive-by of my alma mater, but Dalia insisted that we stop. "It's closed, Dalia," I promised. "Thanksgiving's a national holiday and no one will be here."

"I don't care. I just want to walk around a bit. This is going to be fun."

We made small talk while strolling the perimeter of school, from High Street to 40th, from Van Dorn to 37th. It was predictably cold and windy, and Dalia reached for my hand along the way. "I've never been this cold in my life. Warm me up, please," she implored.

I would very much like to warm you up, I thought. I took her hand like a gentleman and undressed her with my eyes only. As we passed the parking entrance, I heard a friendly double honk. I looked up and saw Frank Dupuis pulling up in his 1977 Pontiac Sunbird. He rolled down the window. "Well, I'll be damned. If it isn't the young Dr. Bahar."

"Hi, Mr. Dupuis," I answered happily. "What are you doing here on Thanksgiving?"

"I should ask you the same question . . . I'm just grading some papers. You know how I hate getting behind." He turned to Dalia and tried (unsuccessfully) to disguise a double take. "Ron, aren't you going to introduce me to your friend?"

"Oh, uh, sorry . . . Mr. Dupuis, this is Dalia Klein. Dalia is visiting from Israel . . . Dalia, this is my all-time favorite teacher, Mr. Frank Dupuis."

"Nice to meet you, Dalia."

"Very pleasant," she answered, only slightly lost in translation.

They exchanged "pleasantries" until I interrupted, "So how's the new crop of students this fall?"

"Eh, they'll never match up to *you*," he answered jokingly.

"I'm sure not . . . hey, what are you doing Saturday night?"

"I guess I'll be eating leftovers with Sheila and Fern. Why?"

"Well, remember Benjie Kushner? I think he was in your

bio class a couple of years ago. Anyway, his band's playing at
PO Pears this Saturday. I think I remember that you like
watching live music . . . you should come. Might be fun seeing
a former student on stage."

"Hmmm . . . I don't know if I could get Sheila to come,
but I might just fly solo. Could be entertaining." He looked at
Dalia before returning his gaze to me. "Nice seeing you, Ron.
Good to know you're back in the saddle again." He rolled up
the window, and I watched him drive toward the staff parking lot. My eyes then wandered to student parking, where I
saw "my" spot, now empty.

Before returning home, I drove Dalia up and down that
same stretch of US Route 77 where Amy, the Duster, and I
became so well acquainted. The moment was surreal: two
worlds, two directions. We barely spoke. Instead, Dalia leaned
against me and we looked out into the horizon. She smelled
as good as she looked, and I must admit it felt "very pleasant" having her hand on my thigh. Somehow, though, I was
still alone.

CHAPTER 35

"I have a picture, pinned to my wall. An image of you and of me and we're laughing and loving it all"

—THE THOMPSON TWINS' "HOLD ME NOW," FROM THE
ALBUM *INTO THE GAP*, RELEASED NOVEMBER 11TH, 1983.
IT PEAKED AT NUMBER THREE ON US BILLBOARD'S HOT
100 SONGS.

My mom outdid herself; who knew Thanksgiving turkey went so well with falafel and hummus? Dalia certainly felt at home with my family, and she had quickly grown on my sisters. Though Zillie and Iris were not the most trusting individuals, they were able to compartmentalize Dalia's motives and take this charismatic girl at face value. By Friday morning, Dalia, my sisters, and my mother went downtown together to do more shopping at The Hitching Post and Wooden Nickel, Lincoln's best attempt at cutting edge fashion. Also, as electronics were nearly unaffordable in Israel, Dalia made a high-fidelity pilgrimage to Target to purchase a Walkman.

While Dalia explored the prairie, I made my own pilgrimage to The Garage. Though I had invited myself, the boys were gracious and sentimental upon my return—arriving with two large Godfather's pizzas helped (consider it a turkey chaser for young adult males). Thankfully, Talent Scout Rex was absent, but he would be attending the show the following evening.

I stayed all four hours of the practice session. The music was, as usual, empowering, and it caused me to circle in a continuous loop my night with Jessica.

I love physiology, knowing how the body works . . . like singing . . . the way the brain plays with the diaphragm, the lungs, and the vocal cords to make music. I love understanding why, if I get nervous, or sad, or angry, or excited, my brain makes my body do all kinds of crazy shit. I love that there's part of that crazy shit that I can't control, but there's also part of that crazy shit that I can control. It's a goddamn miracle.

I came home to Dalia's fashion show of the day's shopping spree. She oozed sexy as she ambled an imaginary catwalk through my living room wearing Esprit, Ralph Lauren, Levi's, and her own namesake, Calvin Klein. Honestly, she would have looked good wearing a Hefty Bag. "I could get used to this . . . how do I look?" she asked, rhetorically.

"Really, really good."

Zillie and Iris watched from the doorway. Both smiled but kept their arms crossed. They knew me.

Sabbath featured a dinner challah specially ordered from Omaha's The Bagel Bin, Nebraska's only kosher bakery. Per family tradition, on the Friday of Thanksgiving Weekend, after blessings over the wine and bread, my father scanned the room to ask us what we were thankful for.

He spoke first. "I'm delighted to have my family together for Thanksgiving, and to share this lovely American tradition with our lovely guest from Israel." Dalia smiled without blushing. My eyes rolled without being noticed.

Dalia volunteered to speak next. "I'm also thankful for spending this weekend with your family, and especially to get to know Ronnie a little better." Adorable? Perhaps. Awkward? Definitely.

Zillie: "Tom Cruise."

Iris: "Eight uninterrupted hours of sleep."

My mother, a notorious lightweight, had already nervously indulged herself with a second glass of Manischewitz, and, as expected, she proclaimed:

Hebrew:	"לא עכשיו. אני חושבת שאני קצת שיכורה."
Transliteration:	"Lo achshav. Ani choshevet sheh ani ketzat shikorah."
Literal Translation:	"Not now. I think I'm a little drunk."
Intended Translation:	"Listen, Ronnie. I know you think we're overbearing and maybe a little nuts. However, we *are* your parents, and we've been around the block a few times. You need to have faith in us that we just understand the world better than you do. Yes, we made you live in Nebraska with unrealistic expectations about your love life and, yes, we suppressed your voice, both literally and figuratively. If we could go back in time, chances are we'd do things a little differently, but unfortunately we don't have that option. It's a rough world out there, and there's no playbook on how to move an Israeli family to the Midwest while preserving both faith and culture. You know we love Amy . . .

Intended Translation:	. . . but you need to let go of her, and Dalia seems like the best way to help you . . .We just want to protect you. So, yeah, I had a couple of drinks to calm my nerves, because if this plan doesn't work out, I'm going to go apeshit. PS. I love you."

My father smiled and turned to me. "Okay, Ronnie, it's your turn."

I paused then spoke. "I'm . . . I'm thankful for whatever happens next."

AFTER dinner, Dalia and I walked the half-mile to Christine's house on Pioneers Boulevard. The crisp air failed to clear my head. Chris was having a party, but she made it clear that this time Amy would not be attending. It was just as well; I longed to see Amy, but until that time, I couldn't imagine a more uncomfortable encounter.

Funny how, when college freshman meet high school friends during Thanksgiving weekend for the first time in three short months, one would think they'd been simultaneously paroled from prison following eighteen years of good behavior. After an enormous and mutually heartfelt hug with Christine, she looked at Dalia, who had been standing behind me.

"Well, hello! Who are *you?*" asked Christine. She was direct as usual.

"I am Dalia. You *arrre Chreeese*, no?"

"No? Oh, yes, I *am* Chris. Come in. Here, let me take your coats." As she did so, she stared at me, out of Dalia's view, with a furrowed brow. "Ron, I've got like ten coats piled up here now. Come help me throw them on my bed."

She glanced at Dalia, this time with a quick head to toe survey. "Hold on, Dalia, we'll be right back." I knew the shit was about to hit the fan.

We entered Christine's bedroom and she slammed the door. "What the *fuck* is going on, Ron? And who's the Goddess of Love out there?"

"Nothing's going on. She's a houseguest."

"Houseguest, my ass. Who *is* she?"

Again, the stare; lying would be futile. I had to return to Dalia soon, so I offered Christine the *Readers' Digest* version. She was able to fill in the gaps.

Dumbfounded, she finally answered. "I thought we had an agreement."

"We do. Don't worry."

Chris and I returned to the family room, where, not so shockingly, my former classmates had already congregated around Dalia to pepper her with questions. "Tell me about the army."

"Have you ever shot anyone?

"Do you ride camels to school?"

"Is everyone really Jewish there?"

"Guys, guys . . . slow down, she just got here!" I announced.

"No, *eeet's* okay, Ronnie . . . I like *eeet*." said Dalia.

"She calls you 'Ronnie'?" asked Mark, laughing. "That's fucking *adorable!*"

Dalia and I stayed at the party for several hours. I regressed to my role as the wallflower in a real-time social experiment featuring Dalia, the fantastically hot girl, engulfing the attention of ogling guys and jealous girls. I later realized that, regardless of geography and religion, every school or town has a Dalia, a Tommy, a Ron, and an Amy.

CHAPTER 36

*"Don't wait for answers
Just take your chances"*

—BILLY JOEL'S "DON'T ASK ME WHY," FROM THE ALBUM
GLASS HOUSES, RELEASED JULY 24TH, 1980.
IT PEAKED AT NUMBER NINETEEN ON US BILLBOARD'S
HOT 100 SONGS.

After the party, Dalia and I walked home. This time I volunteered my hand first; she was, in reality, a great date who always remained clear in her intentions. She may have been manipulative, but she wasn't devious. I envied her straightforwardness very much. "Your friends are sweet, Ronnie. I love it here," she said as we strolled. She was speaking again in Hebrew and could express herself more clearly. "I mean, I would never live here, but I love it."

"Why would you never live here? Remember earlier today you said you could get used to this?" I asked, not so much to challenge her—I had my own issues with Nebraska—but instead to pick her brain.

"I was talking about buying clothes, not moving to Nebraska, silly. I'm an Israeli, and that's where my soul is. This *thing* that we have—and I think we do have a thing—is fun, and I meant it when I said I want to get to know you better . . . better than the childhood playmates we used to be . . . but I think you and I just see the world differently."

"Yes, I agree," I answered, smiling. "And I didn't mean I wanted you to move here. I just wanted to know why you never would."

"I think I know what you mean. Let me explain what *I* mean . . . I'm *mostly* a free spirit, but I won't compromise about certain things, like leaving home for good. You, on the other hand, are mostly *repressed*, but you'll compromise about almost anything, like doing what your heart tells you to do." She put her hand on my chest. Whatever was inside was still beating. She was indeed candid, but, like most Israelis, she had perfected the art of being presumptuous. She only knew part of my story.

Once home, we snuggled on the couch platonically—if there is such a thing—and watched the end of *Letterman* before calling it a night. "Ronnie, you're a very complicated boy," she said finally. "If you want me, you know where to find me, but I might be far away when you finally make up your mind." She kissed me gently on the lips and went to bed.

Once again I spent half the night engaged in a staring contest with the moon. *Goddammit*, I thought. In any other world, Amy would be the kind of girl my mother would dream about, and Dalia would be the kind of girl my mother would warn me about.

DESPITE a collective and desperate plea from my sisters and me to spare us from morning services at the synagogue, my parents forced us to attend. Amidst the expected withering scrutiny of the roughly sixty congregants in attendance, however, my date remained remarkably unaffected.

Old Mrs. Goldberg, who sat directly behind us, simply couldn't endure waiting for services to conclude to snatch a moment of face time with Dalia. During the Torah Service, I felt her tap my shoulder. "Ron, who is this lovely lady?" she asked in what I assumed was the loudest whisper in recorded history.

"Estelle Goldberg, meet Dalia Klein. Dalia, meet Mrs. Goldberg," I answered quietly.

"Hello," said Dalia, speaking softly but smiling widely. She and I then turned to face the altar again.

A conversation between Mrs. Goldberg and her husband Max ensued. As it turns out, it was actually Max who had the loudest whisper in recorded history.

"She has looks to die for, this one," declared Estelle.

"*Oy*, what I would do with that *'shayne maidel'* if I were sixty years younger," answered Max. Somehow using the Yiddish term for "beautiful girl" made his declaration even more painful to my ears.

Estelle continued, "Shut up, you dirty old man."

"What? It's true!"

"I said, shut up!"

By the time Max (and Estelle) finally did shut up, Zillie and Iris were shaking with silent laughter. I cringed before closing my eyes in a fruitless attempt to make the Goldbergs go away through telepathy. Though neither Dalia's English nor her Yiddish was perfect, she understood enough to squeeze my arm, grin, and continue looking forward. After services, Dalia and I were forced to endure a veritable receiving line of templegoers, and we were eventually approached by Benjie's parents, Marcia and Sheldon. "'Bout time we got some new blood around here," quipped Sheldon.

"Shel, be nice," implored Marcia.

"Benjie told me you had a little lady in town, Ron." He turned to Dalia. "Sheldon Kushner," he announced, introducing himself. "Damn glad to meet you."

Dalia looked at him curiously. After a moment, she

skipped the salutation, and instead smiled and said, "I love your funny jacket."

Sheldon was indeed in rare form, sporting a red polyester blazer with a white "*N*" embroidered on the chest pocket to represent his beloved Nebraska Cornhuskers. It was his custom to wear this gem on important football game days. That afternoon the team would play the Oklahoma Sooners in Norman, Oklahoma, and a Cornhusker win would propel them to a berth in the Orange Bowl to compete for the national championship. It had not even occurred to me that his appearance was anything out of the ordinary.

He looked down at his jacket and seemed to realize how its appearance could be considered odd when viewed for the first time. "Oh, this thing? Well, thank you," he answered proudly. He paused as she continued to stare. "But it's not funny; it's tradition. Don't just judge a book by its cover."

"I don't understand," she responded.

"It's a metaphor. You know, just a figure of speech."

"I don't understand," she repeated.

No, she really didn't understand.

Sheldon relented, and though he changed the subject, he continued the banter with Dalia for several minutes before turning his attention to me. I braced myself for the latest in his long line of irreverent comments. "Well, I think Dalia's a keeper, but, then again, that's what I thought about the last one," he chuckled. He was lucky he was one of my favorite people on Earth.

"Sheldon!" yelled Marcia.

"Oh, I'm just teasin'."

Thankfully, he changed the subject. "Dalia, are you coming to my son Benjie's show tonight?"

"Yes, I am. Ronnie told me he *de* best."

"Yes he is if I may say so myself . . . you know, Ron has an excellent voice too."

"Yes I *hearrr* him once. *Dis* is beautiful."

"He's even sung with Benjie's band before."

Dalia then looked at me. "I love to *hearrr dis* one day."

THAT afternoon, Dalia and I joined Sundar and *on-again-off-again-now-long-distance* Anne to watch the Nebraska game at the Rajendran's house. During the course of the twentieth century, college football had woven itself into the fabric and melting pot of American life, so that a Christian, a Hindu, a Jew, and his exotic companion could sit down in front of a twenty-five-inch color TV and snack on samosas and Coca-Cola while gripped by twenty-two men of all races chasing inflated pigskin. By the second quarter, Dalia had completely immersed herself in Husker Nation. Though she still didn't understand me, or any of the rules of football, perhaps she began to understand the red blazer. No blind faith, just hope. After a thrilling, game-ending defensive stand, Nebraska had defeated Oklahoma, 28-21. All was right in the world. Almost.

Immediately after the game, the visitors' sideline could be seen erupting with joy. The team, their coaches, and nearly all traveling VIPs bounced aimlessly in a spontaneous display of excitement. Only one young couple could be seen in an oddly motionless, prolonged embrace, and the cameraman zoomed in to capture the moment. When the two finally separated, faces were revealed; there stood Kimmy and Scott Campbell, whose wedding a full year prior marked my first real attempt at rocking and rolling in front of an audience.

Kimmy smiled and Scott cried. Announcers Gary Bender and Pat Hayden blathered something about the absence of machismo and the presence of unbridled emotion; they clearly didn't recognize Scott, the former Cornhusker, and they clearly didn't understand that he was crying not only out of happiness, but also out of his own unrequited success as a national champion or as a professional athlete.

"So the men with the 'N' . . . they *weeen*?" asked Dalia.

"Yes, they win." I answered, smiling.

This was either going to be my finest hour, or the biggest fucking disaster of all time.

Just hope.

DALIA could sense my nervousness as the four of us drove in the Duster to PO Pears. "What *de* matter?" she asked finally.

"Oh, nothing," I responded, as sweat beaded down my forehead and drenched my T-shirt. I removed my jacket and rolled down the window in an attempt to cool off and to preventatively freshen the air should my colon ignite.

"Ron, what the hell are you doing? It's fuckin' freezing back here. Close the window!" demanded Sundar, as he rubbed his bare hands together and leaned against Anne.

"Oh, sorry guys." I obliged and tried to distract myself by turning on the radio. KLMS was playing George Benson:

". . . *Turn your love around*
Don't you turn me down . . ."

Shit! Not now, I thought. I changed the station. KFOR was playing Bryan Adams:

". . . *Give it to me straight from the heart*
Tell me we can made another start . . ."

Fuck. No FM radio in the Duster, so I turned it off.

"Hey I *liked* that song," complained Anne.

"Sorry, I just can't do 'adult contemporary' right now."

"Who made *you* Casey Kasem?" she snapped, obviously annoyed.

By now, I had become nauseated. Anne could tell I was ill and so she let it go. We reached PO Pears and climbed out of the Duster. "Sundar," I said, "could you and Anne let Dalia in? Here's five bucks for her ticket. I gotta go take care of something."

"Dude, you don't need to speak in code. Just leave some toilet paper for the rest of us."

"No," I answered. "I mean, yes . . . I mean, I gotta go, but then I gotta do something else . . . I'll see you once the show starts."

"What? Dude, what's *wrong* with you?" he demanded. "I know you got stomach issues, but you're acting all mysterious too . . . what gives?"

"Sundar, just trust me." I turned to Dalia. I paused and stared at her for just a moment. *God help me*, I thought.

Hebrew:	".אני אראה אותך בעוד כמה דקות"
Transliteration:	"Ani er-eh otach be' od kamma dakot."
Literal Translation:	"I'll see you in a few minutes."
Intended Translation:	"Dalia, forgive me for what I'm about to do. Maybe someday you'll understand."

CHAPTER 37

*"Did you never call? I waited for your call
These rivers of suggestion are driving me away"*

—R.E.M.'s "So. Central Rain (I'm Sorry)," from
the album *Reckoning*. Performed during their first
national television appearance, October 6th, 1983,
the song itself wasn't released until May 15th, 1984.
It peaked at number eighty-five on US Billboard's
Hot 100 Songs.

I pounded wildly on the back entrance of PO Pears. I was ready to lunge at the door and dislocate a shoulder when it finally creaked open and Benjie appeared.

"Dude, you look like shit," he declared.

"Thanks a lot. And hello to you, too."

"Sorry." He gave me a cursory hug. "But what the hell's wrong with you?"

"Nerves . . . it'll pass—it always does; you know that—I'll be backstage in a minute, I promise." I scurried past Benjie and headed for the men's room. I barely reached the first stall and urgently shut myself inside before I proceeded to spew forth from every orifice of my body. It was ugly, but it was over within seconds. A bar toilet is generally not a great place to collect one's thoughts, and the combined smell of vomit, Clorox, and drunken beer piss splashed on the floor beside the urinals did not help. It did, however, motivate me to leave the stall and "freshen up"—if that were possible—at the sink with the white powdery shit that comes from the soap dispenser.

I quickly bathed my face in a cold brew of said white powdery shit and metallic tap water. Then, mostly recovered, I gathered the determination to look in the mirror, and I opened my eyes. Tommy appeared behind me.

"Fuckin' a, if it isn't my favorite rock doc!"

Not now, I thought. *Anytime—even when you caught me naked with your girlfriend—but not now.* "Tommy!" I said finally. "What are *you* doing here?"

"Listening to live music, just like everyone else, bro . . . actually, Chris and Amy were going to come by themselves, but my poker game fell through at the last minute, so I decided to come. Chris was really upset, like she was on some kinda date with Amy. She made me feel like a goddamn third wheel. Jesus, women are all fuckin' nuts. Amy *is* my girlfriend, for God's sake." Blissfully tanked, he then relieved himself nonchalantly in and around the urinal.

"Totally," I responded. *I'm* totally *fucked,* I thought.

As we walked out of the men's room together, I noticed Dalia wandering the hallway alone. *I may as well get this over with,* I thought. "Dalia!" I yelled and waved her over.

"Who the hell is that?" demanded Tommy. "She's outrageously hot."

Yes, she was outrageously hot. Dalia wanted to fit in, so I persuaded her not to wear the cowboy hat she had also purchased at The Fort. She did, however, insist on showing off the rest of her Western wardrobe. Watch out, Paris: the sultry cowgirl look had made its debut in Lincoln, Nebraska. "She's . . . a guest, from Israel."

"Holy shit, she's your . . . I mean . . . you actually *know* her?"

"Well, not in the biblical sense, if that's what you mean . . . but yes, I've known her for a long time. She's a family friend."

"Dude, I'm happy for you. Honestly."

"But . . ." I stopped myself as Dalia arrived.

"*Derr* you are! I *worrry* about you . . . *arrre* you okay?" she asked as she placed her hands on my pale cheeks.

"Yes, I'm fine." I did need to gargle a Coke to extinguish the residual taste of anxiety puke, but I would survive. It was now or never.

"You *surrre* you don't want to go home? We can *seeet* on *de* couch and watch more *Amerrrican* football *eeef* you want."

"I'm okay . . . really!" I insisted, and quickly changed the subject. "Dalia, let me introduce you to my friend Tommy."

Apparently something interesting happens when two exceptionally attractive people meet each other for the first time. I didn't know whether to be jealous, curious, or simply amused, but I was pretty sure I witnessed the two of them engage in an ephemeral mutual admiration club assessment, followed by a synchronized, knowing head nod. "Hello, my *frrriend*," she said.

Never lacking in self-confidence, Tommy responded with a chuckle and an impersonation. "Hello to you too, my *frrriend!*" After laughing at his own wittiness, he continued, "Hey, Dalia, come meet my girlfriend, Amy. She and Ron go way back."

"What *eeet* means 'way back'?"

"It means . . . it means they've known each other for a long time."

Dalia looked at me curiously. I felt myself blushing. I hoped it had appeared only as though the color had returned to my post-puke pale face. "Hey, Tommy," I said, "Why don't you take Dalia back to meet Amy? I'm going backstage to say 'hi' to Benjie . . . I'll see you all in a few minutes."

"Sure thing, bro." As they walked off, Tommy turned to me, made a dick-rubbing gesture, and took off with Dalia.

I ran backstage to find Benjie. "What the fuck *took* you so long?" he asked, exasperated. "We're on in two minutes." The band had spent so much time performing together that even when they shook their heads in disapproval, Peter, Jeff, Johnny, and Benjie did so in unison.

"Guys, I'm sorry . . . I swear I'm ready." I peeked at the crowd. In the back of the room, by the Budweiser sign, stood Iris. We instantly made eye contact. She was carrying on the long-standing tradition of our mother by wiping away tears. She understood. She was also smiling; she truly understood.

Iris faced Zillie, whose arms were crossed, not in a judgmental way, but in her own "fucking *carpe diem*" way. She also understood. Iris whispered in Zillie's ear, and my older sister immediately turned to me. A simple nod was all that was necessary; she also truly understood.

Front and center, surrounded by Sundar, Anne, Dalia, Christine, and Tommy, stood Amy, wearing a little black dress. Sometimes the heart has the ability to trick the lonely mind to envision an old flame in an unrealistic light. Not in my case. I imagined she smelled like jasmine. Amy's hair, which had grown longer since summer, appeared to dance around her face in a desperate attempt to cover those hazel eyes. She ran her fingers through it the way I had seen so many times in the past but never fully appreciated how incurably cute this maneuver was. Her eyes appeared. My heart didn't lie; it melted.

". . . Behold, you are beautiful, my love; behold, you are beautiful; your eyes are as doves . . ."

A heated discussion behind me ended my trance. "You boys got a reputation to uphold . . . do you realize what you're risking?" It was Rex Dawson, fresh from an extended trip either to the surface of the sun or to the most powerful tanning bed on Planet Earth; he glowed an orange hue rarely found in nature. "You know I can pull the plug on you right here and now!"

"Rex, why are you doing this?" asked Benjie, looking utterly perplexed.

"I'll tell you why I'm doing this . . . I'm doing this because I'm not just a talent scout; I'm a babysitter. Unlike most guys in this cutthroat business, I actually care about the four of you. I know what it takes to be a success in music, and it's not just being able to play the guitar or sing. You gotta have your shit together, and you gotta stay focused. Now what's it gonna be?"

I ran over to Rex and stood directly behind him. "Don't, Benjie." I said. "It's not worth it!"

Rex shifted his gaze between the band members and me. "Listen to the doctor, Benjie. He's the only one here besides me who's makin' any sense."

Benjie looked past Rex and on to me. The dilemma shook both of us. "Ron, I think the guys and I need a minute to talk this over." Guava quickly huddled in a corner, as by then the restless patrons began to clap rhythmically. I felt a surge of anticipatory guilt and disappointment. Fuck!

Within a minute Rex himself grew tired of waiting. "Boys, I've just about had enough."

Guava looked up. "Okay, Rex," said Benjie.

"Okay, *what*?"

Benjie quickly glanced at me and then calmly walked up to Rex. "Look, we know we don't have as much experience as you do, and we appreciate that you care about us, but we're all adults and we don't need a goddamn babysitter; we need an advocate. You know this is important to Ron, and I'm not abandoning my friend . . . not now, not ever. So if you can't be that advocate and support our decisions, well then I guess we're out."

Rex's eyes then bounced repeatedly between Peter, Jeff, and Johnny. Guava didn't flinch. "So you boys are really planning to go along with this bullshit?" he asked, growling.

"Yup," they answered, simultaneously.

Rex didn't look pissed; he looked dumbfounded "So it's 'all for one and one for all?'"

"Yup."

Rex pursed his lips as he silently contemplated his options. The standoff continued for a good, uncomfortable minute before he finally began to nod his head slowly. "Well then," he said, and a resigned smile crept over his face. "I'd be a stupid *sonofabitch* to do anything cruel to a buncha guys with so much loyalty."

"Thanks, Rex," said Benjie. "You won't regret this."

"Yes, I will . . . but what the hell." He shook his head before taking a sip from his scotch. He then addressed me, still befuddled over the confrontation. "You change your mind yet, doctor?"

"What do you mean?" I answered nervously.

"You know what I mean, son. Do you wanna be a professional singer?"

"To tell you the truth, I haven't really been thinking about a career in music lately . . . I've got other things on my mind."

"I gathered as much."

I didn't answer.

"You got a *helluva* friend there, brother . . . a *helluva* friend," he said, now grinning from ear to ear. He took a drag off a Marlboro Light, not-so-accidentally blew smoke in my face, paused, and added, "Well, I didn't think tonight was going to be your audition *anyway* . . . I think I'll just sit back and enjoy the show."

Guava waited for the sound of the audience to come to a crescendo. "Okay boys, it's time," said Benjie. He then grabbed me by the shoulder. "Hey!"

"Hey what?" I asked, not knowing what to expect.

"It's just like band practice . . . when I call your name you're gonna get out there and kick some musical ass!"

I stood stage left as Benjie and the rest of Guava made their entrance to a thunderous applause of Nebraskans, drunk with pleasure from alcohol, the Cornhusker victory, and the impending concert from the hometown band. Benjie then grabbed his guitar and stepped up to the microphone. "Lincoln, are you ready for Guava?" he asked rhetorically.

"Yes!" roared the spectators.

"Well *allllll-right!*" he responded, now toying with the crowd. He then turned to me, smiled, and winked.

Rex witnessed the interaction. "You'll never find out 'what if' until you show the courage to try," he said, smiling again. He then gestured by raising his glass before disappearing into the crowd.

Once the audience quieted, Benjie continued, "We will always have a special place in our hearts for Lincoln. This town is where we grew up—where we got our start—so, as a special tribute you, the good people of Lincoln, Nebraska, we're going to take a trip down Memory Lane . . . do any of you remember a band called The Repeats?"

Pandemonium.

"Well *allllll-right!*" he repeated. *Brace yourself,* I thought. *Here it comes.* "Tonight is The Repeats' swan song, and it's all about cover music . . . and speaking of nostalgia

. . . first, we have a very special guest singer . . . many of you know him . . . some of you even like him!"

I remained out of view. As the audience laughed, I continued to watch Amy. She eyed Christine, who raised her brow and shrugged.

"Direct from Madison, Wisconsin—but still a local hero—the 'medical miracle' . . . the 'rabbi of rock'—put your hands together for Lincoln's own Ron Bahar!"

The crowd cheered. I swallowed hard, put my head down, and walked to the microphone stand that waited patiently for me center stage. Terrified but determined, I looked up, right into Amy's eyes. Neither of us blinked. Without looking away, I said, "Thank you, Benjie, thank you, Repeats, and thank you, Lincoln!" Still watching her, I plucked the microphone from its perch, and continued, "Amy Andrews, this song's for you. It's not infatuation, and it's not an impulse . . . I just love you." I knew Tommy's blood would boil, and that perhaps this time he would kick the shit out of me in a manner that would make my previous pummeling look like child's play. I didn't care.

"Find your passion, find your priorities, and embrace them, no matter what."

A hush spread across the room. My heart began to race and I felt myself trembling ever so slightly as I waited desperately for the music to begin. Then finally, Ambrosia:

"(Sunlight) There's a new sun arisin'
(In your eyes) I can see a new horizon . . ."

I looked away from a shell-shocked Amy and surveyed the room again. Sundar and Anne stood in disbelief while

Christine simultaneously tilted her head and rolled her eyes to her right while giving me the "this is *your* mess, honey" look. My eyes followed Christine's and traveled past the three of them, beyond the end of the stage. Leaning against the wall, with a napkin neatly hugging his Budweiser, was Frank Dupuis. No judgment this time. He simply nodded and raised his drink as if to say, "Now I get it . . . good luck, son." I decided to focus once again on Amy. If my serenade was to be part of a fairy-tale ending, it didn't start smoothly. Her eyes welled, but, unlike Iris, she didn't wipe away tears of joy. Instead, she gave me a death stare as the waterworks ensued.

I tried valiantly but unsuccessfully not to return the favor. Goddammit, no, I thought, as I struggled to hold back tears. Though I was thoroughly embarrassed by my show of emotion, my voice didn't fail me; neither did The Repeats. I could tell that Amy wanted to leave, but Christine held her hand, partly as a show of support, and partly as a gentle means of preventing her escape.

I continued to sing, and the inevitable happened. Tommy nudged his way past Amy and Christine. It was too loud to hear his voice, but I didn't need to be a professional lip reader to understand when he mouthed the words, "I'm going to fucking kill you." He placed his hands on the stage to brace himself before leaping on to it.

As I began to retreat in an attempt to keep him at arm's length, someone grabbed Tommy from behind. He turned, likely anticipating a fight with bouncers. Instead, he encountered Dalia, who wrapped her arms around him and began to dance. In short order, she bumped and grinded him into submission. Conspicuously drunk and reliably horny, Tommy happily reciprocated. Dalia looked up at me, and for the second time this night I was the recipient of an encour-

CHAPTER 38

*"And after all that we've been through
I will make it up to you. I promise to"*

—Chicago's "Hard to Say I'm Sorry," from the album *Chicago 16*, released May 17th, 1982. It peaked at number one on US Billboard's Hot 100 Songs.

Not again. I couldn't let Amy disappear from my life for good without having her hear me out. She was surprisingly fast, but adrenaline, my knowledge of 9th Street downtown, and the muscle memory of my many fifth-place finishes at cross country meets allowed me, in short order, to overtake, circle, and confront Amy face to face, directly beside the Duster.

I tried to touch her hand, but she recoiled. "Ron, What the *fuck* was that? You just embarrassed me in front of hundreds of people!"

It was the first time I had heard Amy swear. While it was refreshing to confirm that she, too, was only human, I knew I was in trouble. I chuckled nervously. "Holy shit, you actually said the word 'fuck!'"

"It's not funny!" she yelled.

"I'm sorry, I'm sorry," I answered quickly. "I . . . I just . . . we need to talk!"

"What's there to talk about? It's *over*."

"Why?"

"You're kidding, right?"

In the background, we heard The Repeats continue without me. In my pursuit of Amy, it was only appropriate that I had completely deserted my cameo as the frontman and the second of two songs that I was to perform at PO Pears. Always the consummate professional, Benjie assumed his rightful place as lead singer, and the band's rendition of The Climax Blues Band's "I Love You" began:

"When I was a younger man, I hadn't a care,
Foolin' around, hitting the town, growing my hair . . ."

"Amy, I was drunk and stupid."

"Well you're right about that . . . but *you* let it happen. You had control over the situation, and you let it happen!" She fought through the tears and continued, "And that's only part of your problem. You don't even know what you want!"

"I know *exactly* what I want . . . I want *you*."

"You know what I'm talking about . . . you don't know what you want out of *life!*"

"Once again, I want *you* . . . the rest is irrelevant."

"You *know* that's not true."

"Okay, let me rephrase that . . . I love medicine and I love singing . . . but I'd give up *everything* for you—that was just a show back there—and I needed to publicly declare that I love you and that I want you back."

"Well that's just pathetic. Why would you give up every-thing, and why would I want to be with you anyway? This isn't a fairytale, Ron . . . it's real life. You betrayed me, so I dumped you. It's as simple as that."

"But . . ."

"But *what?*"

At that moment, I realized that though I had practiced diligently the day before for my performance that night, I had never considered its aftermath. When it came to debate, I had little chance against Amy, even under the best of circumstances. *Once again, I am a complete idiot,* I thought. I fumbled for a response. *Think, goddammit, think!* I considered my countless hours of lonely self-reflection in Madison . . . then, a moment of clarity. "Okay, okay . . . listen . . . Jews are supposed to have the free will to make mistakes, but we also have the ability to try and make up for them. I'm just asking for that chance. Please, I know you still feel something for me, and it's not just the 'guardian angel' stuff Tommy told me about before I left for Wisconsin. I know you talked my parents into sending me to Israel last summer. You told them you wanted to help me sort things out, but I know you weren't just thinking about medicine or music. You were also thinking about *us.*"

Amy responded with a literal and figurative cold shoulder, as she looked away, crossed her arms, and started to shiver in the unsympathetically cold November night. "Amy, just let me hold you . . . you're going to freeze to death out here!" I implored.

"No!" she yelled as she turned back to me with a devastating glare. "And let's just finish this right here and right now. Your religion is also supposed to be your moral compass . . . a lot of good *that* did you!"

Of course she was right, but I persisted. "I know I was an ass—"

"Well, that's an understatement."

"Amy, please, just let me explain . . . there's no way I could justify what I did, and my excuse about being drunk and stupid is just that . . . an excuse. When I was in Wisconsin, I kept reliving what I did to you over and over in my head, and I thought a lot about faith too. Faith is, well, it's not just a belief in God or a religion . . . turns out that faith is mostly about belief in other *people*. You had faith in me, and, just as you said in your letter, I broke your heart. I abandoned you. I never really understood what that kind of faith was until I lost you."

Her watery but penetrating eyes nearly overwhelmed me. "Amy, I'm telling you, I know I fucked up—I'm sorry, I mean, I know I *screwed* up—but I'll do anything I can to make up for my mistake. I honestly feel that fate brought us together and that we were meant *stay* together."

"Do you *really* believe in fate, or are you using fate as an excuse for your bad behavior?"

"That's a fair question, and I would be skeptical if I were you too. The answer is 'yes,' I do believe in fate. I believe in science—in medicine, and test tubes, and physics, and evolution—but I also believe in fate. It all may seem contradictory, or even irrational, but I believe there's a reason you and I met. Amy, I love you, and I think you might still love me too. And it might seem hokey, but I also believe in second chances."

"Ron, I just don't think . . ."

"Amy, if you have feelings for me, then take me back!" I begged. "Come with me to Wisconsin!"

"Wisconsin? Are you out of your mind? I suppose you also want me to convert to Judaism too? Is this all part of the elaborate plan you conceived for that perfect world of yours?"

"Well, if there's one thing I've learned over the last year, it's that the world isn't perfect. It's big, and complicated, and beautiful, but it's far from perfect . . . I think that's what makes life interesting. If everything were easy, no one would care." I paused, if only to try and collect myself in a failed attempt to avoid crying once more. *Good Lord, Ron. Again?* "The only thing I know," I added, "is that I'm still in love with you, and I always will be. I don't care what obstacles we face—*faith* or otherwise. It couldn't be any more difficult than what my family, your family, or any other family has ever faced. I want you . . . I want *us* back."

"I just don't think . . ."

"Amy, stop!"

"Stop what?" she asked, now flustered.

"Stop running away from me . . . I know what I did was terrible. Just let me show you I've grown up. After all we've been through . . . please don't give up on me." She continued to tremble as the tears were now streaming down her face. I reflexively reached for her cheek to wipe them away. She didn't stop me.

"Amy, if you can honestly say you're ready to walk away, once and for all, I won't stand in your way, and you can go back to Tommy . . . once he sobers up." I smiled hopefully and continued. "But if you're willing to give us one more shot, come take another ride with me in The *Good Times Machine*." I opened the door to the Duster, where I had left my jacket during my sweatfest. I then plucked the jacket off the seat and delicately placed it over Amy's shoulders.

Amy glanced at the car and then stared at me, no longer with loathing, but instead with uncertainty. Those eyes; they actually glistened with the combination of tears and the streetlights above. God, she was beautiful. I imagined that, inside PO Pears, as "I Love You" concluded, Benjie was completing the greatest *grab-microphone-clench-fist-in-anguish-shut-eyes* the world had ever seen.

"I'm not asking for a promise," I added. "I'm just asking for another chance." The Earth stood still as my heart pounded with the physiology of both love and anticipation.

She stepped inside, and the music played on.

Just hope.

ACKNOWLEDGMENTS

"... Chapter Two: I think I fell in love with you. You said you'd stand by me in the middle of Chapter Three ..."

—ELVIS COSTELLO AND THE ATTRACTIONS' "EVERY DAY I WRITE THE BOOK," FROM THE ALBUM *PUNCH THE CLOCK,* RELEASED AUGUST 5TH, 1983. IT PEAKED AT NUMBER THIRTY-THREE ON US BILLBOARD'S HOT 100 SONGS.

I would like to take this opportunity to formally apologize to my wife Laurie Bahar. I tortured you by forcing you to listen repeatedly (and I mean repeatedly) for two years to hit songs released between the years 1980 and 1983, and by asking your opinion on which tune you felt was the most appropriate for each chapter of *The Frontman.* I cannot begin to describe my appreciation for the devotion you displayed through your endless patience and thoughtful and insightful editing skills. I love you.

To my sons, Ethan and Matthew Bahar, whom I may have embarrassed with many tall tales of my youth—thank you for steering me towards acting my own age and having my story take place in 1980s Nebraska, rather than in your own twenty-first century California. While I may be a smartphone-wielding pediatrician, I understand little about the relationship between modern music and social media. At the same time, I hope I taught both of you that everyone has a story to tell.

To my parents, Ophira and Ezekiel Bahar, and my sisters, Zillah and Iris Bahar, thank you for allowing me to share a factually inaccurate but emotionally truthful version of *our* sometimes painful, sometimes hilarious adventure as outsiders. I hope that, through us, readers of *The Frontman* will better understand the complexity of the immigrant experience. It's been an interesting ride.

To the *real* Benjamin Kushner, thank you for being the closest thing I ever had to a brother. I will always cherish our time together; while you made me jealous of your skills as a musician, you also made me appreciate music and that, in reality, I was not alone. To the *real* Christine Evans (Millar), thank you for the two years of email banter between California and New Zealand that fortified our relationship. You made me laugh at your sharp wit while you took ownership of the fictional you and forced me to get her right. To the *real* Sundar Rajendran, thank you for demonstrating the power of healthy irreverence in your pursuit of our common goals.

To my writing coach, Nicola Kraus, who expertly dissected early drafts of *The Frontman*, and then tactfully and disarmingly steered me to more-clearly express my message, or "final thought," to readers without making me feel like a buffoon. I'd like to think you were able to squeeze all the writers' juice out of this first-time author.

To my publishing and publicity teams from SparkPress and BookSparks, including Brooke Warner, Crystal Patriarche, Lauren Wise, Savannah Harrelson, Kristin Bustamante, Maggie Ruf, Jennifer Caven, Megan Rynott, Julie Metz, Sarah Lazarovic, and Stacey Aaronson, thank you for truly listening to my story when others would not. I will always appreciate your ability to gently navigate a debut novelist through a process that can sometimes be more difficult than medical school.

To the television writers in my life: Ed Decter, who guided me to make Amy a more complex, believable, sympathetic, and "human" character, rather than simply the shallow object of Ron's infatuation; the *real* Mark Gross, who demonstrated that comedy, perseverance, and introspection count, and who, with his unique perspective as my childhood friend, forced me to go out of my way to try and make the reader as uncomfortable as possible through Ron's bad behavior; Josh Reims, who acquiesced to allow this "nonwriter to write," and who helped me avoid dead ends with my characters.

To the following readers, who allowed me to pretend that I was Charles Dickens by having them read and critique every chapter of *The Frontman* as soon as it was written, and by doing so with the eyes of an adult and the heart of a teenager: Alicia Austerman, Holly Bario, Anne Barnett, Bill Barnett, Brynie Collins, Catherine Chao, Lindsey Cole, Cheryl Doherty, Kevin Dicker, Yoel Ephraim, Gail Field, Peter Field, Mallory Freedman, Robert Gandara, Samantha Gandara, Jeff Glaser, Jane Griffin, Jana Hand, Cathy Hedstrom, Kevin Kaiserman, Marla Lorber, Mini Mehra, Shereen Memarian, Jennifer Morales, Divya Mowji, Julie Ofman, Linda Pachino, Cindy Ramos, Pamela Reims, Eric Rosin, Howard Sherwood, Stephanie Sherwood, Madeline Tien, Sophia Vaccaro, Emily Vargas, Michael Weisberg, and Linda Wolk.

To those people in my life, both living and passed, whose names were used in the rewritten history of *The Frontman*: Hannah Bahar, Silas Bahar, Jim Burton, Frank Dupuis, Charles Evans, Jill Fager (McCook), Eric Freedman, Jonathan Berkoff, Marcia Kushner, Sheldon Kushner, Wesley Lauterbach, Deborah Lipson, Mark Nemeth, Lendy Nickerson, Leonard Nickerson, Haim Pesso, Rakefet Pesso, Sigal Pesso, Shlomit Pesso, Yael Pesso, Anne Read (Zakin), Zalman Rodov, Zillah Rodov, Babu Rajendran, Prema Rajendran, Somasundaram Rajendran, Elaine Snowbell, Jeff Soifer, David Syrett, Peter Syrett, Chris Taylor, and Andy Weigel. Thank you for enriching my life—you made the real enhance the imaginary.

NOTES

Chapter 9

1. N Engl J Med. 1980 Oct 2;303(14):818. Vomiting and diarrhea associated with cryptosporidial infection. Tzipori S, Angus KW, Gray EW, Campbell I.

Chapter 16

1. Words and music of *"Chameleon Man"* by Benjamin Kushner, used by permission from the author. Copyright © 2001 by Benjamin Kushner.

Chapter 17

1. General Foods Corporation, DeLuxe Edition Passover Haggadah. Copyright © 1965 by General Foods Corporation.

Chapter 32

1. Frank H. Netter, A Compilation of Paintings on the Normal and Pathological Anatomy of the Digestive System, Part III, Liver, Biliary Tract and Pancreas. Copyright © 1957, 1964 by Havas MediMedia Icon Learning Systems.

ABOUT THE AUTHOR

credit: Leslie Tally

RON BAHAR was born in Boulder, Colorado, and raised in Lincoln, Nebraska. He attended college at the University of Wisconsin-Madison, and medical school at the University of Nebraska College of Medicine. After completing post-graduate training at The University of California-Los Angeles, he served there for three years as an Assistant Clinical Professor of Pediatrics in the Division of Gastroenterology, Hepatology, and Nutrition. In 2000, he opened a private practice in Encino, California, where he continues to work and live with his wife and two children. *The Frontman* is his first novel.

SELECTED TITLES FROM SPARKPRESS

SparkPress is an independent boutique publisher delivering high-quality, entertaining, and engaging content that enhances readers' lives, with a special focus on female-driven work. Visit us at www.gosparkpress.com

Forks, Knives, and Spoons, Leah DeCesare, $16.95, 978-1-943006-10-6. There are three kinds of guys: forks, knives, and spoons. Beginning in 1988, Amy York takes this lesson to college, analyzes it with her friends through romances and heartbreaks, and along the way, learns to believe in herself without tying her value to men. On the quest to find their perfect steak knives, they learn to believe in themselves—and not to settle in love or life.

25 Sense, Lisa Henthorn. $17, 978-1-940716-30-5. When 25-year-old Claire Malone moves to New York to pursue her dream of being a television writer, she ends up falling in love with her married boss—a move that threatens to end her career before it even starts. *25 Sense* is about the time in a young woman's life when the world starts to view her as a responsible adult—but all she feels is lost.

So Close, Emma McLaughlin and Nicola Kraus. $17, 978-1-940716-76-3. A story about a girl from the trailer parks of Florida and the two powerful men who shape her life—one of whom will raise her up to places she never imagined, the other who will threaten to destroy her. Can a girl like her make it to the White House? When her loyalty is tested will she save the only family member she's ever known—even if it means keeping a terrible secret from the American people?

Star Craving Mad, Elise A. Miller. $17, 978-1-94071-673-2. A middle-aged elite private elementary school teacher's life changes when her celebrity fantasy becomes a reality.

The House of Bradbury, Nicole Meier. $17, 978-1-940716-38-1. After Mia Gladwell's debut novel bombs and her fiancé jumps ship, she purchases the estate of iconic author Ray Bradbury, hoping it will inspire her best work yet. But between mysterious sketches that show up on her door and taking in a pill-popping starlet as a tenant—a favor to her needy ex—life in the Bradbury house is not what she imagined.

About SparkPress

SparkPress is an independent, hybrid imprint focused on merging the best of the traditional publishing model with new and innovative strategies. We deliver high-quality, entertaining, and engaging content that enhances readers' lives. We are proud to bring to market a list of *New York Times* best-selling, award-winning, and debut authors who represent a wide array of genres, as well as our established, industry-wide reputation for creative, results-driven success in working with authors. SparkPress, a BookSparks imprint, is a division of SparkPoint Studio LLC.

Learn more at GoSparkPress.com